W9-CKT-930

PLATOON

HEMDALE FILM CORPORATION presents

An ARNOLD KOPELSON Production   An OLIVER STONE Film   PLATOON   TOM BERENGER   WILLEM DAFOE
CHARLIE SHEEN   Music By GEORGES DELERUE   Co-Producer A. KITMAN HO   Executive Producers
JOHN DALY and DEREK GIBSON   Produced by ARNOLD KOPELSON   Written and Directed by OLIVER STONE

PLATOON

A NOVEL BY
DALE A. DYE
BASED ON A SCREENPLAY BY
OLIVER STONE

C

CHARTER BOOKS, NEW YORK

PLATOON

A Charter Book/published by arrangement with
Ixtlan Corporation

PRINTING HISTORY
Charter edition/December 1986

ISBN: 0-441-67069-5

Charter Books are published by The Berkley Publishing Group,
200 Madison Avenue, New York, New York 10016.
PRINTED IN THE UNITED STATES OF AMERICA

"Rejoice, O young man, in thy youth . . ."

—*Ecclesiastes*

1.

Flaring its sinister hood into a scaly saucer, the serpent flicked a forked tongue to taste the soggy air around its victim. It swayed for a moment seeming to savor the tension and fear that washed off the young man's face in tangible waves. Death was very near and the victim seemed helpless to prevent it.

The strike was swift and sudden. A painful jolt shook the young man's body and he heard a prolonged hiss of pleasure as the snake sank its fangs into the flesh of his cheek. His body spasmed violently and he reached out for support to lever himself away from death.

"Gawdamn, Taylor! Get yer shit together, boy." Private First Class Lemuel Gardner pried at the young man's strong grip on his knee. "If'n yer gonna freak out over a little plane ride up to the war, how the hell you gonna act in combat?" Gardner's oversized belly rippled with laughter but it was hard to hear anything over the roar of the C-130's turbo-prop engines.

Private First Class Chris Taylor wiped stinging sweat

from his raw eye sockets and returned Gardner's grin.
He didn't need to hear the Georgia farmboy's throaty
chuckle. He could recall it precisely from hundreds of
other uneasy moments, in basic training at Fort Jackson and at the replacement depot near Cam Ranh Bay.
It seemed entirely appropriate that Gardner should laugh
again on arrival at Cu Chi, home of the infantry division to which both men had been assigned for the next
365 days.

"Jesus," Taylor commented as the big aircraft taxied
toward a parking apron. "I was dreaming about snakes."
This time he did hear Gardner's snuffle.

"Lawdy, boy. You better get them snakes out of yer
head. We got us a shootin' war to fight heah." Taylor
nodded to end the exchange and began gathering up the
meager belongings the Army allowed him to bring forward from Cam Ranh. He had become Gardner's un-
willing best buddy during the convoluted process of
getting into the Army and over to Vietnam. It was not a
position in life that brought much joy.

Chris had a few moments to contemplate the situation
as the airplane roared and rattled toward the passenger
terminal. He and Gardner should repel each other like
opposite ends of a magnet. Taylor had nearly all of a
college education, had been brought up in a white-
collar family in New York City and considered people
like Gardner clowns; caricatures you found in bad nov-
els. In other circumstances, Chris would be described
as urbane and sophisticated. In the Army, he was type-
cast as a loner, a snob or a shitbird, depending on the
situation and terrain.

Gardner had practically no education other than the
practical knowledge passed along by generations in his
farming family. He'd been raised by folks sharecrop-

ping a cotton patch on a larger Georgia farm and called a single trip to Atlanta the extent of his world travel.

While Taylor joined the Army on a whim, expecting some deep and meaningful insight during a violent rite of passage, Gardner entered service because he was, quite simply, draft-eligible meat with nothing whatsoever to defer him from the grinder in Southeast Asia.

The vast differences had made no difference to Gardner, who had attached himself to Chris like a leech since one unhappy day at Cam Ranh Bay when they'd both been assigned to scrub urinals for the sin of having nothing more productive to do. For no apparent reason at all, Gardner had stopped scrubbing, grinned through the smell of disinfectant and declared that he had, by God, made him a buddy in the Army. For lack of any valid reason to shun the overture, Chris allowed himself to become that buddy. The relationship made him nervous. It seemed almost as if he'd been shamed into adopting a retarded child.

As the C-130 braked to a halt, allowing its four huge engines to windmill, Chris looked at Gardner. The man was grinning around at the forty or so other replacements who had been sent to Cu Chi on the flight. And he was doing what he always did during times of stress: grinning, sweating profusely and contemplating his well-worn snapshots of a girlfriend named Lucy Jean.

With a frightening hiss of decompression, the huge tailgate of the Air Force C-130 jolted toward the ground. Although they were all anxious to see their new home, the replacements staggered backward at first, recoiling from the blast of hot, heavy air that roared into the aircraft bearing visible clouds of red dust. A bored crewman waved them out and Chris picked up his AWOL bag to shuffle toward the rear of the aircraft.

The air was so heavy with humidity and dust that he felt he was wading rather than walking into war.

On the blazing tarmac, Gardner and several of the other new soldiers broke out pocket cameras they'd purchased in the PX at Cam Ranh and began pirouetting like ballerinas, laughing and snapping shots of everything they could see. It wasn't much.

They'd been told to stay close to the aircraft and their baggage until someone from the Division came to pick them up. Chris strolled out from under the tail of the plane for a first look at the combat zone beyond Cam Ranh; beyond the world of spit-shined jungle boots, starched and pressed fatigues and military bureaucrats.

It was certainly not what he'd expected. Heroism and a valiant battle against a storming enemy was hard to imagine here. Where was the hilltop Chris had imagined in his patriotic fantasies? How could a man stage a stirring last stand on a sterile strip of concrete? The imagery would have to improve in a hurry. His father had warned him—full of the smug omniscience of a rear echelon officer—that the infantry was devoid of glamor, but Chris had rebelled against that advice. And he'd rejected the sage counsel of accepting the OCS commission that had been offered in basic training. His father didn't understand and neither did the tactical officers who wanted to talk him out of his destiny.

If you wanted to do your duty for your country, if you wanted to become one with the *real people* fighting for your country, you volunteered for the infantry and you came to Vietnam. The cream would rise to the top. Chris knew that inherently, from deep inside where those stirrings of patriotism and pride remained unaffected by the attitudes and posturings of his schoolmates. They could look down their noses, say they were too good for this and call patriotism an outmoded concept, but there were still people in the world who recognized duty and understood it must be done.

Still, this did not seem like the place for it. Everything seemed to have a reddish tint. The buildings, the vehicles and the men walking slowly around in various states of undress all bore a patina of rust-colored dust. Where the hell is the jungle, he wondered. Weren't we trained for a jungle war?

There was apparently no mistake. The sign over the transient terminal indicated this was the home of the Twenty-fifth Infantry Division ("Tropic Lightning") and that matched the designation on his orders. Maybe those green hills shimmering off in the distance were the jungle. It certainly wasn't here where he'd thought it would be. Why the hell couldn't they have had the consideration to send a volunteer where he wanted to go?

Chris scratched at an itch on his left shoulder and felt the irregular shape of his new division insignia. Some kind of fucking tropical leaf with a lightning bolt through it. Why wasn't his entire deltoid covered with the proud shield of the First Cavalry Division? A man could stir up some emotion; some pride in a symbol like that and when the time came for the cream to rise, he could reach back into the history of a great unit serving a great nation for inspiration.

Chris was contemplating the possibility of a transfer when he was distracted by a low humming sound. His ears locked on it and filtered out the excited babble of the replacements, the muttered curses of the air crewmen unloading baggage and the click of camera shutters. The sound was somehow ominous, like the buzz around high-voltage electric terminals.

He moved to the other side of the aircraft and found the source.

"Is that what I think it is?" Gardner was not laughing now. He stood beside Chris and breathed noisily through his nose. They stared fixedly at a long line of black rubber bags covered with a teeming blanket of blue-black flies. The insects whirred into the air as a shirtless Spec 4 waved them away and knelt beside a bag.

Angrily the man snatched at a buff-colored tag that had been attached to the zipper-pull of the bag. He checked some information and made a note on the clipboard he carried. As he moved on to the next bag, the swarm of flies hungrily descended to feast on some invisible glob of goo that had leaked from the corpse in the body bag.

Chris had read everything he could find concerning Vietnam before he'd made the decision to join the Army. He remembered the references to the gallant dead and the sorrowful-yet-resolute survivors. Why wasn't he seeing that? Were those really dead American soldiers? Or was this some sort of macabre initiation rite for pledges to the military fraternity? He had no further opportunity to contemplate.

"You better get the fuck back on that bird, New Meat . . . *before* they put *you* in one of them bags."

Chris and Gardner glanced up at a ragged gaggle walking toward the now-empty C-130. It wasn't hard to tell they were men finishing up their combat tour and heading home. What was hard to tell was that they were soldiers at all. Compared to the replacements with their fresh military haircuts and newly issued dark green jungle fatigues, the men shouting taunts at them seemed like . . . well, they looked like ragtag guerrillas. Chris even thought for a moment they might be a new enemy. The veterans resembled what he thought veteran Viet Cong jungle fighters must look like. But their language was strong, vibrant and distinctly Anglo-Saxon.

"Whazzat, Dudes? You say three-sixty-five and a wake-up? Man, you gonna love the Nam . . . for-fucking-ever!"

"Fuckin' New Guys, man. Hey, be advised, I got more time on a medevac than you dudes got in the Nam!"

Chris recognized the language but not the vocabulary. He stared in embarrassment at the nearly white leather of the men's jungle boots. Several pairs were held together by OD tape. Their uniforms were bleached by sun and sweat to lime white; modified, torn, ripped and patched beyond anything Chris had ever seen in Army uniform regulations. A few of the men sported dull metallic belt buckles inscribed with a star, and one individual was loaded down with a cracked Yamaha guitar and a weapon that Chris recognized as a Chinese Communist SKS carbine.

Their hair was well beyond regulation length and Chris self-consciously ran a sweaty hand over the stubble that remained on his own neck as a result of the final GI haircut at Cam Ranh. The veterans had all clambered noisily onto the C-130 now and Chris was again distracted by the angry buzz of flies. Support troops were loading the body bags on wooden pallets for transfer inside the cargo bay of the plane.

Chris felt the searing heat of the tarmac through the molded soles of his issue-fresh jungle boots and hoped any interested observer would connect the angry flush reddening his face with the weather. He knew better but he also realized day-one in the combat zone was no time to display temper or discouragement. If he'd learned anything in a brief military career, it was to expect disillusionment.

His uneasy condition had nothing to do with the embarrassing behavior of his fellow replacements. Through basic training and other transitory Army experiences, he'd learned to understand that. Most of the men were younger and less experienced than he was. They reacted like children on the threshold of some relatively grand adventure. Chris admitted to sharing such giddy anticipation. Hemingway had written that war was man's greatest adventure. But there were dark undercurrents here on the brink of war. Was he the only one to recognize that?

Perhaps it was the semi-serious harrassment from the departing veterans that doused his great expectations with such uncomfortably cold water. It was an element of human nature that Chris recognized from his experiences in the quasi-military environments of an all-male preparatory school. Anyone with a week or two longer in alien surroundings than the next person automatically inherited the right to demean and deliver veiled warnings. He'd envisioned that from the veterans he would meet in Vietnam, but he'd expected it from proud survivors of man's greatest adventure uniformed smartly for their return, ready with sage advice for their replacements and bearing medals to mark their achievements.

Perhaps it was the exact opposite vision that contributed to Chris Taylor's disillusionment standing on the blazing taxi-way at Cu Chi. Or perhaps it was the gruesome foreboding of the bodybags and the callous disregard—almost hostile resentment—with which ev-

eryone seemed to treat them. If he made some friends
here other than Gardner—and Chris desperately wanted
to do that—would they hate him if he ended up as the
bloody contents of a body bag?

Surely not, he told himself. Surely not. War dead
should be honored for their service and sacrifice. He'd
been taught that by his father and grandfather. They'd
grudgingly related tales of their own experiences in
World War I and World War II. As educated men,
they'd always wound up such sessions indicating war
was a terrible, gruesome, unnecessary thing . . . but
there was something in their eyes, in their voices, when
they remembered those vital times. It had seemed such
a contradiction until Chris arrived at his own conclusion
about soldiers. They were never more alive than when
they risked death.

It was a conclusion that demanded exploration and
Vietnam was Chris Taylor's only available research
site.

Gardner punched him painfully in the ribs and pointed
to a figure striding purposefully across the parking apron.
The swagger, clearly visible chevrons and pissed-off set
to the man's jaw all spelled "Lifer." The Twenty-fifth
Infantry Division's Official Reception Committee had
arrived to take possession of body, mind and military
personnel records.

"Now you cheesedicks listen up and answer when
your name is called." The staff sergeant scratched idly
at his crotch and eyed the line of replacements as
though they were some particularly vile form of vermin
sent specifically to fuck up his Army. He called names
in the time-honored military fashion: last name, first
name, middle initial. When the roll call was finished,
he called the unit to attention, faced them to the left and

marched them off toward the transient terminal. The
NCO did not bother to call cadence for the marching
unit, figuring correctly that they would never be able to
stay in step anyway.

Inside the steaming terminal, the replacements fell in
on their duffel bags, which had been laid out in a row
similar to the organization of the body bags on the
tarmac outside. Other NCOs grouped around the Lifer
who had marched them indoors and came away holding
several of the manila envelopes containing personnel
records and official orders. They began to shout names
and search for the respondents. The scene reminded
Chris of a cattle auction. He and Gardner answered
"Here, Sergeant" to their names shouted over the bed-
lam and watched as a grinning individual with high
cheekbones and laughing, slightly deranged eyes saun-
tered in their direction.

"Which one's Gardner; which one's Taylor?" Pointing fingers in two directions, Chris had a moment of
panic thinking he had been singled out for service in
some special operations unit. The NCO grinning at
them did not look like what he had been taught to
expect in the way of your average grunt. The man's
jungle fatigue trousers had been tapered tightly around
muscular legs. His blouse had been modified with zip-
pers where the upper pocket flaps should be and bore
both the Combat Infantryman's Badge and parachutist's
wings. Long, silky hair flowed behind his ears from
under a mangled bush-hat decorated with grenade pins.

"I'm Elias," he said in a husky voice, "squad sergeant with second platoon, Bravo Company. You dudes
are assigned to my outfit, third of the twenty-second.
Welcome to the Nam."

The man sounded sincere in the greeting, but there

was something in his green eyes that seemed to say they were not welcome here . . . not at all.

Gardner seemed anxious to make another friend. "This here don't seem so bad, Sarge. Do they ever give us passes to go into Cu Chi?"

Elias turned from contemplating Chris's sweaty face and blinked at Gardner. His voice gained a sharp edge. "Lissen, Cracker, you'll be lucky if you see Cu Chi once more before you DEROS . . . if you DEROS. This place is for transients and REMFs. The fucking grunts are out in the bush, man. That's where you're headed and it's where you'll stay unless you find a way to skate out of it. Now get your shit and haul ass out to that deuce-and-a-half outside. We got to catch a chopper out to the unit."

Gardner and Chris shouldered their gear and followed Sergeant Elias out into the blazing sunlight. Elias helped them get squared away on the hard, wooden benches. The heat didn't seem to bother him at all while both Gardner and Chris oozed a slimy flow through their uniforms. As the truck jolted off into the cloying storm of dust that seemed to surround Cu Chi, Gardner made a final overture.

"Say, Sergeant Elias. I didn't quite catch that thing you said back there. What's a RUMP?"

Elias shook his head and leered out from under the brim of his bush-hat. "It ain't RUMP, Gardner. It's R-E-M-F, pronounced REMF, and it stands for Rear Echelon Mother Fucker . . . something you ain't, as of now."

2.

Trying hard to ignore the stinging, searing pain in the palms of his hands, Pfc Taylor focused his vision tightly. Maybe if he concentrated on each jungle vine as a separate target, he'd forget the raw, bleeding blisters the machete had raised less than fifteen minutes after Sergeant Elias had rotated him up to point.

He just couldn't seem to get the hang of moving through such dense terrain with any facility at all. Straps supporting his pack and fighting equipment bit viciously into his shoulders. His helmet banged painfully against the bridge of his nose as he flailed away at the rubbery vines with the machete. The OD towel around his neck seemed to chafe rather than absorb the sweat that cascaded off his face.

Cu Chi and the brigade headquarters at Dau Tieng had been one thing, but this was *the bush*. Here he was on point on his first day in the jungle. It seemed like insanity for him to be up here. He was having trouble just keeping pace back in the middle of the column and then they put him up ahead of everyone. No special instructions, no words of encouragement, no hello, no good-bye . . . not even a kiss-my-ass, Taylor or whatever your name is. Just get the hell up there on point.

There seemed to be only one sure thing. He was going to die very soon from bleeding blisters, exhaustion and heat prostration. Yet Chris was determined to cut it; to become a functional part of this faceless mob fighting the war. He could not let himself become a burden to the eccentric bush veterans of the second platoon he was blindly leading through the bush. Coaxing his mind away from the pain, he reviewed his status.

Somewhere in the trek to this point he'd gotten a year older. His twenty-first birthday had come and gone in the time-warp of a jet aircraft headed from September 14 to September 16 via the International Date Line. It seemed unfair for him to miss such a momentous event just as it seemed unjust to put him on point his first day in the bush. He wanted to blend into the pastel of common people in this unit, but he'd been splashed once again with that vivid paint that marked him as different; something special. He'd have to work hard to dull that glow; to erase the shiny gloss of a new guy in the Nam.

Chris noted a fence of bamboo ahead and wondered if it might mark the Cambodian border. He was somewhere in the densely jungled hills near Cambodia. Second Lieutenant Wolfe, his eager platoon commander, had mentioned that when Chris and Gardner had met him at an LZ hacked out of the bush somewhere below this high-ground.

From what painfully sparse information Pfc Taylor had been able to determine, Bravo Company was combing the jungle for traces of a North Vietnamese Army unit which someone said was using this area for sanctuary. The ugly, scar-faced Staff Sergeant Barnes, his platoon sergeant, had mentioned that to his RTO before they began the climb into these agonizing hills.

The platoon was pushing hard through the difficult terrain, but not hard enough. During the last break Chris had overheard Captain Harris, the Bravo Company CO, chewing on Lieutenant Wolfe's ass. He was only gradually becoming familiar enough with the language of military communications to understand the exchange.

"Bravo Two, Six." The company commander was calling his second platoon. "What's the delay up there? We've got a link-up at Phase Line Whiskey at one-eight-zero-zero, over." Bravo Company was supposed to meet another unit at some point on the map at 6 P.M. End of conversation.

Chris felt his knees buckle and he lurched forward as the machete in his right hand sliced air. He was standing on the edge of a clearing. He gasped, reached for a canteen and leaned against a gnarled teak tree to keep himself from falling to the ground under the staggering weight of his rifle, ammunition, pack and equipment. He emptied one canteen and reached for another, wondering how much weight he could drink away from the ninety or so pounds strapped to his back and body.

A horrible smell caused him to gag on the mouthful of rancid water. He thought perhaps he was kneeling next to a spot someone had picked to shit out something particularly vile that was contaminating his digestive system. He'd never smelled anything so putrid as to make his stomach churn violently. He gagged, gasped and stood to move away from the stink of this spot. That's when he saw it . . . or what was left of it.

Someone—a North Vietnamese Army trooper from the look of his charred equipment—had been caught in the tangled roots of the tree by napalm or something else that had turned a human being into a barbecue feast for the worms and maggots that now infested every cavity of what had been a normal face and body.

Chris began to heave a bellyfull of C ration ham and eggs, chopped, while leaning on his rifle to avoid falling into his own vomit. Oddly, he thought of the dead men he'd seen in Hollywood war movies. They died cleanly and were quickly covered by some humane individual so audiences did not have to see the worms at work. Why hadn't someone done as much for this . . . this . . . thing that lay ripe and rotting in their direction of march?

He had no time to contemplate the answer. A powerful hand smacked into his back and he was lifted to his feet by someone jerking on his pack straps.

"What the fuck you waitin' on, Taylor?" Chris tried to focus on the hard blue eyes of Staff Sergeant Barnes but he locked on the long, lightning-shaped scar that ran down the right side of the man's face from a puckered bullet wound in his forehead. It contorted the NCO's face as though someone had inserted a screwdriver in the facial muscle and twisted.

Chris refocused and supposed part of the contortion was what passed for a grin in the platoon sergeant's limited range of expression.

A small crowd from Chris's squad had gathered on the point and Staff Sergeant Barnes raised his growl for their benefit.

"That's a good gook, Taylor. Good and dead. He ain't gonna bite you. Now get your shit together and move out . . . or I'll make you stay back here and bury that sorry sack of shit!''

Levering himself along with his rifle and hacking feebly at the bush with the machete, Chris crashed ahead barely noticing the exchange of radio chatter between Barnes, his RTO and Lieutenant Wolfe.

"Two Bravo, this is Two Actual. Move it out. Six says we're jamming 'em up back there. Two Actual out.''

Barnes was concentrating on getting the clustered soldiers spread out and moving. He glanced briefly at the radio handset being profered by SP4 Tony Hoyt.

"Tell that dipshit to get fucked.'' Hoyt grinned and turned away to couch his response in more acceptable language. Barnes turned to Elias who was getting a fresh supply of salt tablets from SP4 Paul Gomez, the tall platoon medic. "Elias, we ain't goin' anywhere soon with that asshole Taylor on point. Let's try the other new meat. Get Gardner up here and give him the machete.''

Elias didn't like the order. He'd argued briefly with Barnes when Taylor had been selected to walk point.

"Let's keep the cherries off point for a while yet, Barnes. This fuckin' terrain is an ass-kicker. They can walk slack and get the hang of movin' through it first.''

Barnes had been typically disinterested and cryptic in his response. "This ain't no fuckin' trainin' outfit, Elias. They learn or they burn.''

It looked to Elias like Taylor was definitely bound to burn. He passed the word back for Gardner to get up on point and walked forward with an easy gait to where Chris was thrashing noisily in the bush. Taking the machete from the young trooper's bloody hand, Elias supported Chris and walked back toward the clearing. Chris was nearly passed out on his feet. He made distracted swiping motions at the back of his neck and wobbled to a halt on rubbery legs.

Barnes was unsympathetic to Taylor's plight. "What the fuck's the matter with you, candy-ass?" He would have added more but Gardner came jolting and clanking into his view. Unsecured equipment and munitions, including an LAAW rocket tube, 250 rounds of extra machine gun ammo and two Claymore mines dangled from his portly frame. Barnes turned his attention from Taylor to the new point-man.

"My Gawd, Gardner, you look like a fuckin' soup sandwich. Get up there on point and relieve Taylor. Now, let's move this lash-up out of here. Elias, take Two Alpha out on the left flank. Move, assholes! We got a war to fight."

Elias dropped his hold on Taylor's arm and headed out of the clearing. He was organizing the first squad's order of march when he heard the crash.

Taylor had passed out clean and was lying facedown in the clearing under a huge pile of equipment. Barnes shook his head in disgust and motioned for the medical corpsman to take a look at the casualty. He aimed a kick at Gardner's ample ass to signal the move and bulled his way into the bush.

Elias sent his squad out on the flank under control of Crawford, his RTO, and returned to help the Doc with Taylor. "Don't think I'm feelin' sorry for his dumb ass, Doc." Elias grunted with the effort of turning the overburdened casualty over so they could see his beet-red face. "But we ain't got a whore's chance in hell of getting a medevac in here."

Doc Gomez had one hand on Taylor's fluttering pulse while he poured water from a canteen over the casualty's head with the other.

"Even if we could get a bird in here, Barnes would never allow it. Not for no fuckin' heat casualty."

Elias stripped Taylor's bulging pack and began to open it.

Before the medic could reply, Chris blinked and began scraping at his neck. "Fuckin' ants," he panted. "Fuckin' ants are bitin' the shit out of me."

Doc peeled the towel from around Taylor's neck. Black ants about the size of a man's fingernail were swarming across the blistered skin of Taylor's upper body. The two bush veterans swept them away gently while Taylor gulped tepid water and salt tablets. Doc Gomez squeezed one of the ants between his fingers.

"These black fuckers are the worst, man. Don't sweat the red ones so much, but watch out for these dudes when you're bullin' the bush."

Elias had pulled an entire stack of items from Taylor's pack and sat back to contemplate his collection. "Ants ain't what kicked his ass, Doc. Look at all this shit he's been humpin'."

Poking at the pile, Elias chuckled. "Jesus Christ, man. A rubber lady, three fucking books and some magazines, a civilian shaving kit, extra fatigues and boots . . . and look at this . . . a goddamn *gas mask* for Christ's sake!"

Doc Gomez helped Taylor to his feet with reassurances that he'd be okay once he got rid of some of the weight in his pack. "Didn't nobody tell you not to hump all that issue shit to the bush?"

Taylor shook his head in an embarrassed silence. He was desperately afraid that word of such foolishness would mark him as a dumb-shit soldier for the rest of his tour. He didn't think he could stand that on top of everything else. Pride had brought him to this point.

Yet it did not seem enough to carry him beyond the pain of the hump. Elias might lighten his pack, but no one could lift the crushing mortification he felt lying on the floor of the jungle. You've got a right to be this way when you're wounded, he reminded himself angrily . . . not before.

Elias breathed a sigh. "Look, we got to catch up with the rest of the platoon. I'll hump this shit for you until we can get it out of the field on a re-supply chopper. And next time you pack your shit for the boonies, check with me first. I'll save you a kicked ass."

Taylor tried to mumble his thanks but Elias had already gathered up the excess equipment and disappeared into the dense bush. Doc Gomez glanced around the clearing and shouldered his platoon medic's kit. "We'd better split, man. Here comes Bunny and he's walkin' Tail End Charlie."

Chris shrugged into the lightened pack and picked up his M-16. He was about to follow the Doc into the jungle when he was distracted by a girlish giggle and a strange splashing sound.

Bunny, the eighteen-year-old, apple-cheeked grunt with no visible beard beneath fifty-year-old eyes, was pissing into the dead man's empty eye socket.

3.

Bravo Company finally got the word to dig in on a barren hilltop overlooking a blue ribbon of water that formed the only interruption in the vibrant green of the landscape below the high-ground. It was just another jungle stream like a hundred others that meandered through these mountains, but it was a landmark. That made the stream special to Chris. It was a point of reference, the only one he'd made able to determine in an effort to find out where he was.

In fact, Chris reflected as he halted the machinelike motions he'd been making for the past hour in an effort to fill a small portion of the sandbags the re-supply chopper had brought into their LZ, he could not say for sure whether or not they were still in Vietnam. They might be in Cambodia, Laos . . . or goddamn Cincinnati for all he knew. After the hump, he'd asked a few of the veterans about the border. Did they know when they crossed it? Where was this hilltop? Where would they be going tomorrow? How far had they come today? Did they accomplish some mission or were they on their way to do that?

The sum total of the information he gleaned from such questions included one "How the hell should I know?", one "Fuck off, asshole!", and a disinterested belch. It seemed incredible. Didn't anyone else care what they were doing out here? How the hell would second platoon know if they were doing well or badly if they had no yardsticks?

Maybe it was the business of being a New Guy, Chris speculated. No one has time to answer questions for a man so low on the scum-scale that he doesn't even have a need to know what day it is. No one on the hilltop seemed to have the energy or inclination to ask or answer questions about their status. Feed any of these guys a full-scale briefing on the military situation in III Corps with special emphasis on the mission of their own squad and you'd get the same response: "Yeah, right. Whatever, man, whatever."

Certainly Chris would get no information from Junior or Big Harold, the two black troopers who had been tasked with helping dig and fortify the fighting hole on the platoon perimeter. They had opted to let the New Guy do the digging while they heated and ate a C ration supper.

Junior, the militant black man from Cleveland, was wrapping an Aunt Jemima-style bandanna carefully around his shaped Afro and trying to talk Big Harold, the huge lop-eyed farmer from rural Mississippi, out of a can of beans and franks. The way they were going at the horse-trade indicated it was much more important than the topic of NVA sanctuary areas.

"Hey, Harold. Souvenir me them muthah-fuckin'

beans and weenies, man. It's against my religion to eat these pork slices, dude.''

Without looking up, Big Harold poured another generous dollop of hot sauce on the meal he had cooking over a heat tablet burning inside a ration can fashioned to make a stove. "Git the fuck out of my area, bitch. Ah ain't souvenirin' you jack-shit.''

Junior looked hurt. "Awww, muthah-fuckah, now how you gonna act? Huh? Didn't I souvenir you dat ham and lima beans shit when you wanted my turkey loaf las' week? How about some payback, dude?''

"Junior, don't gimme your jive-ass bullshit, man. You know de only reason you got up off dat turkey loaf is 'cause cain't nobody but me eat dat shit.''

"Muthah-fuckah, you know dey name streets after dudes like you back where I come from in the World. One Way. Dead End. I hope Manny get that laundry gig back in the rear before you do. I hope they keep you ass out here, man. You need to hump some of that shit off you belly, man.''

"Manny just think he gonna grab that skate befo' ah do, man. Brothuh ah knows in the reah, he gonna put mah name in soon's that dude that got the laundry duty DEROS.''

"Bullshit, my man. Pure-dee bullshit. Chuck dudes be grabbin' all them jobs in the rear just to keep soul brothers in the bush.''

Chris buried his entrenching tool in the loose dirt outside the foxhole and shook his head over the exchange. Military numberspeak and radio jargon were not the only new languages he'd have to learn to survive in the Nam. He watched Rodriguez, the wiry, silent Mexican kid from San Antonio stringing a Claymore mine outside the perimeter and got in some language practice. His eyes swept the perimeter from the Company Command Post on a rise above them (Bravo CP) across the line of half-finished holes where sweaty men cleaned or loaded weapons.

There was the huge lion-headed black man, King, on his machine gun (M-60). And Sanderson oiling his grenade launcher (M-79 or Blooper) next to Sergeant O'Neill of Two Charlie (third squad, second platoon) talking to someone on the radio (AN/PRC-25 or Prick 25). Rhah, the maniac with the gravelly voice and the Hell's Angels tattoos was juggling three hand grenades (M-26). Here came Rodriguez into the hole trailing the wire he would plug into the firing device for the Claymore anti-personnel mine (M-18). And there was Doc Gomez digging into his medic's kit (Unit One) for something to treat a pair of smelly feet that threatened to rot right off the ankles of Fu Sheng, the Hawaiian kid.

Chris had seen pictures of Fu Sheng dressed in captured NVA uniform and equipment. He'd heard tales that the young oriental charged five bucks MPC (Military Payment Certificate) to don his enemy drag so platoon members could send home a shot of themselves and a grinning enemy soldier. Watching the Doc work on Fu Sheng's feet reminded Chris of the painful blisters on his hand. Several of them appeared to be getting infected. He stepped out of the hole to see if the medic could do something about it.

Junior looked up from his meal to note Taylor was no longer working diligently on the hole they would have to use for protection if the enemy struck this night.

"Hey, White Boy, get yer dick-skinners back on that e-tool. That hole ain't gonna dig itself." Taylor held up his bleeding palms and motioned toward the medic.

"You lucky that's all that be wrong with you, Taylor. I saved yer life yestiddy, dude. I kilt a shit-eatin' dog."

Big Harold jumped up from his sandbag seat and grabbed an e-tool. "Dat reminds me, Junior. I gots to take me a shit." Chris was quickly forgotten in the beginnings of another heated exchange.

"You gonna wipe yer ass dis time, man?"

"Yeah, hell yes, Junior. If'n you lends me yo' shirt."

Adding his own sweat to the humidity of the still air, Chris strolled toward the medical aid man and listened for a sterile pause in the conversation that would allow him to inquire about infected blisters. He stood mortified for the second time on his first day in the bush. Was there nothing about being a grunt in Vietnam that the Army had adequately prepared him for? No, Chris supposed, there wasn't. How could anyone who wasn't actually living this life explain it?

It seemed so bad that veterans would likely erase the day-to-day memories from their mind the moment they were granted a reprieve. Chris felt terribly abused and alienated. No wonder there's such hostility here, he thought. But why is it all focused on me? I can't help it if I'm a Fucking New Guy. Everyone has to start somewhere at some time. Don't they understand I'm doing my best? Why don't they help me? Can't they see that I'm trying to do my part and help win the war?

Chris Taylor stood beside the engrossed medic, wincing at the smell of Fu Sheng's tortured feet, and wondering why the grunts didn't focus their anger on the enemy rather than each other. Like everyone else in the second platoon of Bravo Company, Doc Gomez seemed totally disinterested in Chris's concerns or conclusions.

"Started out as jungle rot between them toes, Fu. I told you to keep changin' yer socks and be sure to use lots of foot powder. Now you got a bad case of immersion foot. I'll have to tell Barnes yer a medevac. You go out tomorrow when the chopper comes in to pick up the water cans."

Fu Sheng struggled to an upright position and rubbed at his feet. "Shit, Doc. Don't go tellin' Barnes nothin'. That crazy motherfucker will swear I did this on purpose. You know he don't let nobody out of the field less they missin' an arm or a leg."

"You gonna be missin' both feet if you don't get off them for a few days. Just count yerself lucky I don't have to call in no special dust-off for you. El-tee Wolfe would shit his drawers if the cap'n found out he wasn't takin' care of his troopies."

"Wish to fuck we had the captain for a platoon commander instead of that fuckin' Wolfe. Dude from personnel told me Captain Harris was a grunt hisself. Said he worked his way up through the ranks. Bet that fucker knows how to take care of his troops."

Doc Gomez stuffed ointments back into his Unit One. "Yeah, well, Fu, you just do what the rest of us do out here. You wish in one hand and shit in the other. You'll see which one fills up first."

Taylor forgot about his infected blisters, borrowed a couple of medical slings to wrap around his hands and went back to filling sandbags.

At the company CP, Captain Bradley Harris was trying to concentrate on his tactical situation map and thinking that on his third tour in Nam, he should have learned to ignore the squawk of four radios. It had been so much easier when he was a Special Forces team leader back in '64. Now he was pestered by the constant grope of responsibility for nearly two hundred men and plagued by a growing conviction that his country would lose a war of attrition unless someone unlocked the political handcuffs that restricted logical tactical decisions.

He gulped cold coffee from his canteen cup and glanced around at the three platoon commanders he'd called up for a briefing. Where the fuck did they get these guys, he wondered. His tired eyes settled on Second Lieutenant Mark Wolfe. Harris laid mental odds that the intense young man with the beatle brows would prove to be the worst of a bad lot. Wolfe could not read a compass and consistently got his platoon lost when the bush got heavy. There had been a number of embarrassing messages from the battalion commander concerning speed of movement while Bravo Company searched for a fix on the lost second platoon.

Harris contemplated relieving Wolfe and turning the platoon over to Staff Sergeant Barnes, the man who really ran the show, but he realized the bureaucracy would never allow him to dismiss an officer from the field without at least a metric ton of accompanying paperwork. In a crunch, Barnes would call the shots for second platoon anyway, so he could let Wolfe fumble along until he'd completed his six months in the bush and rotated back to a job in the rear.

"Gentlemen, here's the situation as I know it. Follow along and update your maps. Sky Six reports a fresh company of NVA moving across this blue line. That's the river just below our current position."

Harris paused to point out the river on Lieutenant Wolfe's map so there would be no chance the officer would miss the significance of his information. Second

Platoon was dug in on the portion of the perimeter facing the river.

"We've got a good chance to light 'em up tonight. We catch their asses before they can get lost up in these hills and we save a lot of grief for everyone. Weapons and third platoon will hold the perimeter tonight.

"I want good platoon ambushes in this area and right here. Lieutenant Hawkins you put your people near that old rubber plantation and cover all access trails. Lieutenant Wolfe, your people 'bush around those old Buddhist temple ruins that we passed on the hump in here. We move 'em out at dusk. That's in about one hour. Any questions?"

While the other officers stood to return to their platoons, Wolfe stayed in a squat, worrying over his map. Harris glanced at him and shook his head.

"I asked if there were any questions, Lieutenant Wolfe. Is something bothering you?"

Wolfe seemed startled, surprised that the briefing was over. "Uh, nossir. No problem with second platoon, sir." He stood, folded his plastic-covered map and walked away from the Company CP.

Captain Harris watched the sweating officer depart and paused before asking for a radio to make his report to battalion. Yeah, he thought, there's a problem with second platoon, lieutenant . . . and you're it. He recalled looking over 2d Lt. Mark Wolfe's 201 file when the officer had joined Bravo Company.

Okay, Uncle Sam, he thought. For the price of one ROTC scholarship so Mark Wolfe could complete his degree in agricultural business administration, you may wind up killing a lot of your soldiers.

• • •

When Chris Taylor finished constructing what Junior called a "piss-poor excuse for a foxhole," there had been an elegant moment of release. Without harrassment, ridicule or interference, he'd been allowed to walk away from the banter and bullshit to eat his C ration meal. Sitting quietly in the late afternoon shade, he relished the semi-solitude and told himself that moments like these would be extremely few and very far between in Vietnam. It was another unwelcome disillusionment.

This is no place for a loner, he thought as he painfully maneuvered the P-38 opener suspended from his dogtag chain around the rim of a ration can. Even in the forced congeniality of private school dormitories Chris had sought solitude in the library or disappeared inside his own mind to grapple with thoughts that transcended sports and grades and getting laid. And those deep thoughts had ultimately led him here, to Vietnam— where there was no time or opportunity to contemplate motivations or meanings. Chris grinned and shook his head at the thought of bringing books and news magazines to the field.

Did I suppose we would fight a fierce—but mercifully brief—battle and I'd be allowed to rest on my rucksack and ponder the meaning of it all? Did I think there would be time to wander around inside my brain, walking point and searching for pockets of new understanding while someone else dug the holes and filled the sandbags? You wanted wisdom and you wound up getting whacked so hard by reality that your brain is numb.

Chris contemplated the congealed lumps of fat that peeked from the folds of meat stuffed inside his can of turkey loaf and thought of his grandmother, the kind

lady who knew so much and demanded so little. She
had delighted in cooking holiday turkey dinners for
him. She loved to listen after dinner when Chris wanted
to talk. She seemed to calmly accept Chris's decision to
join the Army and go to Vietnam when he parents had
been shocked, angered that their son would opt out of a
promising academic career and join an uneducated rabble
trying to cope with an unreasonable war halfway around
the world.

Grandmother had understood there were things Chris
needed to know that could not be discovered in books
no matter how hard he looked. He should take this rare
opportunity to write to his grandmother, Chris realized,
but the turkey loaf and a rifle that badly needed cleaning seemed more important. Besides, he rationalized,
how can I tell her about being a grunt in Vietnam? If
hell is the impossibility of reason, then Vietnam is hell.

How could he tell anyone about a life that centered
on careening through nearly impenetrable jungle searching for an invisible enemy with soldiers who wanted
nothing more than to avoid contact with the people they
had been sent to find? There it is, Chris thought. The
impossibility of reason.

Who could reasonably be expected to understand put-
ting a new and confused soldier on point for the entire
platoon and giving him no more instruction than walk
this way, walk that way and watch out for gooks?
Watch out for gooks? What did gooks look like? Certainly they'd be in better shape than the putrid corpse
he'd seen that morning. What did Bunny call it? A
"Crispy Critter"? With me on point, a gook could be
standing three feet away and I'd never know it.

Where is the reason in exhausting us to the point that
we couldn't fight the gooks if we did find them? My

father and my grandfather never mentioned getting up at
sunrise, humping all day while carrying enough weight
to cripple a strong mule, digging foxholes and eating
rations that would gag a maggot.

What reasonable person would understand going
through all that and being denied sleep to go out on a
night ambush or three-man listening post in the jungle?
How can grunts take this? And how can I learn to be a
grunt?

No one is going to help. That's for sure. When
you're a New Guy, no one cares. They don't even want
to know my name. The rule is simple and I've learned
it already. A New Guy's life isn't worth as much. He
hasn't put in enough time to make him valuable. It's
unreasonable. How can I get beyond being a New Guy
if no one's willing to help?

Chris remembered what he'd heard two veterans say
when they were sure he could hear. "If you're gonna
get killed in the Nam, it's better to get it in the first few
weeks. That way you don't suffer too much."

That's reasonable, Chris thought. It's about the only
thing that's reasonable so far. Chris did some mental
calculations and realized he still had almost a full year
to do as a grunt in Vietnam.

Even if we never find the enemy, he reasoned, I
probably won't make it that long.

4.

Lieutenant Wolfe had been contemplating his future in longer terms than the platoon night activities when the company commander's briefing broke up. He'd calculated that his mandatory six months with a line outfit would be up at the end of January. Just four short months to stay alive and he'd get a skate job as someone's flunky assistant back at battalion.

That would insure a smooth and uneventful DEROS and he could get out of the Army with his credentials as a patriotic American firmly established. Such things carried a lot of weight back in Indiana. More than one state senator or representative had done time as a platoon leader in World War II or Korea. The key was to play it cool and keep his ass off the skyline.

Sergeant Barnes could take the ambushes out tonight. Barnes wouldn't bitch if the platoon commander decided to stay inside the perimeter. Hell, Barnes loved nothing better than to crawl around in the fucking jungle just on the off-chance he might find a gook to murder. That scar-faced sonofabitch was crazy anyway. Why not use that to your own advantage?

Mark Wolfe reassured himself it wasn't cowardice or a lack of leadership on his part. He'd been active in all sorts of college campus groups. He had leadership to spare. Unlike Barnes, however, he realized effective leadership was a delicate mixture of conservative judgment and prudent caution in difficult situations. He thought it might be wise to make that point with Sergeant Barnes sometime in the near future. The man acted as though he ran second platoon and that was plainly not the case.

Wolfe interrupted the siesta being enjoyed by Ace, his shiftless RTO, and told the man to call for all squad leaders and the platoon sergeant to join him at the CP. Stretching muscles cramped by the day's hump, he opened a can of cold C rations, hoping to finish a meal before his NCOs arrived to hear the bad news.

First to interrupt his meal was Sergeant Elias. Wolfe counted himself lucky to have two such vets in his platoon. Elias was on a second tour; Barnes on a third. Certainly Elias had come through it much better than Barnes. The man bore some wound scars. Wolfe had noticed them when Elias stripped down to dig in along the perimeter, but his mind seemed unaffected by the war. Maybe the man just liked being here, unlike Barnes who positively *loved* it.

Sgt. Leon Warren, squad sergeant for Two Bravo, Wolfe's second squad, arrived next. The tall black man had difficulty arranging his size 16 jungle boots in a comfortable position and concentrated hard on the task before speaking to anyone. Wolfe thought, as he had many times before, that there was something wrong with the man. Something vacant and vacuous in those liquid brown eyes. He put it down to an obsession with religion that the man had been displaying lately.

Wolfe grinned, recalling that most of the troops had been using pages from the religious tracts Warren distributed for shit-paper out in the bush. Still, the man was not totally with the program and Wolfe made a mental note to have Two Bravo remain inside the perimeter while the other squads went out on ambush.

Sergeant Warren removed a chewed matchstick from his mouth and grinned at Elias. "Barnes and O'Neill been over talkin' to them ARVN scouts that come in on the chopper this afternoon. They said they'd be 'long anytime now."

As Warren finished his lazy pronouncement, Wolfe caught sight of O'Neill trailing Barnes on their way down the hill toward the CP. There was no question about what was wrong with Sergeant O'Neill, the cocky, crass Boston Irishman who followed Barnes around like a mewling puppy. The man had been in the Army too long. Wolfe didn't have the full story, but he knew O'Neill had been caught in some shady dealings while stationed in Germany. Rather than face a court-martial, the man had grudgingly accepted orders to Vietnam. Wolfe admitted some sympathy with the man's plight. O'Neill was working as hard at surviving for a safe job in the rear area as he was. O'Neill thought Barnes was the answer to that but Wolfe suspected otherwise. Barnes thought everyone wearing stripes or bars should be obsessed with the war.

Barnes bulled into the center of the CP and placed his own map over the one the lieutenant had prepared for the briefing. He stabbed a blunt finger at a spot near the river and smiled around the circle of soldiers.

"We got boo-coo fuckin' movement out there, troops.

We'll be tanglin' assholes with them gook bastards before long or I'll shit in my own messkit.'' Barnes shifted his finger an inch to the east.

"Third battalion got the shit smacked out of 'em about fifteen kliks north of here. When the dinks broke contact, they headed in our direction."

O'Neill caught the senior man's enthusiasm for the bad news and tried to echo it. "Yeah, shit. Fuckers had them lollipop Claymores up in trees. ARVN say they blew a whole goddamn platoon apart. Now *that* is some baaaaad shit!'' He turned a gleeful grin toward Wolfe and noted that the man's furry eyebrows had knitted into a solid line of worry over the intelligence on enemy movements. "We heard the little cocksuckers blew away two lieutenants and a fucking captain!"

Wolfe cleared his throat and ignored O'Neill's wicked stare. They'd not get the pleasure of seeing him squirm just because some officers from another battalion had been killed. That was someone else's misfortune.

"Well, the CO wants most of Bravo Two out on ambush tonight in this area near those old gook ruins. . . ."

Barnes accepted a light for his cigarette from O'Neill's zippo and blew a distracting stream of smoke into Wolfe's eyes. "Well, no shit, El-tee. How the hell else we gonna fire their asses up? You got to bring some to get some. Alright Elias and Warren, you two go with your squads on ambush. O'Neill stays in on the perimeter . . ."

Wolfe decided it was time to re-establish control. "Uh, Sergeant Barnes . . . I had already decided that Sergeant Warren's squad would remain back on the perimeter. The ambushes should be composed of people from Two Alpha and Two Bravo."

Barnes squinted up at Wolfe wearing what passed for a smile with him. Wolfe watched the network of scar tissue on the man's face contort under the effort and focused on a tobacco-stained incisor that was revealed in the process. Barnes's expression was caught somewhere between a grimace and a sneer. He silently took a long drag on his cigarette.

O'Neill ignored the lieutenant's gaze and whined at Barnes. "Bullshit, Bob. You know Morehouse and Sal are short. Fu Sheng's goin' in on a medevac tomorrow and Sanderson's due for R&R. You don't want to send their asses out on an ambush tonight. Elias has got the new meat. Let him and Warren cover the night activities."

Barnes turned his grimace on Warren but the black NCO didn't seem to care one way or the other. He was staring at his gigantic boots and rocking back and forth. Only when his gaze landed on Elias was there any further discussion.

"Those fuckin' new guys don't know shit, Barnes. Chances are we're gonna run into somethin' out there tonight and . . ."

O'Neill grabbed Barnes's elbow still purposefully ignoring the lieutenant. "So? So, what the fuck am I supposed to do? Get one of my guys zapped just so some fresh-faced fuck can get his beauty sleep? Bullshit! No way, man. No way!"

Elias realized one way or the other his men were going out on ambush tonight. He rose to leave but not before he let O'Neill know what he thought of a man who tried to skate out on his turn in the bush.

"You ought to give it a rest, O'Neill. There's nothing in the regs says you have to be a prick every day of your fuckin' life." He gathered up his rifle and left the

CP to let his troops know there would be little sleep this night.

Barnes eyed the somnolent Warren once more, shook his head and turned to O'Neill. "Red, your people that ain't short or otherwise got some sorry-assed problem will fill in with Elias tonight. That includes you. Warren stays inside the perimeter."

O'Neill didn't want to risk the platoon sergeant's anger any further. "Sure, Bob. That's fair. That's all I ask is a fair shot. I'll go let 'em know who's up tonight."

Warren ambled out of the CP area along with O'Neill. He did not seem to appreciate the victory that had been handed to him by Barnes and Wolfe. He did not seem to mind anything other than the rocks in the trail leading down to his squad area.

Barnes revealed the incisor again and flipped his smoke into the bushes outside the CP. "Warren's got himself a little problem, lootenant. In his condition, he ain't fit to be outside the perimeter."

Wolfe jumped at what he presumed was an overture. "Then you agree that I should make these decisions in *my* platoon, Sergeant Barnes?"

"Not a bit of it. Ah said ah agreed Warren don't belong on no fuckin' ambush tonight. You do what you think you have to do, lootenant. And ah'll do what has to be done with this fuckin' platoon."

Wolfe wanted to argue but something in the set of Barnes's misshapen jaw told him it was not a conversation judgment or the act of a man exercising prudent caution.

In the last fading rays of sunlight, Chris finished a cursory note to his parents and wondered what the hell to do with the envelope. He'd been told to simply write "Free" in the corner where the stamp would normally be placed, but no one had specified where you found a mailbox in the middle of the jungle.

His eyes settled on two black men reclining on sandbags a couple of holes away from his own. He recognized King from the flash of a gold tooth stuck prominently in the man's mouth. The other man would be Francis, the kid with the lovely falsetto singing voice that Chris had admired doing Motown tunes back in the rear. King appeared to be writing a letter also and Chris approached to ask about mailing facilities.

As he approached, Francis was jabbing his finger at the crinkled, stained paper which contained King's nearly illegible scrawl. "Shit, King. It ain't d-e-r-e. It's d-e-a-r. And Sara don't have no two rs in it. Shame on you, fool."

King grinned again and let Francis bask in the flash of his gold tooth. "Don't mattuh, my man. She know what it mean. Ah' she don't read any bettuh than ah write nohow. . . ."

Taylor's shadow fell across King's paper. The big black machine-gunner grinned up at him. It was one of the friendliest, most open expressions Chris had seen in the Nam.

"Taylor, my man. How you doin'? Ah heah you goin' out on ambush with us tonight, dude. That raht? You got to keep yo' head and yo' ass wired together out there. Mistuh Charlie can play rough at night."

For some reason Taylor felt better hearing that King would be along. There was something solid about the man. And he would be a second machinegun to add to the firepower of Tex, the M-60 gunner from Two Charlie. Taylor grinned, shrugged his shoulders and showed King the envelope he carried.

"What you lookin' fuh, Taylor? A mailbox? Ain't none a them out heah, man. You just give that letter to my main man Francis heah. Francis ain't goin' tonight. Doc say he catchin' pee-monia. You just let Francis take that letter back to the rear wit' him."

Francis hacked confirmation of his condition and spat the glob of phlegm out onto the ground. "Yeah, White Boy. And you keep an eye on the King Pin out there in the bush tonight. He'll help get you through it."

Chris Taylor nearly cried on his way back to load up for the night ambush. Those were the kindest words anyone had spoken to him in Vietnam.

Barnes stood next to King at the head of a loose column on the edge of Bravo Company's perimeter. In the glow of a red-lensed flashlight, both men planned a route that would take them quickly and quietly a distance of slightly over a kilometer where they would intersect a little-used trail between the river and their hilltop position.

Elias had spotted the potential ambush site during the march to the perimeter and pointed it out to his platoon sergeant. With practised eyes both soldiers had scanned the temple ruins. There was enough structural debris— including a twelve-foot stone Buddha, several freestanding sections of wall and a massive archway spanning the trail—to silhouette an enemy in the moonlight as well as increase the shrapnel effect of their weapons. In most places the jungle cleared by the original builders of the temple had not been able to match the lush growth of the surrounding terrain. That meant visibility and fields of fire for the good guys and lack of cover for the bad guys. It was almost perfect.

"Ah reckon them gooks might just walk wide of that place, Sarge." King was tracing the wide loop he intended to take while walking point and bringing the ambush party into a U-shaped final position near the temple ruins. "They knows a good ambush spot as well as we does."

Barnes cocked an ear at a soft peel of distant thunder. Snapping off the flashlight, he stared into King's wide, white eyes which seemed distended and fearful against the ebony of the man's cheeks. Was it merely a combination of pigment and the deepening gloom of dusk? Or was King getting some ill wind up his ass after ten solid months in the bush. Barnes decided it was simply a matter of King hating to give up his beloved machine gun and being stuck on point.

"Lissen to me, King. I put you on point because you're solid, experienced and one-eighty out from them other jive-ass niggers in this platoon." Unseen in the dusk, King winced at the epithet. There was no use calling it at this point. He'd served with S. Sgt. Robert E. Lee Barnes of Clifton, Tennessee long enough to know "nigger" was just another descriptive term in the man's limited vocabulary. It was something his brothers back in Birmingham would never understand.

"In mah book, you a soldier, King. Ah don't see you as no other color 'cept olive drab so ah'm gonna tell you somethin' ah learned about these fuckin' gooks a long time ago. They ain't supermen, so don't go out-smartin' yerself by thinkin' they don't fuck up and walk into ambushes jes' like we do. And they ain't afraid of us no matter how much firepower we got ready to bring down on 'em. So don't think they'll tiptoe around us or di-di when we lock horns with 'em. You keep them things in mind, King, and you'll kill boo-coo gooks before you go on back to the World.''

A light drizzle had begun to fall and Tex, the angry M-60 gunner from Waco, was worried about the five hundred rounds of spare ammo being carried by his assistant, Junior Williams. He spat a stream of tobacco juice toward the man with whom he'd been unwillingly paired by the voracious appetite of his automatic weapon and thought about what his old man had said that day when Tex left the machine shop for the Army.

''Ah know y'all will prob'ly have to serve with some Meskins, but ah hope you ain't called on to fight next to no niggers. Yuh cain't rely on 'em worth a shit.''

Tex checked the 50-round teaser belt in the gun, made sure the bolt was to the rear and muscled the weapon onto his shoulder. ''Junior, you gonna get that ammo under yer poncho or just let it rust? Don't they teach niggers nothin'?''

Junior had been through it all before and usually gave as good as he got from a bigot, but this was no time to be fighting with Tex. There was just too much the man could do to fuck him over in a firefight.

''You worried about dis extra ammo, man, you get some othuh muthah-fuckah to carry it. We got dat new meat wit' us tonight. Give the fuckin' ammo to one of them.''

''They wouldn't know which end of the round comes out the muzzle. You jist cover up that ammo and stay where I can see you tonight, boy.''

Junior turned to Manny and Big Harold standing next to him in the muster area. ''Look heah, brothuhs. I be standin' right heah wit' a big dick and a basketfull of balls and this honkey muthah-fuckah call me a boy. Ain't dat some shit?''

Up the line and out of earshot, Chris Taylor stood next to Lem Gardner busily checking his equipment and trying to avoid conversation. He was nervous and wanted to concentrate on his gear before Sergeant Elias arrived to check it. He knew Gardner was still having trouble fitting in with the platoon and clung to his oldest Army friend.

Gardner had patronized the souvenir shop outside their base camp where he purchased strings of psychedelic beads, a large silver peace medallion and a wide watchband made of water buffalo hide in an effort to look less like new meat, but the platoon still held short of any kind words or helpful advice. Like every other student in the University of the Nam, Gardner would learn by doing or die taking one of the exams. Until it went one way or the other, he consoled himself with Chris and the ever-present picture of Lucy Jean.

"Say, Chris, ah reckon there's just enough light left fer me to show you mah favorite picture of Lucy Jean.'' Gardner thrust his wallet at Chris and he reluctantly accepted. It wasn't hard to understand the pairing. Lucy Jean had a lot in common with Gardner. She was corn-fed with the contented gaze of a cow in green pastures. For both of them, understanding of—and concern with—the affairs of the world ended just beyond the south forty. Lucy Jean was also bone ugly.

"You're a lucky guy, Gardner. She's real . . . uh, cute." Chris tried to avoid further conversation but Gardner was insensitive to anything but his own reverie.

"Yep, she's the one fer me all right. We gettin' hitched soon's ah get home and get out of the Army.'' Gardner seemed to notice he was losing Taylor's attention to a minute inspection of weapons and grenades. He replaced the wallet, waved his hands briefly over his own gear and tried again.

"How 'bout you, Chris? You got some gal waitin' at home fer you?"

Chris was annoyed and trying hard not to show it. No use distracting Gardner any more than necessary from the task ahead. The man just couldn't seem to make his presence felt in second platoon, but that was hardly Chris's fault. Why irritate me with all this swarmy crap about Lucy Jean and the great life they'll have back on the farm after the Nam? Shit, we've got to survive the Nam first.

Gardner was still staring expectantly, wanting to hear about someone pining away at home for Chris Taylor. Well, he'd wait a long damn time for that.

"Naw, Gardner. There's no one, man. . . ."

Gardner went back to his mental masturbation and Chris checked the tension on his magazine springs. It was fortunate he didn't have to explain his love life—or lack of one—to the rest of second platoon. To them a lack of steady pussy spelled dipshit and virgin equated with faggot. For a moment, Chris wondered what he'd do if anyone in this outfit ever cared enough to ask him about sex. He'd lie, he supposed, as he'd done before when the question arose.

Certainly his parents had tried to link him amorously with suitable girls, hoping physical attraction would lead Chris into a normal pattern of achievement, marriage and procreation. And he *had* been attracted. Wet dreams and sexual fantasies had been a big part of Chris Taylor's adolescent life. But the grapplings remained in his dreams, subjugated to an almost zenlike devotion to cerebral concerns.

There was plenty of time, Chris reminded himself.
I'll know who and how and why about women when
I've learned what there is to know about surviving with
my own sex.

Gardner was close to launching one of his eternal
fantasies about life with Lucy Jean after Nam when
Chris cut him short.

"Here comes Elias, man. You better look over your
gear again."

With quick hand movements, Elias spun both new
men around and picked off several items of equipment
they would not need on the night ambush. He insured
each man had a poncho against the coming rain and
hauled Taylor away toward the head of the formation.

"Tex, you got Taylor here on your position tonight.
Keep an eye on him. He'll stand watch with you and
Junior."

The raw-boned machine gunner was not happy. First
a nigger, then a fucking recruit. "Goddamn, Elias. You
know this gun's boss out on ambush. Ah ain't got no
time fer babysittin'. Put that fucker somewheres else."

"Shut the fuck up and stop bitchin', Tex. You been
wantin' a new A-gunner. Start training one. You got
Taylor."

Elias ignored the insubordinate squirt of tobacco juice
and turned an infectious grin on Taylor. "Look, man,
just stay cool tonight. Tex is a pain in the ass, but he
knows what he's doin' out there. If you get separated or
lost in the dark don't start yellin' and don't panic. Just
sit tight and we'll find you."

Chris nodded and wondered what the difference was
between himself and Gardner. For the second time this
night, someone had offered him kind words and reassurance. Gardner was getting no such treatment. Elias

merely jabbed the other man in the shoulder and pointed
toward Hoyt packing the squad radio. ''You stick with
Tony and set in with him. 'Bout time you learned to
stand radio watch.''

Chris had just enough time and light to notice the
hurt expression on Gardner's face before King led the
ambush off into the dark and threatening jungle.

A hiss of wind in the high canopy and the rattle of
rain against the giant rubbery leaves around the ambush
site covered the sound of the unit moving into position.
Tex had taken first trick while Junior and Chris curled
up under their ponchos, squirmed around to make a soft
depression in the mud and tried to sleep away the
misery of cold and wet conditions. Before allowing
them any respite, the machine gunner had personally
checked to insure both Claymore mines were properly
positioned to send a hail of steel balls down the trail
toward the looming arches that had previously marked
the entrance to the courtyard of the old Buddhist temple. He had personally plugged the arming wires into
the firing magnetos, checked the safeties to insure no
one could accidentally squeeze the firing handles and
pointed out the positions of the rest of the ambush
party.

Machine guns manned by Tex and Sal, a former
numbers runner from Newark, were at the two feet of
the horseshoe-shaped formation on either side of the
trail. Barnes with Hoyt, the radio, and Gardner had set
himself in the center and slightly to the rear. Closest to
Chris was a three-man position occupied by Sergeant
O'Neill, Sanderson with the Blooper and Bunny with a
Remington 12-gauge shotgun. The rest of the men had
placed themselves in positions where they could ob-

serve the trail without being seen and placed their spare magazines and grenades at hand. One man in each position watched the trail for two hours before waking his relief.

The steady rain had raised a cloud steam from the dank, warm earth of the jungle floor. Inside that eerie mist were swarms of mosquitoes that made sleep impossible for Chris. He'd covered his face with a towel, wrapped the poncho around his head and shoulders until he nearly choked and still they buzzed and dive-bombed to suck his blood in a ravenous assault. The issue mosquito repellent, or "bug juice," was long washed away in the flow of water that cascaded onto his face and hands from every crease in the poncho. Taylor ran a water-wrinkled hand over his face and felt the huge welts left by the insects. His left eye was nearly swollen shut from a bite on the lid. Would this misery ever end?

Chris reached into his pocket for the luminous watch Elias had made him remove before they set out on the ambush. It was nearly midnight. He had ten minutes before his turn on watch.

Tex either didn't know that or didn't care. Chris felt a hand shake his shoulder and sat up to notice the rain had slacked a bit and a half-moon was trying to peek through the clouds. The mist hugging the ground reminded him of a set for a low-budget horror movie.

Tex was poking him in the thigh with the tube of a light-intensifying device known as a Starlite Scope. Resembling a telescopic rifle sight, the scope magnified the tiniest amount of reflected light and gave the viewer some ability to identify glowing green shapes in the dark. Conditions of weather, power and ambient light had to be just right for the Starlite to be worth its weight. Apparently the conditions were not right tonight.

"This thing ain't worth a fuck," Tex whispered. "Cain't see nothin' but a greasy green smear out there." He dropped the scope in the mud and began to pull a poncho over his head. His chin rested on the feed cover of the machinegun.

"Hey, man. You're ten minutes early wakin' me up for the watch." Chris caught the flash of teeth in a tight grin.

"*Xin Loi*, motherfucker. Ah'm gettin' me some *z*s. You sure you know how to work them fuckin' Claymores?"

Chris felt around at his feet for the electrical firing devices shaped like miniature industrial staplers. Each was fitted with a wire clip that could be wedged under the handle to prevent accidental firing. To detonate the deadly mine, you simply flipped back the clip and squeezed on the handle. A small jolt of electricity traveled through the wire and set off a blasting cap inside the mine. That touched off the C-4 plastic explosive packed inside the body of the device and sent a hail of ball bearings out to a range of seventy-five yards. Chris recalled the details from training and assured Tex he could handle the mines.

"Don't be coppin' no eyes on me, New Meat. I catch you sleepin' and ah'll turn you ever way but loose. You wake Junior up at oh-two-hunnert hours . . . and you make sure that fuckin' nigger's awake!"

Chris peered into the gloom, hugged his rifle and grappled with the mob of irrelevant thoughts that had been swarming inside his brain with the same ferocity as the mosquitoes on the outside of his skull. He was miserable—more miserable than he could imagine ever being—and yet he was alive and functional. He was not prostrate, mentally or physically, under the strain of it all. He was, in fact, quite a bit more than the man he thought of as Chris Taylor before Vietnam.

He grinned into the dark and relished visions of some day back in the World when a limp-dick civilian would ask him if he'd done his share for his country. Come what may, Chris realized, no one will ever be able to say I didn't do my part; do what's expected of all Americans when the country calls.

Chris warmed to his reverie and the wet chill of the night against his itchy skin disappeared. He supposed it wouldn't be too presumptuous to put himself in the same category with Thomas Jefferson. He'd always admired the patriot for saying, ''I hold that a little rebellion now and then is a good thing. . . .'' Given the circumstances, Chris felt he qualified as a rebel. He'd taken a hard turn away from the goals his parents had set: respectability, a job with a modest salary, a house of his own and a family. They'd be happy with just another white boy on Wall Street but Chris wanted more . . . or less. It didn't matter. What seemed important in his rebellion was control over his own destiny. If that involved outrageous behavior—such as joining the Army and coming to Vietnam—so be it. A little rebellion now and then . . .

The longer he sat in the misery of the ambush site, waiting to kill someone on cue, the more Chris became convinced he could handle being a simple grunt; involved at the visceral gut-level in *the* war of his generation. The virtual anonymity of it all pleased him. Most of his life, he'd been pampered and sheltered, singled out by intellect or good fortune as a kid who shouldn't have to deal with the seamy side of surviving the factionalism of a confused generation. There were the haves and the have-nots—and the special people like

Chris Taylor who wandered around in the middle of it all, immune unless they chose to become infected by one side or the other.

People like his parents who struggle up through anonymity could never understand it, but that sort of life made you beg for a place in the faceless mob of humanity. It bred sympathy for the devil and made you want to test your mettle at enduring the fires of hell.

Other people could point to their degrees, accolades, achievements and bank accounts. Chris could point to his time as a grunt in the Nam. He'd remember these hard times among an incredible collection of men the nation had abandoned to their fate in Vietnam. Chris was beginning to form a clear picture of the grunts. His own face had not entirely appeared on the canvas as yet, but he knew something was very special about these men who lay sleeping or trembling around him.

They were the bottom of the American barrel. The grunts knew that; even prided themselves on it in a perverse way when the subject of more privileged civilians arose. Chris considered the hometowns he'd seen scrawled on helmet covers. Pulaski, Tennessee; Brandon, Mississippi; Pork Bend, Utah; Wampum, Pennsylvania. From such unknown and inconsequential places, the grunts came to Vietnam. They were poor, uneducated and about as far from the trappings of the Great Society as you could get. Yet they were over here, fighting to support America, freedom as they knew it, and some vague set of principles to which they'd been told they owed allegiance.

Say what you will, Chris told the shocked crowd at an imaginary cocktail party, the grunts are the backbone of this country. They are the heart and soul; the men who helped me find my own heart and soul out there in the mud and blood of Vietnam.

Chris wiggled his numb buttocks deeper into the mud and realized he was sitting at the bottom of the American barrel for the first time in his life. Maybe from down here I can start up again, he thought. Maybe now I can be someone special without having to fake it. Certainly I will have seen things I could not have seen before. Maybe I'll learn those nagging things I do not know.

To his rear a branch cracked in the wet wind and Chris was startled out of his concentration. With a glance at his watch, he realized he'd been lost in his head for nearly two hours. Had his eyes been open? Had he been asleep? Had he missed a gang of gooks crawling around out there in the mist?

No. Better men were awake and alert on the other positions. They'd have let him know if it was time to fight. Waiting a full fifteen minutes until his watch showed 2 A.M., Chris moved to wake Junior.

It wasn't easy. He thought at first the black man might be dead; knifed by some slithering gook infiltrator while Chris composed his thoughts. Junior eventually responded to Taylor's prodding and glared from under his poncho with one dead eye. He rolled over, pried his rifle from the mud and slowly crawled toward the trunk of a bush where the Claymore handles had been placed.

Chris made a futile attempt to smear on some more mosquito repellent, closed his eyes and dropped off to sleep in the pouring rain.

So did Junior.

•　　•　　•

Chris pried his swollen left eye open with his fingers
and peeked out from beneath a corner of the towel that
swathed his head. Something about the night sounds
had changed. What was it? The drone of ravenous
mosquitoes was still in his ears but he could sense
something altered. The chirrup of the tree frogs had
stopped but there was something else. The rain. The
rain had stopped. He could no longer hear the constant
thrum of raindrops on the vegetation.

The air transmitted something eerie. It was like the
expectant silence from a noisy audience just before the
curtain goes up in a theater. He sat up in a pool of
muddy slime to check with Junior. Tex was breathing
rhythmically beneath his poncho and Junior . . . Junior
was asleep too! The asshole had gone to sleep on his
watch!

Shifting his eyes to the trail, Chris thought he saw
something. There. That shadow. It looked like a man
wearing a helmet . . . but there was something about
the shape. It must be a tree or a bush. No human could
stand that still. It must be a bush but . . .

Chris heard rather than felt the blood pounding in his
head. In an instant he knew the difference between wet
from sweat and wet from rain. In the same instant, he
realized he was looking at a gook trooper standing just
fifteen yards from his position.

As though to confirm Chris's judgment, the NVA
soldier shifted his AK-47 and made a slight sweeping
motion to someone at his rear. Chris was paralyzed by a
combination of fear and indecision. Why didn't someone open fire? Could they all be asleep like Junior?
Didn't anyone else sense the danger?

Chris swiveled his head cautiously. His rifle seemed
like it was buried in mud at least a mile away from his

grasp. Tex and Junior showed no signs of awakening. What the fuck should he do?

The enemy point-man moved cautiously down the trail. Chris caught a glimpse of other shapes passing through the arches. There was no sound. The shapes seemed to glide rather than pace. He re-focused on the point-man who had come abreast of his position. The reluctant moon beamed through a hole in the scudding rain clouds and Chris saw the face of the enemy.

The gook was soaking wet and water dripped from the rim of his Soviet-style helmet. He had cold, dark eyes. Chris watched, riveted by those eyes. He felt hypnotized against his will. Every synapse that sparked in his tingling brain screamed for him to move, to go for the Claymore handles or scramble for his rifle. He nearly moaned aloud with the agony of his utter paralysis. Why couldn't he do the right thing now that he was facing the enemy for the first time? Why couldn't he do anything?

The frozen silence continued while the young American watched the older North Vietnamese turn to continue his journey through the night. And then a flash of reddish white light blinded Chris. Had someone thrown a grenade? Or had the gook killed him?

Chris was blown flat. He felt a numb pressure around his forehead and eyes. He heard the raking cough of automatic weapons. Another explosion jolted him from the rear and tore the helmet off his head. Tex was screaming and scramblinig through the mud to get his machine gun in action.

"The Claymores! Blow the Claymores! Get those cocksuckers!" Chris swam through mud and tore at branches to reach the Claymore firing handles. Junior was up on his hands and knees but scrambling away from the trail. Using both hands to squeeze the handles, Chris trembled and waited for the blast of the mines. He couldn't get the fucking things to fire!

Above the bark of the M-60, Chris could hear Tex screaming something at him.

"The safeties, you shit-head! Take the fucking safeties off!"

Dropping the stock of the gun, Tex lunged and grabbed the Claymore firing handles from Chris. He flicked off the safeties and squeezed. Taylor was jarred for the third time in as many minutes by the red-orange flash of dual detonations. Squinting to regain his night vision and shouldering his M-16, Chris thought he saw one of the enemy soldiers near the archway explode like a water balloon filled with thick red liquid.

Ignoring the carnage and a dull ache in the back of his head, Chris began to squeeze the trigger of his rifle. The solid jolt of the weapon against his shoulder was reassuring amid the deafening din of the firefight.

In the center of the ambush site, Gardner had been sleeping when the fight began. He convulsed into a sitting position and reached for his upper pocket where he kept the wallet wrapped in plastic and containing Lucy Jean's picture. He felt he should protect her image in this time of danger . . . or do something. But how? And what should he do? What would these soldiers expect of him now that there was an opportunity to gain their approval?

Staff Sergeant Barnes had scrambled out of sleep and forward toward the fight almost before the second shot had been fired. Gardner had just caught a glimpse of his ass wiggling away through the mud. Hoyt, the RTO, was hugging the ground and shouting into the handset trying to notify second platoon that their ambush had been sprung. What could he do that wasn't already being done by someone more experienced?

Wait. No one was actually firing at the enemy from this position. If he could lay out some fire and kill him a few gooks, Gardner thought he'd shed the New Guy image once and for all. He could define no target in the muzzle flashes and burst of grenades to his front but he'd been trained to fight, by God, and fight he would.

Gardner rose to his knees and thumbed the selector switch of his rifle back onto full automatic. He stood to fire, ignoring something Tony screamed from his position on the muddy ground. As he'd been taught in basic training, Gardner aimed down the trail and squeezed on the trigger. He was rewarded by the jolt of the weapon rattling away into the dark. He was pleased by the muzzle flash and sure that the rest of the platoon would know he was not cowering. Gardner was helping his outfit fight the gooks.

He hoped his favorite picture of Lucy Jean was okay as he staggered backward and tried to catch his breath. Something had slugged him solidly in the chest. And there was a burning . . . almost like the time he'd dropped a hot soldering iron on himself. But this was different. It was so goldarned hard to breathe.

Sergeant O'Neill could see gook troopers scrambling for cover in the bright blast of light each time Bunny fired his shotgun. The fucking kid was laughing; enjoying this shit! Sanderson was hugging the ground with the Blooper beneath him. What if the gooks were trying to work their way around the flank? They'd have to come right through his position and O'Neill knew the shotgun wouldn't be enough to stop any such move. He reached a freckled hand out to feel around in the slop. Frags. A few quick grenades out there and the gooks would look for some other way to escape the murderous fire of the ambush.

He came up with an M-26, wrapped his thumb firmly around the safety lever, jerked the pin free and heaved. O'Neill didn't care where the damn thing landed as long as it made enough noise and threw out enough shrapnel to keep the gooks off his ass.

Tex was firing his M-60 with one hand while reaching back for Junior with the other. "Feed me, you sonofabitch! Where's that extra ammo?"

Realizing continued fire from the gun was more important than his own rounds, Chris grabbed the muddy belt of 7.62mm ammo from the place where Junior had left it and crawled toward Tex. The gunner was cursing in a continuous roar. In the bright light of another Claymore detonation, Chris could see he had raised the feed cover of the weapon with his right hand. He was waiting for the ammo.

A detonation threw Chris forward across Tex and he banged his head painfully on the open cover of the gun. Tex was thrashing underneath him but the man's discomfort had nothing to do with Chris.

"My arm! Jesus Christ! My fucking arm!"

Chris rolled off the screaming machine gunner and tried to pin the man to the ground. Tex brought up his right hand to push Chris off but there was only ground meat and bone where the fingers should have been.

Chris knew he'd also been hit in the blast. He could feel warm blood coursing down the back of his neck. But it hardly seemed important compared to the warm gouts splashing over his face from the stump where Tex's right hand used to be.

Screaming obscenities at the necessity of such a move, Junior crawled forward and got the M-60 back in action. He did yell for the medic but the humane plea was lost among his curses.

"Don't quit on me now, Gardner, goddamn you! Don't quit on me now! You got to help me, man!"

Doc Gomez knew screaming at the man who lay gasping for air beneath him wasn't doing any good. Neither was the mouth-to-mouth resuscitation he'd been trying for the last several minutes. Why didn't God design some sort of better protection for the human chest cavity? When it got torn open, there was not much a combat medic could do. And all that internal bleeding caused by bullets or frags. How the fuck was he supposed to keep a guy with a sucking chest wound from drowning in his own blood?

Tony Hoyt scrambled forward with the plastic coating from his spare radio battery. The Doc had sent him for it while he fought to breathe into Gardner's starved lungs. Maybe they could seal the chest with the plastic well enough to hold some air in the injured man.

Before they could complete the seal, working with wet surgical tape against the blood-matted skin of Gardner's ribcage, Lucy Jean's intended went into cardiac arrest and died.

No amount of closed-chest massage or adrenaline injected into the heart could bring him back to life. Doc Gomez sobbed and choked back the bile churning upward from his stomach. Why the fuck did shit like this have to happen, he wondered for the fifteenth or twentieth time since he'd left medical school and tried to earn his tuition via the GI Bill. As though to answer the unspoken question, Tony put a hand on the medic's shoulder and shouted over the dwindling sounds of broken contact.

"Fuckin' guy. He just stood straight up in the middle of a firefight. Fuckin' guy, man."

Barnes glanced only briefly at Gardner's corpse before snatching Doc's arm in a powerful grasp and hauling him away to have a look at Tex. The firefight was over but the platoon sergeant could still hear the bang and rattle of Bunny cycling shells through his shotgun. That little fucker would learn a thing or two about fire discipline or Barnes vowed to shove that 12-gauge up his skinny ass.

It didn't take long to learn Tex would lose what was left of his right hand. Doc Gomez stopped the bleeding with a length of surgical tubing he always carried on his field equipment and jabbed a syrette of morphine into the wounded man's thigh. The shot quickly reduced the machine gunner's cries to a less irritating level and Barnes swung around from his examination of the casualty to face Chris and Junior.

"You assholes controlled the first line of Claymores. You want to tell me how those gooks got that close?"

Chris was beginning to feel some sharp pain in the back of his neck. He tried to ignore it and look at Barnes's face. He could feel the snarl long before he was able to see anything in the moonlight. It was hard to think.

"That dumb fuck didn't blow the Claymores!" Junior was panting and wheezing at his side. The black man rose to his knees and pointed an accusing finger at

Chris. "He let 'em walk right up on us. The mothah-fuckah was sleepin' on his shift!"

Chris tried to form the words of denial but realized he'd only mumbled as he started to fall face forward in the mud. Big Harold, who had crossed the trail from his ambush post on the other side, tried to grab Taylor by the collar of his jungle fatigues and drew back a handful of blood.

"Shit, Doc. Taylor's hit too!"

The big soldier flopped down in the mud and rolled Chris across his ample lap. The Doc hurried over and snapped on a red-lensed flashlight.

"You caught some frag in the neck, Taylor. Nothing to worry about." The medic snatched another morphine syrette from his kit, broke the seal and squeezed the pain-killer into Chris's bicep. The sting of the needle made Chris start and he tried again to tell the truth.

"Sergeant Barnes . . . I . . . I wasn't asleep. It was Junior's shift. . . . I woke up and saw . . ."

Worrying now about shock, Doc Gomez interrupted the narrative. "Self-preservation's the first law of nature, man. You got to learn to work your shit, Taylor." He applied a field dressing and turned to Big Harold. "Keep him sittin' up, man. I think he's gettin' shocky on us."

Tex began to moan loudly again and Harold wrapped his huge paws around Taylor's ears. "Don't you worry none now, Taylor. Barnes done gone to call a Dust-Off bird and Elias scoutin' an LZ. We get you out of here raht shortly."

Taylor stared at the black face above his eyes and tried to convince himself he wasn't dying. Big Harold seemed to be getting farther and farther away. "Do you . . . do you know when you're gonna die, Harold? Does it feel like everything's gonna be fine . . . and then . . ."

"Don't you be takin' on like that now, Taylor. Everythin' *is* gonna be fine. You be gettin' outa the field, man. Three hot meals and clean sheets . . . and them white nurses be givin' you blowjobs if you pay 'em enough. I heard dat from a dude come back from the 95th Ee-vack las' month. You just save yo' strength, Taylor my man."

Junior felt he was losing the edge of protection provided by righteous anger to sympathy for the wounded man. He heard Barnes returning from calling the medevac and decided to reinforce his position. "Don't babytalk the dude, Harold. The cocksucker fell asleep, man. He let them gooks walk right up on us. He didn't do shit."

Barnes burst into the circle. His voice had an icy edge. "Knock this shit off. Elias found a paddy we can use for an LZ about a hundred meters over there on the right, behind that Buddha. You people police up your ammo and frags and get the wounded over there. Chopper'll be here in about two-zero mikes."

Tex began to wail again as Sanderson and Bunny moved to pick him up for the hump to the chosen LZ. The keening seemed to trigger something in Barnes that had been pent up during the firefight. He grabbed the wounded man, wrapping his entire jaw in a tight grip and bent to put his face only inches from the man's incredulous eyes. It looked for a moment as though he intended to kiss Tex on the mouth.

"Take the pain," he hissed and let his voice swell to an evil growl. "You just shut the fuck up and *take the pain*!"

Releasing his hold on a shocked and silent Tex, Barnes stood and addressed his remaining men. The calm had returned to his voice. "O'Neill, you start movin' 'em over to that LZ and send Elias back here to me. Bunny, you and Rhah check out the gook bodies. Junior, you go on with Doc and carry Gardner to the LZ."

Junior already felt overburdened by having to carry the machine gun that Tex could no longer handle. "Bullshit, man! Let Taylor carry his white ass. He the dude that got him fucked up in the first place. Who'd be humpin' that KIA out if'n it was a brothuh got kilt?"

King loomed up in the darkness beside Junior and cut him short by slapping him in the chest with a folded poncho. "Seem to me it don' mattuh what color he is now, Junior. Seem to me he done paid his dues and qualified to become a brothuh."

Bunny had just stripped a bloody NVA belt off a gook killed by someone's Claymore. He was fondling the prized souvenir and critically measuring the mangled corpse with his pale eyes.

"That ain't no NVA, man. That's a chink, Rhah. Look at the size of that cocksucker. He's six and a half feet tall. Look at his gear, man. That shit's as good as ours."

Rhah was busy digging through the man's bloody rucksack. "Ain't no Chink, man. Just some dumb NVA grunt got caught in the struggle between love and hate." He dangled bloody hands in front of Bunny's face. The two words were crudely tattooed on the knuckles of his hands. Bunny didn't attempt to look. He'd seen them before . . . and heard Rhah's deranged rap about why they were there.

"Let's get the fuck outa here, man. Ain't nothin' in that pack 'cept fish-heads and rice."

Rhah kept digging until he found what he'd been looking for when he started checking the bodies left in the wake of the ambush. There had been only four and it wasn't until he checked the last man that he found the stash of Cambodian Red. The strong dope would be catalyst for a good party when he got back to his domain in the Underworld.

Elias found Barnes standing in concentration over a wounded gook near the archway. He'd walked into the ambush area on the trail the gooks had used and found no other bodies. Barnes paid no attention as Elias approached. He was poking the gut-shot enemy soldier with the muzzle of his rifle. The squad leader stopped and raised his weapon when he saw the wounded NVA open his eyes and stare up at the platoon sergeant. The man made small grunting noises as though he was asking for help.

Staff Sergeant Barnes stared intently into the wounded enemy's dark eyes. Somewhere in there might be a secret he could use. The NVA had been around awhile. Barnes could tell from the condition of his uniform and the sleek, no-nonsense cut of the equipment stripped to bare essentials. Maybe the man was one of the long-service NVA bush vets who regularly guided fresh troops across from Cambodia and into the fight.

"C'mon, gook," he whispered. "Sharpen my edge before you die." The NVA seemed to be an older man, not one of the baby-faced teenagers Barnes had encountered when he'd first come to Vietnam. He whispered again and prodded the casualty with the muzzle of his rifle. "It's gotten to be big time now, ain't it, old sarge? We ain't fuckin' around no more, are we?"

Barnes growled and remembered a time down in War

Zone C when his entire world had changed. Had this gook been around when he graduated from simple soldier doing a job to a man with a mission?

"Did you train that slopeheaded sonofabitch that shot me in the face?" Barnes raised his rifle and remembered a time when he'd been wounded and lay bleeding to death on the edge of a rice paddy. All the other soldiers in his squad had died within seconds when the VC unit popped the ambush. He remembered the mad eyes of the grinning kid in black pajamas who had checked the bodies, cut off Barnes's boots and jolted in fear when he discovered one big American was still alive.

"You should have taught him to shoot straighter." Barnes sighted over the barrel of his M-16 and brought the front sight to rest on a spot just above the wounded man's left eyebrow. He remembered staring into the muzzle of the VC's M-1 carbine that terrible day in War Zone C and thinking he was going to die before he could really begin his Army career. "Your boy tried to finish me off . . . but he fucked it up, sarge." Barnes shifted his aim from the point where he'd been shot by the VC over to the center of the NVA's forehead.

"Ah won't fuck it up," he whispered. "You won't have to wear no mask through the rest of your life. You won't have to fret over them kids or fight no more."

Barnes fired twice into the man's head, stared for a moment longer and then turned to face down the trail. He recognized Elias and walked to join him.

"Why'd you do that, Barnes?"

"You know we ain't got time for no fuckin' prisoners, Elias."

"No. I mean why'd you keep pokin' at him? Why

not just shoot the sonofabitch where he lay and be done with it?"

"Wanted that bastard to see me first."

Elias was about to pursue the matter but he heard the distant clatter of an inbound Huey.

"Bird's on the way. We better get on over to the LZ."

"You check out the area?"

"Yeah. Blood trails keep going on down there. But no bodies."

"Now how the fuck did they get away like that? We shoulda got a lot more of 'em."

"Yeah, well. They're hard-core NVA, Barnes. They returned fire as soon as we lit 'em up and then unassed the area. Can't say they didn't have their shit together."

"No, I cain't. But it don't mean nothin'. Hard-core or raggedy-ass rice farmer, they all die the same in the end."

Barnes and Elias found a sodden, sorrowful group clustered around the prone figures of Tex and Gardner. Both men were lying on ponchos, but the fabric beneath the dead man had been pulled over his face. That did not keep Chris from staring down at him as he hung dazedly onto Big Harold's frame.

While the chopper and its gunship escort made precautionary passes over the rice paddy to get bearings before attempting a landing in the dark, Barnes pushed and shoved at the troopers, molding them into a loose line for easy loading. As he passed Gardner's lifeless form, he nudged it with his muddy jungle boot.

"Y'all take a good look at this lump of shit. Remember what it looks like. You fuck up in a firefight and ah guaran-goddamn-tee you a trip out of the bush . . . *in a body bag*! Out here, assholes, you keep your shit wired tight at all times!''

He paused before Chris and glared directly into the new man's heavy eyes. ''That goes double for you, shit-fer-brains. You don't sleep on no fuckin' ambush!''

The Dust-Off chopper settled noisily into the rice paddy and several men moved to pick up the platoon's casualties. Barnes raised his voice against the roar of the engine and blades.

''Be advised, the next sumbitch ah catch coppin' *z*s in the bush, ah'm personally gonna take an interest in seein' him suffer. Ah shit you not!''

Chris was being dragged across the paddy by Big Harold but he turned to catch Barnes's attention. A slow burn was eating away at his intense embarrassment. ''I didn't fall asleep, Sergeant. It was Junior . . . he . . .''

Sergeant O'Neill loomed into his line of sight headed for the helicopter at a fast trot. ''Excuses are like assholes, Taylor. Everybody's got one.''

Chris started to protest but Bunny cut him off with a hard shove. ''Shut your face, chicken-shit! You in big trouble, boy.''

There was gleeful anticipation in Bunny's eyes. Chris had seen it before on the face of a schoolyard snitch who ran for the teacher when he saw one of his playmates do something that would yield public punishment.

Fighting hard against the numbing effect of the morphine, Chris forced his legs to follow Big Harold through the rice paddy and toward the waiting helicopter. Anger coursed through his veins and helped counter the wooziness. Why am I pissed off at myself, he wondered vaguely. I should be pissed off at Junior. Where did that lying bastard get the idea he could blame me for his mistake? And what about Barnes? How could he look at the two of us and believe I'd fuck up and Junior wouldn't? It wasn't fair, goddamnit!

He didn't do anything so wrong, but Chris was now going to be blamed for the blown ambush, Gardner's death and Tex's wound. How could S. Sgt. Barnes say shit like that? The man was tough, but he was also a fine, experienced soldier. He should know better. He should know that Chris Taylor was trying hard to do his part and would never fall asleep on an ambush.

How many fucking wars did a man have to fight? He just wanted to remain anonymous and do his part but they seemed to be singling him out at every turn . . . and for all the wrong reasons. They were trying to fight the gooks . . . but they wound up fighting each other. Why? Why did you have men like Elias, King, Barnes and Big Harold on one side and assholes like Bunny, O'Neill and Junior on the other? Wasn't one fucking enemy enough?

Chris felt himself dumped roughly into the belly of the helicopter and remembered what he'd been thinking out there on the ambush site. I thought I had passed the initiation, he moaned inwardly. Now I'll have to do it all over again. Chris wanted to roll off the shuddering aircraft and disappear quietly into the jungle below. He would survive the wound, but the mortification of his failure to fight well in the first encounter with the enemy was much more painful and damaging. Why couldn't he have unstuck himself and reached the Claymore handles? Why couldn't he have fired when he first saw the enemy? Maybe Gardner would still be alive and Tex would not have been wounded.

For the first time in his life, Chris felt the full, agonizing impact of personal failure. Out here there are no make-ups for failed exams. In the bush, you take the test, pass or fail, live or die. If you fail to measure up, you live with that mark for the rest of your life. Chris drew his knees up to his chest and tried to hide.

The first helo had departed and a second landed to pick up the remaining members of the ambush party before Elias finally started across the paddy. He passed Barnes, who would be the last man to board. He paused and knelt briefly next to the platoon sergeant. Elias had seen hundreds of casualties during two tours in the Nam, but something about Gardner, the way the man died and the bewildered smile that had frozen on his face seemed extra pathetic.

"This thing with Gardner was a waste, Barnes. That man would be alive if he had had a few more days to learn something."

If Barnes even heard the comment over the clatter of rotor blades, he gave no indication.

5.

For lack of anything more productive to do while waiting for his release from Charlie Ward of the 95th Evacuation Hospital Annex at Cu Chi, Chris Taylor rattled the plastic vial containing the three pieces of ragged shrapnel the surgeon had dug out of his neck.

They didn't seem like much to cause the pain and stiffness he felt up and down his spine. The ache seemed to radiate from the top of his head to the small of his back. Chris touched the sterile dressing covering the wounds and wondered if two nights sleeping on clean sheets in air-conditioned comfort had been worth it. He thought there would surely be more, but the ward orderly who gave him this little bottle of souvenirs said they needed the space. Taylor would be picked up by someone from third of the 22nd this afternoon and taken to his unit for a week of "light duty" before returning to the field.

The normal calm of the ward was disturbed by the tromp of heavy boots in the hallway. Chris caught sight of two faces peering through the swinging doors that led to the ward. He was surprised to see Sergeant Elias and SP4 Johnny Lerner, the Army language school graduate who served as interpreter for the platoon.

"Damn, Taylor. Seems like I'm always picking you up from one place or another. Docs tell me you're being released in a couple of hours." Elias and Lerner parked themselves on the edge of Taylor's bed. He could smell the sweat and dirt competing with the antiseptic odor of the hospital.

"Hell, we thought you'd be here a few more days, man. Guess you won't be needin' this." Elias tossed a manila envelope onto Taylor's stomach and stood to leave. "I brought you one of them books you was humpin' your first time out in the bush . . . but you ain't got time to read now. I'll go check with the dispatcher to see about a ride for us back to Brigade."

Lerner seemed to bask in the air-conditioned comfort of the ward. "Legal says there ain't nothin' more I can do, Sarge. I'll hang out here until Taylor's ready to go."

Chris was happy for the company. Tex had been taken all the way back to Saigon and he knew no one else at the hospital. "What the hell you guys doing this far in the rear?"

Lerner chugged the entire contents of the metal water pitcher next to Taylor's bed, wiped his chin and grinned. "What a cluster-fuck, man. They pulled us out of the field the day after you got hit. I ain't no sooner off the chopper than I get a letter from my wife sayin' she wants a fuckin' divorce. What a bummer, man! If they don't get you in the bush, they get you in the rear."

Taylor hadn't even known Lerner was married. He didn't know what to say since he couldn't tell how

Lerner felt about the situation. Maybe if he changed the subject.

"Wow, man. That is a stone bummer. So, what's Elias doing back at Division?"

Lerner was toying with the vial of shrapnel from Chris's neck. "Well, dig it, man. I knew Elias had been through this divorce shit before, so I asked him what a guy can do when he's stuck over here in the Nam. He didn't know, but he's got a buddy in Division Legal, so he brought me in here to ask a few questions."

"Get any answers?"

"Well, I found out it ain't as simple as a 'Dear John,' wham-bam, thank you, ma'am. See, the dude at Legal told me they got a law that's been on the books since World War II or somethin'. Anyway, it's designed to protect a GI from having his morale fucked up while he's doin' his thing overseas. The nitty-gritty is that your wife can't shit-can you while you're in the Nam unless you sign a paper that says she can."

"You gonna sign?" A ward orderly arrived to tell Taylor he could collect his uniform and belongings to begin checking out of the hospital. Lerner stood and stretched, hoping some of the cool air would be absorbed into his skin and tired muscles.

"Think I'll just wait awhile, man. Who knows? I may get blown away and save all the paperwork."

Still unsure of Lerner's true feelings over the domestic crisis, Chris picked up the envelope Elias had left. The book was a collection of classic short stories given to Chris by his Grandma before he left for the Nam. But there was something else inside. Chris examined the blue, leather-covered box and then opened the lid.

Lying inside a velour frame was a Purple Heart Medal. Taylor recognized the heart-shape and the pur-

ple ribbon from which the decoration derived its name.
On the front was a golden bust of George Washington,
the general who had designed and authorized the medal
during the American Revolution, and on the back was
an inscription: "For Military Merit."

There was a note folded tightly inside the box and
Chris straightened it to study the loose scrawl.

"Taylor, take a close look at this thing. It's one of
mine. Purple Hearts are made out of plastic, but they
sure as hell ain't cheap! One is all you'll ever need.
Elias."

Lerner was looking over Taylor's shoulder to read
the note. "That Elias, man. He's somethin' else, ain't
he?"

"I don't know, man. It's hard to figure a guy wearin'
stripes. What's his story anyway?"

"Well, he ain't no Lifer. That's fer damn sure. Shit,
Elias smokes and jokes in the rear with all the troopers,
but he's been around, man."

"I heard he extended his tour. . . ."

"Extended's ass, man. Only ones I know with more
time in the Nam than Elias is Barnes and the fuckin'
ARVN. You ever seen that jacket he wears in the rear?
He earned them patches. He's been hooked up with the
173rd Airborne, the First Cav and the Big Red One
before he come up to us. That dude's seen some shit,
man. Been out here somethin' like two years."

"Jesus Christ! Why?"

"I heard him rappin' with some dude a long time
ago. He's from Oklahoma and he made a bunch of
money workin' in the oil fields. He splits from that shit
and winds up in L.A., see? He's trippin' around the
area and then he meets this actress broad. They get

married and he gets a job, but she's all into this psychedelic thing.

"She blows all his bread on gurus, LSD and shit like
that until she gets busted by the narcs. Then she cops a
plea and turns Elias in on a drug rap!"

"Oh, wow, man. Talk about a bummer. . . ."

"There it is. Anyway, Elias cops his own plea and
draws a reduced sentence or parole or some such shit.
Next thing you know, he's divorced and over here in
the Nam."

"But why the Army, man? And why Nam?"

"Hey, who the fuck knows, man? Maybe he's an
adrenaline junkie. You ever notice his hair and them
cheekbones. I figure Elias is more than a little Indian.
The dude moves in the bush like he was born there. I
figure it's what he likes to do more than anything else
that's available."

"How the fuck can anybody like this shit?"

Lerner shrugged and led Taylor out of the hospital
ward. "I talked to a guy one time just after he re-upped
for six years. I couldn't believe it, y'know? He said it
beat the shit out of working in a factory for the rest of
his life."

Before Lerner and Elias took the weapons carrier
they'd borrowed back to the motor pool, they dropped
Chris off near the Bravo Company CP. He squinted at
the sunlight reflecting off the corrugated tin roof of the
hardback hooches and decided he was home. Rounding
a stack of ready sandbags that marked the entrance to
second platoon's area, he caught sight of a familiar
face.

Pfc King was decked out in a cut-off jungle fatigue
shirt and wore a bright red bandanna around his fore-

head. The muscles in his huge arms rippled as he hefted a case of Budweiser beer. Sun glinted off his big gold tooth as he smiled a greeting at Taylor.

"Mah man! What's in the breeze, Taylor?"

King seemed genuinely happy to see him but Taylor was worried about his welcome. Would the platoon hold him responsible for Gardner's death and the loss of Tex? Was King a true barometer or was the big black soldier simply friendly to everyone?

"I'm okay, man. They let me out of the hospital and put me on light duty for a few days."

King shifted the case of beer into the crook of one massive elbow. "Ain't that a bitch? And here we is back in base camp anyway."

King seemed genuinely sorry that Chris would not be able to use his status as an escape from the field. Maybe he really was welcome back into the fold.

"What you got there, King Pin? Beer?"

"Aww, yeah. We fixin' to have us a little party tonight. Ah stole this shit from the Top's private supply. That dude always stealin' it from us anyways." King caught a flash of movement in his peripheral vision. He shifted the case to the front of his body and whispered.

"Chuck's comin, man. We better di-di."

Chris turned stiffly to follow King around a corner but a bark brought them up short. He recognized the broad accent of Sergeant O'Neill before he saw the man approaching with Corporal Sanderson, the grenadier.

"Hey, Taylor. You back among the living?"

"Uh, looks like it, Sergeant O'Neill." From the lop-sided grins on their faces, Taylor could tell both men had been drinking. He wanted very much to get drunk himself and wondered where they found the liquor. Sanderson, a tall dark-haired man with a sagging mouth and dull eyes, echoed O'Neill's Boston Irish accent. Chris supposed that was one reason the two were always seen together.

"Where'd you get that beer, King? The PX ain't open."

King broadened his smile and glanced at the beer as though it was the first time he noticed it under his arm. "Ah found this brew sittin' on some sandbags raht ovuh there, Sanderson."

"Found it, my ass. You goin' on report. Gimme that shit."

Sanderson grabbed the beer and O'Neill stepped in to grab both men by the elbows.

"You troops got enough time to drink beer, you got enough time to handle a little special job I got for you." He began to lead Taylor and King away from the line of hooches.

Chris waved a sheaf of orders at the NCO that he'd been given when he left the hospital. "I got light duty, Sarge. Doctor said to take it easy for a couple of days."

"That's tough shit, Taylor. But we got a cure for tough shit."

In the hot afternoon sun Chris Taylor stood studying the back wall of the small building which soldiers in this sector of the base camp visited when they had to shit. It was covered with scrawls left by men who wanted to immortalize some facet of their lives. There was always a name—either the writer's or his girl's—and a number indicating the amount of time left in the Nam. Chris tried to find a number larger than the days he had left, but nothing was close.

He shifted his gaze to a project undertaken by

Crawford, the blond Southern California surfer with the shark's tooth necklace who carried the radio in Elias's squad. Crawford had drawn an arrow pointing toward the hinged doors that gave access to the cut-down fifty-foot-gallon drums placed under each seat of the outhouse. Above the arrow he had written "LIFER LUNCHEONETTE" in large letters.

King arrived behind the shitter carrying two five-gallon cans of fuel oil just as a smiling soldier walked out of the facility buttoning his jungle fatigue trousers. He was sweating profusely and definitely not in the mood to appreciate Crawford's joke.

"Motha-fuckah! Mothah-fuckah, man! I'm too short to be dealin' with this shit!" It was the first time Chris had seen the black man wearing any other expression but a smile.

Slamming his burden to the ground, King began to help Crawford lift the hinged lids at the back of the shitter and haul out half-barrels full of human waste. Cringing at the smell, Chris followed behind and rolled an empty receptacle into each vacancy. Crawford and King trundled the heavy barrels to a large scorched area behind the shitter and began to pour fuel oil into each one.

"They keep fuckin' wit' us, man. They ain't never no let up. . . ."

Crawford picked up a broomstick and looked out over the dusty base camp while he stirred. "It's fuckin' politics, man. O'Neill's got his nose so far up Top's ass he gotta be Pinocchio."

King dropped a match into the first barrel and stood back against the roiling heat. He stared at the greasy smoke with a dreamy look in his dark eyes, as though he saw something more than burning shit.

Taylor and Crawford lit the remaining barrels and stood back to examine their handiwork. King fished in his pocket for a plastic cigarette case like the one most of them carried to keep their smokes dry in the bush.

"Man, forty-two and a wake-up and ah'm a gone mothah-fuckah. Back to the World!"

Crawford leaned his chin on the broomstick. "Don't half-step gettin' on that Freedom Bird, dude. I broke a hundred last week. You're lookin' at a double-digit midget, man. Ninety-two and a hook! DEROS April 17, man. California this summer. Surfin's gonna be goooooood!"

King was lost in his own mental images. "Dig it, man. March in Alabama. Sniff the pines. Sniff the cross-mounted pussy walkin' down by the river . . ." He shook his sweaty head as though the picture was too much to contemplate amid the choking fumes.

"What you got, Taylor? Lessee, three hundred and *what . . . ?*"

Chris looked away from the roiling black smoke and massaged the throb under the bandage on his neck. "Thirty-two. Three hundred and thirty-two days."

King and Crawford grabbed each other and shook with loud hoots.

"*Xin Loi*, mah boy!"

"There it is, dude. Sorry 'bout that. I can't even remember back when I was 3-3-2, man. Maybe you should count the other way, Taylor . . . like you got forty days *in* or something. Think positive, dude."

King disengaged and lit a C ration match to what looked like a hand-rolled cigarette. "Taylor, you talk like you educated. What the fuck you doin' ovuh heah?"

Taylor poked at the burning shit and showed a shy smile. He knew what was coming. "I volunteered."

King choked on smoke and passed the cigarette to Crawford. "Say what? Say again, Taylor."

"There it is. I dropped out of college, went to see the man and told him I wanted infantry, combat and the Nam."

Crawford exhaled loudly and giggled. Chris had watched him inhale smoke but nothing came out of his mouth.

"You volunteered for *this* shit, man?"

Chris stirred once more at a smoking can. If you couldn't talk straight with a man while burning shit, when *could* you say what was on your mind?

"You had to see it from my side. College didn't make much sense. I wasn't learning anything. And why should just the poor kids go to war while the college kids get away with it?"

King laughed loudly and turned to look at Crawford. "Ah b'lieve we got us a Crusader here, my man." Crawford just shook his head and sucked down another mouthful of smoke. King took the cigarette from his hand and turned to face Chris.

"Shit, Taylor. You gotta be rich in the first place to think like that. Evahbody knows the poor always bein' fucked over by the rich. Always have; always will."

Sweat from his scalp had leaked under the bandage on Taylor's neck and the raw wounds were stinging badly. He grimaced and massaged the area with his fingertips.

"You okay, man? That thing on yo neck botherin' you?"

"Nah. Just stings a little. . . ."

King profered the cigarette he'd been sharing with Crawford. It was sweaty, squashed and not very inviting. "Heah. Have some of this. You won't feel a thing after a few hits."

The comment confirmed what Chris had suspected. The smoke was grass. He'd heard a lot back on campus about how the troops in Nam smoked dope all the time. This was the first time he'd seen it. He suspected that was because no one trusted New Guys not to squeal to the Lifers. Still it didn't seem like a good idea to take a chance on losing control, even in the base camp.

"Nah . . . you guys go ahead. I'm not used to that shit. . . ."

Crawford smiled and giggled enough to extinguish the match he was holding to a new joint. "You better *get* used to it, dude. It's the only thing that kills the smell of the shit."

King tossed the old joint into a burning drum and took the new one from Crawford. "Go 'head on, man. What the fuck you got to lose? You here in the Nam now."

Chris stared at the sleepy smiles and decided King was right. This was here and this was now. Who the fuck knew what was going to happen tomorrow? He took the joint, sucked at it and swallowed the acrid smoke.

King and Crawford stood coaching from the sidelines. "There it is. Suck that shit down deep. That's it . . . now, let it out slow."

Chris contemplated for a moment. If the dope was having any effect on him, he couldn't identify it. "I don't feel it, man." He tried to pass the joint back.

King retrieved the joint and inhaled. "Dat's what dey all say."

Chris squinted and thought he saw something new in the faces staring at him through the smoke. You had to study the expressions carefully. There was a certain softness. Maybe it was the dope . . . or maybe there really was something beneath the iron exterior of these two men that would let them understand the painful embarrassment he felt over the ambush incident.

"You know that night we got hit . . . I . . ."

King raised a giant hand from the broomstick he was holding. "Fuck it. Don't mean nothin'. No such thing here as a coward. You done your best, man. Next time you'll do better."

Crawford displayed a stoned grin and waved a hand in front of his face. "History, man. History."

Chris was surprised at the response. Was that all there was to setting the record straight? He'd been psyched up, prepared to offer a full explanation of what happened that night. He let his aching shoulders sag and relaxed into a warm cushion of well-being.

"I think I'm starting to feel that stuff. . . ."

King chuckled and tossed the tiny joint into a can of burning shit. "You gettin' there, Taylor. Be cool now and I'll introduce you round to some of the heads."

"What are heads?"

It seemed a reasonable question but King and Crawford did not seem ready to answer. They turned and started back in the direction of second platoon's hooches. King merely waved a hand over his shoulder.

"Later."

By day, the sprawling Brigade base camp outside the Dau Tieng perimeter seemed to be slowly stagnating in a tropical stupor. Artillerymen from the Fire Support Battery covered their howitzers with ponchos and sat sweltering under canvas. Armor crewmen abandoned their vehicles when the sun made metal skins too hot to touch. Mostly they played cards or read mail from home down by the maintenance shed.

When the brigade's complement of grunts were in the base camp, they were generally allowed a certain degree of slack. They burned shitters and bussed ammo boxes when required, but they were mostly excused from the tedious donkey-work to rest and recover some of the equilibrium lost during weeks in the jungles. Showers and a messhall that served something resembling hot food helped a bit. Bunks, beer and sturdy bunkers against the occasional incoming mortar round or rocket did the rest.

By night, Brigade base camp came to life. Chris Taylor polished off the dregs in a rusty can of Carling's Black Label and stepped out to see if he could find some more.

As he strolled, feeling smugly superior to the rear-echelon denizens of the base camp, Chris breathed in the muggy night air and told himself everything was all right with his world. No one he'd encountered since his return from the hospital seemed to remember the foiled ambush, much less blame Chris for the casualties. Everyone seemed anxious to put that time in the past—consider it just one more day to be marked off a short-timer's calendar—and deal with the future. Those that did talk about the incident, people like Bunny, collected a crowd of REMFs and told boastful stories of their own combat prowess that were in total opposition to the facts.

He remembered the effect of Bunny's story on a fascinated group of artillerymen waiting in the chow line. "I seen this big Chink comin' around the flank, see? So I pops up in the middle of all this incomin' and I nails the cocksucker dead in the chest wit' a shotgun

slug. You shoulda seen it, man! I blew that motherfucker's spine right out his asshole. So the gook is
layin' there tryin' to suck air through the hole in his
chest. Shit, man. I thought about goin' up there, droppin'
my dick in the wound and gettin' a quick blowjob,
y'know?''

The artillerymen had been duly impressed. Bunny
felt like a big man. Chris felt slightly embarrassed by
his association with a teenager so clearly caught on the
cusp of the lunatic fringe. All soldiers are killers, he
supposed, but the opposite did not always hold true.

He paused by the side of an APC to stare at his face
reflected by lantern light from the polished aluminum
surface of a shaving mirror. A slightly altered Chris
Taylor stared back and he wondered if he was staring at
a killer or a soldier. He burned through two magazines
during the ambush but he certainly couldn't claim to
have killed anyone. He'd been wounded in the fighting
but that didn't automatically make you a good soldier,
not in comparison with men like Elias and Barnes.

So what was changed? What was different? On the
surface it was easy enough to spot. He was lean these
days, like a thoroughbred put through spring paces to
get rid of winter fat for the racing season. There were
hollows beneath his cheekbones and thick fingers of
muscle ran up his neck from his shoulders to just below
his ears. There were unusual lines around the corners of
his mouth . . . and his eyes. His eyes had narrowed
somehow. The soft roundness had been stretched into a
taut oval shape.

Chris stared in fascination at his eyes. I'm either
becoming a gook, he mused . . . or a grunt. It sounded
good to associate his own name with the term. I am a
grunt, he told his reflection, and I can take anything. A

grunt can take anything. Before it's over, he reassured himself, I'll be marked down in the same column with Sergeant Barnes and Sergeant Elias . . . good soldiers. Most people died without being able to say as much about themselves.

Chris walked on through the base camp basking in a glow of self-assurance. When it was all over, he could say he helped his country win a war. And he would help, by God. From now on, he could—and would—do it right.

In a dim pool of yellow light spilling through the screens of one of Bravo Two's hooches, Sgt. Leon Warren leaned his aching back against the cool metal wall of a ConEx box and stared up at an astounding blanket of blue-white stars. He removed the wooden cross that hung from his neck by a piece of surgical tubing and held it at arm's length before his eyes.

I'll see something like that one of these days up there in the sky, he thought, and then I'll know my Jesus is coming. For what seemed like the thousandth time since the day the Lord came into Warren's heart during a mortar attack down at Dong Tam, he wondered why God gave him such huge feet.

"How the fuck's a black man gonna play basketball when he's got size 16 feet," Warren mumbled. "It'd be different if I was seven feet tall, but ain't no coach gonna fool with no player only stands six-three and got to have special shoes made."

He'd thought maybe the problem of his outsized feet would keep him out of Vietnam when he'd been drafted, but the Army had no trouble coming up with size 16 jungle boots. Warren blamed his feet for his predicament and credited the Lord with his salvation. In between, there was the morphine he bought from a brother who was a medic over at the base camp dispensary. It was expensive but Warren had nothing else on which to spend his Army pay. In fact, Warren reckoned, he had nothing else to live for but God . . . and the morphine which brought you closer to Him.

Reaching into a uniform pocket, Warren produced a cloth roll and readied the reusable syringe he'd purchased from his friend the medic. He'd sterilized the works in a canteen cup of boiling water. It was enough of a risk shooting up around all the Lifers here in base camp. He didn't want to upset the odds by flirting with hepatitis. He nursed the needle into the soft seal covering the vial of morpine and examined the hypo for air bubbles.

He was wrapping the surgical tubing around his bicep to pop a vein when he saw someone approaching through the gloom. Whoever it was appeared to be coming from the direction of Brigade headquarters. Warren quickly stuffed the needle behind his back. The improvised tourniquet snapped loudly in the still air and the stranger altered his path to check on the noise.

Lt. Wolfe walked into the pool of light and recognized Sergeant Warren. "Good evening, Scrgcant."

Warren was scared to death the officer might want him to stand and salute. That would reveal the hypodermic . . . and probably send him to jail. Officers wouldn't understand it was God sent him morphine.

"Ev'nin', sir. They got some nice stars out tonight."

Wolfe glanced upward and then back down at his second squad sergeant. What the hell was wrong with Warren? The man's eyes were wide and white as though he was frightened . . . or excited. Jesus Christ, Wolfe had an errant thought. Had the man been sitting out

here masturbating? Well, no matter. He'd come down
here from the officers' area to be among the men; show
them how a good leader cares for his troops. Wolfe
certainly didn't intend to interfere with their private
fantasies.

"Yes, they . . . uh, they certainly did put some nice
stars out tonight. Goodnight, Sergeant Warren."

"Night, sir." Warren stared at the departing officer's
newly shined jungle boots. Eight-and-a-half tops, he
thought. Fuckin' officers.

Warren recovered his hypodermic, rewrapped his arm
and got closer to the Lord.

Bunny was having trouble with the yo-yo he'd bought
for a hundred pee at the Vietnamese souvenir stand
just outside the base camp perimeter. He could usually
do cat's-cradle and walk-the-dog but tonight the goddamn thing just laid there like . . .

He eyed Junior, flat on his back in the next bunk,
blowing smoke rings from a Kool at the tin roof of their
hooch.

. . . kinda like that lazy-assed fuckin' Junior. Bunny
giggled and coughed out a mammoth belch. When the
yo-yo failed to function after a final try, Bunny heaved
it across the hooch and kicked at the empty beer cans
lying around his bunk. The opener was around somewhere and he still had two six-packs to go before he
finished the case.

Junior swiveled his head to stare at the skinny white
boy from upstate New York. Duuuuumb-ass white boy,
he thought. Bunny looked like he should be playin' in a
sandbox instead of humpin' in the bush.

"Y'all might make that yo-yo work if you laid off
that beer."

"Bullshit, Junior, I been drinkin' this shit since I was a kid. I can handle the beer. You know what I can't handle?" Bunny staggered over to a tape player and turned up the volume on Merle Haggard.

Junior wrapped his camouflage poncho liner around his ears.

"Aww, man. Fuck dat redneck shit. All dem dudes be rappin' 'bout how dey losin' dey wimmen and dey ain't got no bread for beer an' shit. Fuck dat honky noise. I *got* to get me some Motown jams!"

Bunny returned to lean over Junior and breathe beer into the black, acne-scarred face. "I ast you if you knew what it was I couldn't stand, man."

From past experience Junior knew it was either hear Bunny out or have to fight him later in the evening. Bunny was a mean kid who became a vicious drunk. "What is it you cain't stand, man?"

"Them fuckin' hopheads, man. That's what I can't stand." Bunny reeled to his own bunk and opened another beer. "You ever smoke any of that shit, Junior?"

Using a guttering candle to light another Kool, Junior pointed a long black finger in the air. "Dat's white devil's poison. Y'all be tryin' to string the black man out and keep him down wit' dat nahcotics shit. Day be comin', my man, when de black man's gonna throw off dat yoke."

Bunny nodded and blew foam off the warm beer. "I can dig it, man. Smoke that shit and everything gets kinda weird, y'know? You hear that story 'bout how the gooks are puttin' chemicals in the grass so we become pacifists? You smoke enough of that shit and you don't wanna fight no more."

Junior blew out the candle and wished the country and western tape would break. "Don't pay it no mind,

Bunny. Ain't nobody makin' no pass-uh-fuss outa you.
You a stone killer man.''

Bunny still had a six-pack at his feet. "Yeah, but I
still like a piece of pussy once in a while. Man, there
ain't nothin' like a good piece of ass . . . 'cept maybe
the Indy 500.''

Groaning at the comparison Junior thought about
escaping to the shitter. "Bunny, you is *so* fucked up,
man.''

"I'm fucked up? You ever look in a mirror, man.
You're uglier than a dick on a dog, Junior.''

"Awww, man. Get up off my case. Here you sit
comparin' a car race with a piece of pussy. You probably think pussy come out the end of that shotgun you
carry.''

"Naw it don't, man. And I probably been laid a lot
more than you have.''

"Yeah. Uh-huh. And you stick you dick between her
knees thinkin' you home free.''

"Don't ast me fer none of this fuckin' beer, Junior.''

"Go to sleep, Bunny. The only way you be gettin'
any pussy is if some bitch die and will it to you.''

They'll be glad to see an officer down here checking
on them now that we're out of the bush and a little of
the strain has been eased. Lieutenant Wolfe reassured
himself as he pushed open the screen door of the hooch
and let his eyes adjust to the dim yellow lighting.

Doc Gomez and Tony Hoyt were playing some sort
of dice game on top of an old ammo box. From the
looks of the litter on the floor around them, the stakes
involved beer. Fu Sheng was picking at his rotting feet
and reading a letter. Rodriguez, the quiet, intense Mexican kid who hadn't said five words in the four months

Wolfe had known him lay on his bunk reading some religious tract. Candles burned in the personal altar the man had constructed from an ammo box.

The main action was clearly at the other end of the hooch where Barnes, O'Neill, Sanderson, Sal, Ace and Morehouse, a punk from somewhere near St. Louis, were locked in a poker game. Wolfe could tell Barnes had tied on a full load since the last time he'd seen the NCO at sundown.

The man's cold eyes sparked like icicles in the sun and there was a certain fleshy slack in his scarred face. Barnes looked almost hospitable, like a friendly host enjoying himself at a party with friends. Still there was that lurking sheen of tension under the man's rippling muscles. And Wolfe had long since decided Barnes had no friends.

He made his way down the middle aisle of the hooch, approaching the poker game with caution and recalling the time several months ago when he'd been on an inspection tour and had occasion to look in on Staff Sergeant Barnes's hooch. The man lived like a monk in some fanatic military order. The only personal belongings Wolfe had found were several bottles of Jack Daniel's whiskey and a year-old copy of *Reader's Digest*. When he'd picked the magazine up, it fell open to the "Humor in Uniform" page.

No one seemed to be showing much interest in the commissioned visitor. Wolfe decided it would be gracious to make the first overture and stopped by the foot of Rodriguez's bunk.

"That's a, uh . . . that's a nice altar you've got there, Rodriguez."

The wiry Mexican quickly crossed himself and Wolfe cringed, hoping he hadn't stupidly interrupted a prayer.

"Thank you, sir." Apparently Rodriguez was not inclined to continue the conversation. Wolfe heard O'Neill at his back launch into some raucous story about a time when he'd been stationed in Germany. They were between hands at the table. A good time to make his approach.

"You, uh . . . you need anything there, Rodriguez?" Wolfe began backing away, smiling into the soldier's confused stare.

"Ah, fine. Well, good. You, uh . . . you let me know if you do."

Wolfe watched Ace and Morehouse guzzle whiskey and chase it with beer before he pulled up an ammo box and scooted toward the table.

O'Neill cut his story short with some visible irritation and ignored Sanderson's correction of some pertinent facts. The card players had fallen silent to stare expectantly at the officer. Wolfe wished they'd just go ahead and play so he could watch for a while. It was as if they were waiting for him to issue an order. He considered it momentarily but "Carry on, men" seemed a bit much with Barnes and O'Neill in attendance. Casting about for something to say, he recalled that O'Neill had a nickname.

"How's it goin' tonight, Red?"

O'Neill jabbed a freckled finger at Barnes and shook his head. "This cocksucker's got all the cards tonight."

Wolfe eyed the stack of MPC and Vietnamese piastres near Barnes. "Looks like you're doing all right, Sergeant."

Barnes tried a grin and managed a sneer. "Shit, ah ain't even cheatin' yet."

Wolfe shifted his gaze to Sanderson. The man seemed unsure what to do with the bottle of Jim Beam he'd lifted halfway to his mouth. Checking the level, Sanderson decided there might be enough to allow for hospitality.

"How about a gust of Kentucky Windage, El-tee."

Wolfe gratefully accepted the bottle and took a small nip. He could feel Barnes's cold glare on his face. He turned to look and confirmed that the sneer had not softened into a smile.

"You wanna play a few hands, Lootenant?"

The lieutenant could think of nothing that would make him more uncomfortable just now. "Nah. I wouldn't want to get raped by you guys."

O'Neill tossed a one dollar MPC note onto the green GI blanket that served as a playing surface to restart the game.

"What the fuck you saving up to be, El-tee . . . Jewish?"

The laughter around the table seemed to provide an opportunity for a semidignified departure. Wolfe stood to take it.

"Got some stuff to do up around the CP. Catch you men later. Take it easy."

He hadn't turned a card but Lieutenant Wolfe felt he'd been raped anyway.

Shortly after Lieutenant Wolfe left the hooch, O'Neill raked in the pot from a quick hand of five-card stud. With the uninvolved hand he pressed his flickering zippo under Barnes's unlit cigarette.

"Sorry-ass motherfucker ain't he, Bob? You think he's gonna make it?"

Barnes inhaled cigarette smoke, belched and cocked an ear at the country music blaring through a radio tuned to the American Forces Vietnam Network in

Saigon. Uttering a grunt, Barnes made a small, almost imperceptible movement of his head and bent to pick up the hand he'd just been dealt.

O'Neill glanced around the table nodding. "See? That's what I figure. Some dudes you just look in their faces and *you know*, man. You *know* they ain't gonna make it."

Barnes laid a two dollar bet in the center of the table and stared directly into O'Neill's face.

Exhaling a cloud of smoke and watching O'Neill's twitchy eyes, Staff Sergeant Barnes wondered if the man could understand how right he was. You *could* see death in some people's eyes. If you ask me, he thought, ain't none of these fuckers gonna make it out of the Nam. That's what they all want—out of the Nam as soon as possible—but they ain't figured out the secret of survivin' yet.

That's what'll kill 'em. They don't understand you don't survive by runnin' and hidin'. You survive like I do. You look for them little yellow bastards and then you outfight 'em. You kill so many that they don't want to fight no more.

Barnes reached roughly for the whiskey bottle to help dull the thudding ache over his right eye. Ah carry a reminder of the truth around on mah face, he thought, blinking in anger at the rowdy card players around the table, but y'all shouldn't need nothin' like that to make you fight. Y'all should understand that politics, religion, principles and all that don't mean shit. You don't fight for them things. If you want to survive, you got to make it *personal*. You got to boil all that shit away like hog fat and get to the meat. It's you and some other asshole that's tryin' to kill you. First killer lives to kill another day. Why don't you dipshits understand that?

Robert Barnes knew he didn't have the words to tell his troops the truth. He hoped they would learn from his example and from guys like Elias who also seemed to understand.

But they never did. He sighed and picked up his cards. The throb had returned to the wound scar over his eye and whiskey wasn't going to help anymore tonight. They never learn and they never change, Barnes thought. They been sendin' the same brand of sorry-ass kid over here since 1964 when they sent me to Vietnam. And ah cain't do nothin' much to help. Ah cain't do nothin' much more than kill gooks for 'em and watch 'em die.

Fewer people seemed to be actively trying to rush themselves into total oblivion down by the old abandoned artillery site that now served the base camp as a quarry for sandbag dirt. Chris walked in that direction, torn between a desire for solitude and a concern for reinforcing his own situation in the platoon.

The sound of high falsetto singing backed by *a cappella* harmony caught his ear as it floated in the muggy air of the base camp. A group of blacks somewhere was trying to bring the Motown sound to the Land of the Lotus Eaters. Chris sat on a pile of empty sandbags and contemplated the birth of the blues. If nothing else, he thought, some genuinely original soul music should come out of this war. With the heavy preponderance of poor, uneducated blacks doing the fighting, it seemed inevitable.

A hundred years ago, their ancestors had sat in forced servitude, in difficult, dangerous situations, and sang themselves away from the pain and frustration. Chris was contemplating potential lyrics when he saw King swing onto the trail leading down to the old artillery site. After a few giant strides, he spotted Chris and his smile split the dark.

"Taylor? That you, man? Where the fuck you been? I been humpin' all over this AO looking fer yo ass, man. You ready to party hearty?"

King grabbed him by an elbow and they turned down a disused trail leading away from the artillery site. "They's an old ammo bunker them Redlegs never tore down ovah here, man. We calls it the Underworld. Lifers don' know nothin' 'bout it and we plan on keepin' it dat way, dig?"

King started humming loudly. His version of an Otis Redding original motivated someone to loom out of the dark. It was Manny, a mostly black Puerto Rican soldier who was said to be the best man in the platoon with a Blooper. Despite the inky dark, he and King perfectly executed a complicted, carefully-structured greeting ritual known as "the Dap." When the intricate series of grips, slaps, slides, glides and manual contortions had ended, Manny reported the area clear of Lifer hazard and King pulled Chris toward a poncho-covered entrance to what looked like the standard field artillery ammuntion bunker.

Inside was another world . . . the Underworld.

It took some time for Taylor's eyes to adjust to the hazy, dim atmosphere. The soft yellow light that illuminated the Underworld came from dozens of GI candles that flickered and flared haphazardly from practically every flat surface. Chris wanted to identify the faces staring up at him but he could concentrate on nothing but the surroundings. His mind said III Corps, Vietnam but his eyes insisted on Haight-Ashbury, San Francisco.

The denizens of the Underworld smiled silently and let Chris drink it all in. Stacked neatly in corners were the assembled contents of "care packages" from home. There were tins of crackers, boxes of cookies, canned meat and cheese from Stateside and cases of PX beer to wash it all down when the heads got a case of the Mojaves. Stateside posters featuring Janis Joplin and the Doors were pinned to the walls. There were two miniature Japanese refrigerators, a large electric fan and a sophisticated tape deck.

Chris shook his head and rubbed at his watering eyes. The air of the Underworld was one part oxygen and three parts dope smoke—either previously inhaled or about to be inhaled. There was no other way to breathe. Squinting in shock at the incredible scene, Taylor was able to discern about seven familiar faces. There was Lerner with his guitar, Crawford, Fu Sheng, Big Harold, Francis, Huffmeister, the kid from Milwaukee who carried Sergeant O'Neill's radio, and Flash, the bug-eyed black with the velvet skin who proudly proclaimed in British-accented English that he came from the U.S. Virgin Islands.

Chris was nearly certain of his identifications . . . except for the clothes. Despite their apparent harmony of purpose, the heads had clearly opted out of military sameness. Chris saw beads, bracelets, bangles and baubles on practically every part of practically every body. There were granny glasses in all tints, bandannas, broad belts and sashes. Uniform items had been cut, modified, crocheted, embroidered and emblazoned with all sorts of nonregulation accoutrements.

Some military items had even been adapted for unintended use by the heads of the Underworld. Chris watched Huffmeister take a huge drag from a bubbling hookah and breathe a gout of dope smoke inside an M-37 gas mask worn by Francis. He watched the man's wide, white eyes disappear behind the lenses of the mask until someone deep inside the mist called his name.

"What you doin' in the Underworld, Taylor?"

King pushed him forward to the center of the bunker and formally announced their arrival.

"This here ain't Taylor, dudes. Taylor been shot. This here is Chris and he been resurrected."

Taylor grinned weakly and looked up at the man who had called his name.

Rhah had shaved most of the bush beard except for a pointy goatee which gave his face an odd, lozenge shape. He wore a sleeveless denim jacket festooned with heavy chains. Tattoos of some esoteric, mystical significance covered both arms. Chris recognized the familiar Hell's Angels symbol on the right deltoid. The man's eyes were wide, red-rimmed and maniacal, and Chris found it hard to look at them. He was fascinated by a gaudy necklace that suspended two amulets on Rhah's sweaty chest. One was a white ivory cross and the other an ebony wood skull.

From his position in the Underworld, it was clear to Taylor that Rhah was the King of the Heads. He sat on a raised throne arrangement made from ammo boxes and the jump seat from an Armored Personnel Carrier. Rhah sucked smoke from a two-foot Montagnard pipe and repeated his question.

"What is the resurrected *Chris* doin' in the Underworld?"

"Uh . . . I, uh . . . I just came down with King and . . ."

Rhah didn't seem interested in the rest of the answer. He jabbed the stem of the brightly decorated pipe at Chris and exhaled smoke in a throaty growl. "Baaaa-aaaaaa!"

Chris grinned at what was apparently an in-house joke and wondered what to do next. He stared cross-eyed at the pipe stem.

"You lame Taylor?"

"What?"

"I ast if you was lame or somethin'."

King grasped the pipe and moved it closer to Taylor's mouth. "Go 'head on, man. Smoke it."

Chris drew a deep drag into his lungs. The effect of the virulent dope, laced with hashish oil, was immediate. He coughed, choked and grabbed a beer from Lerner's nearby hand in an effort to regain his breath.

Rhah chuckled and began to load another pipe. The Heads began to relax with the visitor and joints were passed around the circle. Chris coughed over another mouthful of dope smoke and drew the King's attention momentarily.

"You're shit's in the wind, troop. Baaaaaa!" The expression, delivereed in varying tones and tenors, seemed to be Rhah's utility comment on anything and everything.

At the foot of the throne, Lerner strummed his guitar and watched as Manny escorted Doc Gomez into the Underworld. The Doc accepted a joint and squatted on an empty ammo box. Lerner strummed a noisy dischord and stared up at Rhah with glazed eyes.

"Baaaaa back on you, man. Whyn't you learn to fuckin' express yourself?"

Rhah gazed over the assembled Heads with evil eyes. Flickering light from the candles made his dilated pupils seem yellow. He breathed deeply, leaned back in his throne and bellowed.

"Baaaaaaaaaaaaaaaaaaaaaaaaaaaaaaa!"

Doc shook his head at Chris and passed over a half-smoked joint. "I ought to have that fucker's brain pickled and take it back to med school with me in the fall."

Chris knew he'd not be able to carry on a rational conversation much longer. The dope was making him dream.

"You goin' back to school when you get out of here, Doc?"

"Yeah. I want to finish. Gonna be a gynecologist."

Manny looked up from his minute examination of a strand of multicolored beads. "What de fuck is dat?"

Francis removed his "grass mask" and volunteered the information in a disjointed monologue. "A gyna . . . a groina . . . dat's a fuckin' pussy doctor, man. Doc . . . Doc, he gonna be a snatch sniffin' specialist. Ain't dat right, Doc? You gonna be Doctor Feelgood, man."

The Underworld exploded in coughs and laughter. The Heads were getting into it now. Chris chortled somewhere deep in his chest wondering what the fuck was so funny about a gynecologist. Someone switched on the tape recorder and Chris began swaying his body in time to the sound of the Jefferson Airplane doing "White Rabbit": "Go ask Alice . . ."

He felt better than he had at any time since he came to the Nam. The dope smoke drove away the deep ache in his neck muscles where the doctor had probed to remove the shrapnel. He fetched the vial of fragments from his pocket, showed it to Lerner, who was strumming on his guitar, and then began to shake it like a maraca in time to the driving music.

Chris giggled and dribbled a mouthful of smoke into the cloying atmosphere. This is it, man. I'm at home in the hobo jungle of Vietnam. These are my *brothers*, man! What was it the King Pin said? Taylor's been shot. This here is Chris who has been resurrected. Oh, wow, man! That's heavy! He's right. What I was is dead and I'm a new thing now, man. I'm a soldier among these soldiers.

The tape segued into the Beatles' *Magical Mystery Tour*. Something about a walrus, man. Reminded him of Sergeant Barnes. He tried to concentrate on the lyrics. "I am you and you are me and we are they and we are all together . . ." There it is. We are all together and we are gonna make it, man!

And, you know, fuckin' Rhah seemed like a good head. Crazy as a fucking loon, man! Old addle-brained brother. Chris struggled to his feet, stepped unsteadily over the chanting crowd and approached the throne of the Underworld.

"Hey, Rhah . . . this is great, man! All the brothers here . . . and together . . . like . . . like . . ."

Rhah sucked noisily on his Montagnard pipe and eyed Chris from under heavy lids.

". . . I mean . . . it's soldiers here . . . and we're like brothers . . . and the good soldiers should be here with the brothers. . . . I mean, where's Barnes . . . and . . ."

Rhah leaned over to hiss in Taylor's face. "Barnes ain't nobody's brother, man."

Chris concentrated on the message he wanted to convey. It was hard to vocalize. "Hey, I mean he's a Lifer and all that shit . . . but he's one of us, y'know? I mean he's a damn good soldier, right? He may be a little fucked up and everything but he leads us and keeps us going. Right, Rhah? I mean you gotta respect that. . . ."

Reeling under a load of dope and euphoria, Chris crossed the dirt floor of the bunker and sat down next to Lerner. He became fascinated by the way the man's hands danced on the fretboard of the guitar. It was beautiful, man. Gator seemed to have eight . . . no, nine fingers on his left hand.

The evil snick of a weapon's bolt going home brought him out of a trance. Chris looked around and directly into a leer painted across the face of Elias. He'd apparently been off in a corner somewhere and he must have been doing something with the shotgun that was pointed directly at Taylor's face. Why would Elias want to blow him away? Chris felt himself suddenly getting very paranoid. The spider monkey chattering and clicking from his perch on Elias's shoulder didn't make the scene any easier to digest.

"I . . . I didn't do nothin', Sarge. . . ."

The grin widened and the monkey screeched. "Just put your mouth on that muzzle, Taylor." Elias poked the gaping business end of the shotgun toward Chris.

It was a matter of trust, Chris supposed. Either you were with 'em or you were against 'em. He cautiously pressed his lips against the cold muzzle of the weapon and blinked at the cheers from around the circle of heads.

Elias sucked smoke from his joint and blew it through the ejection port of the 12-gauge. The billowing cloud gathered momentum as it squeezed through the chamber and barrel and directly into Taylor's swelling lungs. Chris felt a warm flush from his armpits to the top of his skull. He closed his eyes and barely heard King's exclamation.

"Can you dig it? In one night mah man Chris be goin' from a little toke to shotgunnin' dope. Ah bleeve the man has arrived."

Elias scooted into a seat beside Chris and lifted his chin. "First time for you?"

"Yeah. First time for a lot of things these days."

"Well, the worm has definitely turned for you, Taylor."

"Feels pretty good. No pain in my neck. Feels good, man."

"Feelin' good's good enough."

Elias blew dope smoke into the chattering monkey's face and laughed as the animal tried to escape the fumes. He was distracted by Lerner playing chords for an impromptu rendition of "Tracks of My Tears" being handled by Manny, Francis and Big Harold.

"Hey, Lerner. How come you got that, 'Dear John,' man? Couldn't she wait?"

Lerner stopped his strumming, which did nothing to discourage the singers. "Nah, man. Intel I get from my buddies back on the block is that she sold me out for some lame-ass 4-F fucker."

"What'd you say your old lady's name was?"

Lerner stared at something in the distance. The dopers sensed a serious rap and stopped singing. Everyone seemed to be waiting, leaning forward to hear what Lerner had to say.

"Her name . . . her name . . . I swear to God, man . . . is Daisy Mae."

Francis rapped out a rhythm on his thighs. "Daisy Mae . . . ain't got no pain . . . wit' dem 4-F fuckers . . . and she pullin' a train."

Lerner sucked viciously on a joint while the other Heads cackled. "Fuck Daisy Mae and anybody who looks like her!"

Elias seemed to like the sound of the word. He leaned back against a wooden upright and closed his eyes.

"I fucked this chick while I was on R&R in Hawaii a while ago, man. She was clearly outasight! Looked like Grace Slick, man. I shit you not."

The Heads joined in the disjointed reverie as the mood impelled them. It was Elias's story but in his condition, they'd have to pry it out of him.

"Where'd you meet a stone fox like that, man? You find a high-class whorehouse down on Hotel Street?"

"What fuckin' whorehouse, man? I spotted her on the beach."

"Yeah, Elias. And you just scooted up and showed her your dick, right?"

"Naw, man. I just scoped her out real good. By this time my swimmin' suit looks lik an upright pup-tent, right? I got one of them blue-steel throbbers . . ."

"There it is, man. I know dat feelin'."

". . . so, I'm thinkin' to myself, Elias you walk away from this and you're gonna regret it for the rest of your life. So I go on up the beach after her. . . ."

The Heads were all locked into the story now, living it along with Elias. The expectant silence was broken only by the serpentine sucking noises of people hitting on joints.

"Well, what the fuck happened, Elias?"

"Well, she was picking up her kids. . . ."

"Uh oh, dat's dat!"

"No, dat ain't dat. . . ."

"Get outa here, Elias. No trooper on R&R don't score wit' no married chick in Hawaii, man."

"I did, man. We got it on like two dogs in heat."

Almost as a unit, the Heads groaned with imagined delight. They were not about to let the details slip away untold.

"Yeah, but what did she *do* to you, man?"

Elias let a hand fall to his crotch and widened his sleepy grin.

"What *didn't* she do, man? She fucked the living shit out of me. Beat on my chest and did it again."

Crawford broke the match he was using to try and light another joint. Even Rhah was lost in reverie.

"See, this chick was a cross breed. Chinese and Polish."

"And she as livin' in Hawaii, man?"

"She had long blond hair and almond-shaped eyes. . . ."

"Hey, man. I thought you said she had black hair."

"She had blond hair, man. And long, tan legs. She wore them leather sandals, y'know. With the thongs that wrapped around her calves and ran up to her knees. She put this sweet smellin' oil on her legs, man. It was great when she wrapped 'em around my face."

There was an extended, painful groan from the Heads . . . and then silence for several minutes.

Elias inhaled dope smoke, exhaled with sensuous pleasure and resumed his narrative. "Her name was . . ." He frowned in concentration, trying to hook a specific title to the passionate memories coursing through his brain. He tried to strike a mental match against the grass blackout. The Heads couldn't wait to name their fantasy.

"Was it Susan, man?" Elias deepened the furrows in his brow and shook his head. No, not Susan.

"Tamara?" He continued to roll his head from side to side. They hadn't hit it yet.

"Elizabeth?"

"Patty?"

"Inga?"

"Jennifer?"

"Connie?"

Elias sat up and snapped his fingers loudly.

"Dawn! Her fuckin' name was Dawn, man!"

Chris whispered it quietly, lovingly to himself. The air inside the Underworld was still for long moments.

They were out there, somewhere in the smoke and the energy created by desire and desperation. Somewhere in the mists of the Underworld were the women the Heads could not have. They looked just as the men imagined, wore whatever the men favored and were ready to do whatever the men wanted.

Maybe the noise kept them at bay . . . maybe if the Heads just ached in silence for a moment . . . the visions would materialize.

6.

Santa Claus and Staff Sergeant Barnes, the man who kept rotating him up on point with frightening regularity, had left Pfc Chris Taylor with a touch more self-confidence and field savvy for the trek into 1968. With the new year came new orders for Bravo Company, third of the Twenty-second Infantry. They were assigned to sweep a spooky range of jungle-covered hills dominated by an obscenely rugged peak known as the Black Virgin.

Somewhere in those hills, according to the intelligence officers whose speculations prodded the grunts into the bush, the entire 141st North Vietnamese Army Regiment was preparing for some unspecified major offensive. The intelligence officers wanted the specifics and thought perhaps Bravo Company could help.

Maybe they could, but Pfc Taylor didn't see how. All he could see as he climbed out of the waist-deep jungle stream was a rugged, rocky hillside covered by triple canopy jungle and split by babbling rivulets that fed the stream from the high-ground. As point-man, he'd have to select the route up that hill and into the jungle. He gave the signal to move forward and glanced around to note Sergeant Barnes and his RTO had moved up behind him. Probably checking to make sure I don't fuck it up, Chris thought, as he cautiously began to work his way up through the slippery rocks.

As he approached a fallen, rotting log that intersected the trail, Chris heard Barnes hiss through his teeth. As he'd learned to do, Taylor froze and dropped to one knee with his rifle at the ready. Barnes edged forward and jabbed the muzzle of his weapon at a spot to the right of the tree. He leaned toward Taylor's helmet and whispered.

"Bunker."

Chris stared and thought he saw palm logs arranged in an irregular shape. If it was a bunker, it must be unoccupied. They squatted less than twenty yards from the entrance.

Barnes pointed to a position on the left of the bunker which would allow Chris to see over the fallen tree and motioned for him to move. Trailed by Hoyt, the RTO, the platoon sergeant duck-walked forward and slipped inside the bunker. It was unoccupied, as were several others Chris began to discern. Dotting the clearing on a flat stretch of hillside were four or five bunkers and a thatch lean-to containing some sort of primitive machinery.

Barnes whispered for Chris to bring up the rest of the platoon and left Hoyt to cover him as he crept along a trenchline that ran like a large artery through the heart of the bunker complex.

It seemed as though they'd stumbled onto a ghost town, but the ghosts were not far away or long gone.

Freshly laundered NVA uniforms swayed in a slight breeze as they hung suspended from a jungle clothesline made from vines. Bulging NVA rucksacks were arranged in a neat squad formation and the smoke from a cooking fire curled up toward the ceiling of the jungle.

While Lieutenant Wolfe paused on the periphery of the clearing to notify the company commander of their find, the second platoon fanned out to get a firsthand look at how the other half lived.

Bunny probed cautiously at the heavy, six-foot bamboo rectangle, avoiding the sharpened bamboo spikes that jutted from the bottom. Like everyone else probing the bunker complex, he somehow felt compelled to speak in whispers.

"What the fuck is this thing?"

Sergeant Warren moved it with practiced ease to reveal yet another bunker entrance. "They call it a Malay Gate. I seen plenty of 'em down around Dong Tam when I was wit' the Fourth Division. They hang the fucker over a trail and rig it to a tripwire. When you break the wire, it falls and you get skewered by them spikes."

Bunny squeezed his slight frame through the bunker entrance after running a hand around it to feel for tripwires. The bunker was apparently an arms store. Bunny picked out stacks of AK-47 ammo, several RPD machine guns, piles of potato-masher-style ChiCom grenades and several of the thatch-woven NVA Claymore Mines. He was examining an RPG-2 rocket launcher when Warren called to him from ground level.

"Don't be messin' with that stuff, Bunny. They boobytraps a lot of it."

Bunny grinned and shook his head. It was like being

in a toy store and not having to buy anything. He fondled the cone-shaped warheads for the RPG and wondered how much he could carry out of here.

"Come on in, Warren. They got some great stuff in here, man. All kinds of weapons and neat shit!"

"Come on, Bunny. Barnes want us to check out dis other bunker over here."

"You check it, man. There's a tunnel entrance down here."

Using two bayonets as climbing spikes, Rhah clawed his way up a huge teak tree and pulled himself up onto a bamboo platform that sat in the fork. He extended his rifle down to King and the machine gunner pulled himself up to stand ten feet above the floor of the jungle.

Five tall urns shared the perch with them. Rhah cautiously lifted the cover of one and discovered uncooked rice. He began to dig around frantically in the rice with one of his knives.

King latched on to his wrist. "What the fuck you doin', man? You know they might have had time to boobytrap this shit."

Rhah jerked his hand away and resumed the search. "You ain't thinkin', King. If you was a gook trooper and you wanted to stash some extra fine dope where no one else would find it, where would you put it?"

King grinned and dug his huge paw into a pile of rice.

Barnes snapped a long length of green rope around Elias's waist and motioned for Hoyt to use the radio. While the squad sergeant rolled down his sleeves, borrowed Barnes's flashlight and checked the chamber on his .45 pistol, the RTO let the platoon commander know someone was headed underground to see what lay below the surface of the bunker complex.

"Bravo Two, two-five. Be advised Two Alpha Actual is headin' down at this time, over." Elias grinned up into Barnes's scarred face as he nosed toward the hole of a tunnel entrance.

"You gonna authorize an extra R&R for me if I hit the jackpot down here?"

Barnes grunted and wondered how any man could *like* crawling into dark, deadly holes. He wanted to kill gooks up where the world could watch but Elias . . . he seemed to love this kind of shit.

"You just make sure you don't hit anything else down there, Elias. You 'member how them fuckers used to trap them tunnels in the Ia Drang. The dinks ain't been gone long and they might have left some troops behind. They don't give up a place like this that easy."

Elias flashed his lop-sided grin and levered himself into the hole. "If I tug twice, you pull my ass out of here."

Ten feet into the musty tunnel, the roof rose to allow Elias breathing room. He could get to his feet and duck-walk through the muddy water that had collected on the floor of the tunnel. The flash revealed a dark corridor that seemed to stretch well beyond the beam of light.

Elias cautiously worked his way down the tunnel, sweeping away cobwebs and kicking at rats that scurried away from his boots. He held the light well to the left of his body. If a gook wanted to use it as an aiming point, the first round would likely pass wide and allow Elias to get off a return shot. His grin widened as he contemplated a one-on-one with the enemy in such tight quarters. Only the strongest survive shit like that, he thought.

A gust of cold air on Elias's sweaty face brought him up short and he noticed a flicker of yellow light that seemed to dance on the ceiling of the tunnel. Sweeping the beam of his flashlight upward he spotted a hole that might be an entrance to a chamber above him.

Snapping off his light and pausing to let his eyes adjust to the dark, Elias worked his way forward and carefully pulled his head and shoulders up into the light. The room was long, linear and intersected with dark green NVA jungle hammocks. Elias blinked in the yellow glow of lantern light and pulled the rest of his body up into the chamber. His eyes fell on a low table covered with blood-stained sheets. A wooden shelf above it held bottles of saline solution, glucose and plasma. Elias thought about the hundreds of blood-trails he'd seen leading away from countless firefights. They carry the wounded back to places like this, he thought.

Not too shabby, he whispered into the gloom, noticing the American parachute that lined the ceiling to prevent falling dirt, the shaft for forced-air ventilation from the surface and the bottles of medicine bearing labels in Chinese, Russian, German and English. Elias pocketed several samples, snapped on his flashlight and moved down the room toward another corridor that led out of the NVA hospital.

As a precaution measure, Elias flicked his light into each one of the hammocks, pointing the muzzle of his pistol wherever his eyes roamed. It was spooky, intense, like walking a tightrope over a pit full of hungry alligators. Elias thought it was one of the most intense highs imaginable. How the fuck you gonna go back to the World and punch a time clock after this, he wondered.

In the third hammock he checked, Elias found a dead NVA trooper riddled with festering shrapnel holes. From the size of the frag wounds, Elias determined the man had been wounded by a Claymore or an M-26 and brought here to die.

Probing into the second tunnel entrance with his light, Elias saw the ripple of dirty water and the beady eyes of swimming rats. It would be scary as hell crawling through that . . . and who knew what was on the other side of that mess? No one did. Unless he had the balls to find out. Elias grinned and edged forward into the slime.

The water was up to his neck before he felt the muddy surface beneath his feet begin to rise. He'd already decided to turn back if he came nose-to-nose with one more rat or if the water came over his head. My luck holds, he thought, remembering the time when he was a boy and his Navajo grandfather had marked his forehead with a special paint to bring him safely through dangerous situations.

He felt a single tug on the rope wrapped around his waist. Barnes was checking to see if he was okay. Elias gave a single tug in return and locked his eyes on a circle of light at the end of the tunnel. He could hear a hissing sound . . . like an unsquelched radio.

Elias sensed another human presence before he actually saw the NVA officer. He poked his head through the tunnel entrance and realized immediately he'd hit the jackpot. This was the CP! He spotted the source of the hiss from a powerful Soviet-style radio transceiver in the corner. The operator spun to face Elias with a look of shock registering on his face. Before the man could strip off his earphones and rise, Elias put two .45 caliber slugs into his chest.

The boom of the weapon in the underground chamber was nearly deafening.

Lieutenant Wolfe dragged his radio operator by the handset over to the tunnel entrance where Barnes and Hoyt sat minding Elias's lifeline. Barnes had heard the shots but didn't seem at all concerned.

"Ah 'spect Elias has found him a rat . . . or a gook down there, lootenant."

Tense as a bowstring in this eerie place, Wolfe found himself voicing his concern before he could stop himself.

"Shit, it's probably a gook. The cooking fires are still hot. They just left this place and Six is ordering us to stick around and get a full count of weapons and equipment. He's even sending some correspondent up with a camera. We're too damn vulnerable in here."

Barnes calmly lit a cigarette. "How 'bout the flanks, lootenant? You got anybody out on the flanks?"

Wolfe cursed himself for his tactical stupidity. They sat surrounded on all sides by dense jungle and he hadn't thought to put anyone out there on watch. The gooks could be sneaking back in to blow them away right now!

Catching sight of Taylor and Manny digging through the line of NVA rucksacks, he sought to correct the error. "Manny, get out there about thirty meters on the right flank. Taylor you cover the left side and let us know if you see or hear anything."

Wolfe walked toward the center of the bunker complex wishing Elias would surface so he could move out of this place.

•   •   •

Sanderson and Sal sat side by side in the broad, flat bunker puzzling over the posters and printed materials pinned to the walls. Sanderson recognized Ho Chi Minh's face on one of the placards and thought they must be in some sort of propaganda or political headquarters. Sal agreed and pointed at an antiquated mimeograph machine in a corner.

"Dat looks like the machine we used to print the number slips up on back in Newark." Sanderson was pawing through a pile of pamphlets printed in Vietnamese but containing line drawings of U.S. soldiers.

"Can you really make any money doin' that shit, man?"

"Yeah, shit yeah, Sandy. Sometimes you make two, three hundred a week . . . and you can shake down the winners if you got the muscle. Now let's get the fuck outa this place. This shit makes me nervous, man."

"Relax, Sal. It's just paper and shit. So, you gonna get me some of the action when we get outa the Nam, man?"

"I'll get you any fuckin' thing you want, man. Let's just get outa here in one piece. They boobytrap a lot of this shit."

There was a mean streak in Sanderson and he enjoyed seeing Sal, the tough-guy street hood, squirm. "Naw, man. We got to check this out. Look at all them papers over there in that ammo box. That looks like maps and shit."

Leaning uneasily against the vine-shrouded trunk of a tree on the left flank of the bunker complex, Chris felt a peal of thunder from his intestines. He thought it was likely prompted by the wild scallions Elias had given him that morning to go with the ham and motherfuckers.

He reached up and felt around the elastic camouflage band that ringed his helmet. The wad of toilet paper was still there.

He leaned his rifle against the tree in easy reach, dropped his trousers and squatted to relieve himself. It seemed like nerves always kept you bound up and straining. He'd have to relax. Chris shifted his gaze downward and studied the verdant floor of the jungle.

It looked like a vine at first. And then Chris spotted the regular bands of lime green, black and orange. Jesus God! Pit viper or krait! He couldn't match the image with the pictures he'd been shown in training, but he remembered the stories. "They call 'em two-step snakes," the instructor had laughed. "Cause you only take two steps after they bite you before you fall on your face, stone-ass dead!"

Chris stared in petrified horror as the serpent slithered steadily toward a spot between his legs. He couldn't make himself move and if the damn thing kept coming, it would brush right by his dick! What if the snake thought his dick was a mouse or some other form of prey and bit him. How the hell did you treat a snakebite on the dick?

But the snake didn't seem interested in Chris or his dick. Whatever it was that prompted him to leave his nest and disrupt the pressing bowel movement of an American soldier lay elsewhere in the jungle. The snake flicked a forked tongue to taste the air and made a looping left turn away from Chris.

He breathed deeply, stood on shaky legs and wondered if he'd ever shit again.

Out on the other flank, Manny stared at the tangled wall of greenery, decided he'd hear any gooks long before they saw him and dug in his pocket for a plastic bag containing three smokes he'd been told by a ten-year-old peddler in Cu Chi were genuine Thai Sticks. He sucked down a mouthful of velvety smoke, held it and smiled when the colors of the jungle became richer and developed a certain texture he'd not noticed at first.

Consulting the calendar he'd scrawled on his helmet cover, Manny decided he was getting close to becoming a double-digit midget. One hundred and four . . . maybe 102 days, man. And then he'd be back on the block. Fine threads in bright colors rather than this OD bull-shit. His kicks with the stacked heels and the pointy toes sharp enough to be dangerous in a fight. No more fuckin' jungle boots, man.

The hot night, the salsa music . . . and the juicy *Puertorequeñas*, man! Awww, man, how he wanted to bury himself in some *Puertorequeña*'s tits, man! Any of them would do: Marlena, Rosita, Lucinda, any of them, man. Manny groped at his crotch, unbuttoned his fly and began to massage his swollen member. It wouldn't take long, man.

But there was not enough time. Long before he felt the warmth of Lucinda's thighs, Manny felt the cold, painful nick of a razor-sharp blade beneath his left ear.

"Leave it alone willya, man! It's just gook shit!" Sal was trying hard to keep Sanderson from digging any farther through the ammo box full of maps and docu-ments. He didn't understand any of the writing on the papers, but Sanderson was dragging the search out for the pleasure of Sal's discomfort.

"Hey, tough-guy, lighten up. This is probably im-portant shit." Sanderson grabbed the ammo box by the handles and started to lift. "I'm gonna take this shit into S-2 when we get back and probably get me a fuckin' medal.''

Sal had seen enough important documents captured in the bush by unsuspecting grunts to realize Sanderson was probably right, but he wanted out of these spooky confines *now*. He told Sanderson where to shove his medal and stepped across the ammo box headed for the exit.

It was a tragic mistake.

In the headquarters chamber of the underground bunker complex, Elias felt the blast before he heard it. He stuffed maps and papers into his soggy pockets, unsnapped his lifeline and rushed for a tunnel that led to the surface.

He emerged dripping slime and blinked twice in the dim sunlight. Elias could see the black smoke rising toward the canopy and debris floating downward. Boobytrap! But who had kicked it?

From cover they had sought when the boobytrap had rocked the jungle clearing, Bravo Two grunts began moving toward the scene of the explosion. Barnes dropped the rope he'd been tending and bounded toward the smoking pit that had been a bunker. His mind barely registered the complete human arm, torn off at the shoulder, that lay in his path. A thin layer of chalky white ash and cordite was settling on the vegetation when Barnes reached the center of the clearing.

He watched in a black rage as Sanderson struggled up from the debris. Both arms had been blown off and the man was pumping geysers of his life's blood into the air with every beat of his heart. Barnes screamed for a medic and ran forward as Sanderson crumpled to the ground, his wide eyes staring up into the jungle canopy. Doc Gomez arrived but did not bother to step down into the ashen pit of the bunker.

Rhah pointed his rifle at a coal-black torso minus both legs. "This must be what's left of Sal. Boobytrap, Sarge. Must have been a big one."

Barnes did not seem to hear. He gazed intently into Sanderson's dead eyes as though he might be able to stare some life into the crushed form. Doc Gomez backed slowly away from the panting platoon sergeant. Something volatile was seething in Barnes. It was as if the man was about to heave . . . or explode.

Chris ran in from the left flank just in time to see Barnes leap into the smoking hole, kneel beside the dead man and scream out his rage.

"Goddamnit! Are you fucking kids ever gonna learn? Don't you understand how easy it is to die?"

Elias arrived to assess the situation and realized Barnes would be of no help until he got back in control. He spun on Lieutenant Wolfe who was babbling incoherently into a radio handset trying to describe what had happened to the company commander. Elias jerked the handset away from his mouth and stared into the man's frightened eyes.

"Tell Six we need engineers up here ASAP. This fuckin' place is crawlin' with boobytraps!" Elias turned to scan the frightened, pale faces of the second platoon soldiers. He caught O'Neill's slack-mouthed gaze and jerked his head toward the stunned group.

"Doc, get ponchos over the bodies. O'Neill, get 'em organized and let's get set to move out of here!"

The sound of authority in Elias's voice touched something ingrained in O'Neill. He snapped his mouth shut, shook his head and aimed a kick at the nearest trooper. "Spread it out! Stop millin' around, goddamnit! One round in here would get you all. Form up over on the right. Two Charlies on point!"

As the troopers sidled slowly out of the bunker area, Elias turned to Wolfe and found him consulting his map. He seemed to be searching for something with his finger. Ace, the RTO, informed Elias the engineers were on their way from the Company CP group to their rear.

Wolfe finally jabbed his finger at the map and stared at Elias. The man was fighting hard to control the tremble in his voice. "Six says there's a gook village about half a klik downriver from here. Battalion thinks the gooks may have headed for it when they left. They want us to move in and search it right now."

"Okay, lootenant. We got to get 'em back together now. Tell Gomez and two men for security to stay back here with the casualties until the engineers come up. I'll start 'em back down to the river. It'll be the fastest way to get to that ville."

Chris was headed out of the bunker complex to join Elias when he caught the glow of a cigarette in the ruins of the hole where Sal and Sanderson had died. He ducked down to look and stared almost directly into the twisted face of Staff Sergeant Barnes. The NCO was looking at him but did not seem to know he was there.

Pfc Taylor felt a cold chill under the glare of naked hate and rage that flowed from the man's eyes. He noticed a tic in the facial muscle near the round, puckered scar that dented Barnes's forehead.

More than three years, Barnes recalled, since the ambush that left me marked this way. But the real scars are inside where no one can see 'em. For four years now, the gooks been chippin' away at the muscle that keeps me goin'. The bastards been killin' my troops since ah put the first stripe on mah sleeves. And ah been allowin' it. Ah been lettin' it happen 'cause the fuckin' Army says I got to play by the rules. Well, ah believe it's time to change them rules.

Barnes felt his face soften. The pain nearly went away for a few seconds. That always happened when he thought of Nobuko, the Japanese woman he'd married while he was in the hospital at Camp Zama recovering from the head wound. Ugly and scarred up as he was, Barnes had been afraid to meet her parents. He'd thought it strange that neither she nor they had been put off by his face. And then he'd learned about the live-in couple; the aunt and uncle who had been at Hiroshima in August, 1945. You live every day with two distorted slugs like that, Barnes had decided, and a guy like me looks fairly normal.

But he wasn't normal. Barnes knew that and so did Nobuko. She did not cry when he'd left her with only an allotment from his Army pay and a promise to be back "when he was through fightin'."

Ah ain't through fightin' by a long stretch, Barnes told himself. In fact, you might say ah'm just fixin' to begin. This here platoon's a fightin' machine from now on and ah'm the head mechanic. You been fuckin' with mah machine, gooks, and now ah'm gonna feed you to it!

Barnes reached up to rub the scar and finally noticed Taylor watching him. His eyes flicked downward as though he was embarrassed to be caught in a private moment. Chris felt a strange wave of sympathy for the disfigured man.

"Uh, you okay, Sarge? Need some help?"

Taylor heard a rumble deep in Barnes's diaphragm. The cold eyes blinked once, twice.

"You gonna sit there and play with yourself, Taylor? Or you gonna be a part of my war?"

Before he could respond, Chris watched Barnes shiver and rise rigidly out of the ashes.

"Awright, saddle up. Pull them flanks in and let's get movin'!"

"I was out on the left, Sarge. Manny had the right flank."

"Well, where the fuck is he? Elias! O'Neill, Warren! You got everybody?"

Elias ducked back into the clearing. "We can't find Manny, Barnes. He's probably out there somewhere fuckin' off. Let me take Alpha and find his ass. We'll like up with you at the ville."

Barnes nodded and stormed toward the head of the formation. "You tell that sumbitch when you find him that he'll be burnin' shitters for the rest of his life. Move it out on point!"

None of the first squad troopers could know it, but the search for Manny in the dense jungle around the NVA bunker complex was a waste of their time.

Walking point for the main body of the platoon, King finally found Manny.

The platoon was strung out in a loose column, emerging from the cold, clear river and headed up a hillside to the village Lieutenant Wolfe had finally located on his map. King snaked his way around a rock formation toward a waterfall and then flashed the "hold" signal. The word was passed to the rear for the platoon commander to come forward. No one could tell what might prompt the shocked expression on King's face.

Lieutenant Wolfe and Barnes saw it at about the same time. No one thought to keep the remainder of the platoon from coming forward to look. They should have. Bravo Two was not ready for the sight after what happened to Sanderson and Sal.

Manny was trussed to a dead tree near the waterfall. His arms were bound behind him with U.S. military communications wire. But no one really noticed that detail. They were all staring at Manny's face. It appeared to have two mouths. One hung slack to reveal gold-capped teeth. The other gaped under his chin and drooled blood over his filthy uniform. Manny's throat— that instrument that had entertained his buddies during musical interludes in the Underworld—had been slashed from ear to ear.

Lieutenant Wolfe was in shock and speechless. Barnes grabbed his elbow and moved the officer away from the grisly scene. "Get yer shit together, lootenant. We can't stand around all day and stare at a dead man. Have him cut down and we'll hump the body into the ville."

The platoon commander seemed relieved to have some direction. It was all becoming too much to handle. How would he explain these losses to Captain Harris? He shouted the orders and the platoon began to slowly move toward high ground.

Barnes shoved King to the rear and led his RTO onto point. Hoyt heard the NCO's mumbled comment as he set a murderous pace up the hillside.

"That'll cost you, motherfuckers."

Hoyt was afraid to ask who and how much, although he had a strong suspicion he knew the answers.

7.

Halfway up the rugged hillside, Barnes and Hoyt broke a cart trail and, checking carefully for mines or boobytraps, they followed it toward the top of the rise. Wolfe's map indicated the village was in a flat spot along the military crest of the high-ground. Barnes suspected that was accurate. He could smell the camphorwood gooks used for cooking fires and a downhill breeze carried the scent of water-boo shit.

Barnes had stepped off the trail to take a leak and give the following troops, gasping to keep up with his withering pace, a chance to catch their breath, when Hoyt spotted the farmer.

"There's the top, Sarge. That old fart must be standin' on the edge of the ville up there."

Barnes stepped back onto the trail buttoning his fly and readjusting his web equipment. He glanced quickly back down the trail at the panting troops and noted he could clearly see the riverbank. Tail End Charlie was somebody from Warren's squad but no one was visible

down there. They must have all caught up by now. He
squinted up the hill where Hoyt indicated and saw the
back-lit silhouette of a gnarled and wizened Vietnamese
peasant. The man was resting on a hoe or rake with one
calloused foot draped over the implement. He looked
like some ancient flamingo.

Surely the old man could see the Americans approaching. Still, he made no move to bolt or warn
anyone else in the ville. Hoyt thought that was a good
omen and said so. Barnes called him a dipshit.

"Them fuckers got an act they ought to take to
Hollywood. Just 'cause they act like they ain't got
anything to hide don't mean they ain't got anything to
hide. Let's go."

Hoyt struggled up under the weight of his radio and
gave the hand signal down the trail. When they reached
the top, the old man still had not moved. They were on
the outskirts of the ville. Hoyt could see the tops of
hooches and hear Vietnamese women and kids babbling. Maybe the old guy was blind. Barnes was staring
directly into the farmer's rheumy eyes waiting for the
man to make some sort of move.

Finally, the old villager held up a knobby hand grip-
ping a handmade cigarette and popped it in his mouth to
hang from lips stained ruby-red from betel nut juice.
"He wants a light. Give him one, Tony."

Hoyt struck a match but had no chance to light the
man's mangled cigarette. Barnes bulled him out of the
way and snapped back the folding stock of the shorty
M-16 he carried. The weapon was in the NCO's shoulder before Tony could look down the line of fire and
see what the man was aiming for as he sighted downhill. He caught a blur of movement near the riverbank
about three hundred meters below them and made out a

Vietnamese in peasant garb running toward a second trail that led up the hillside in a different direction.

Barnes fired once, automatically adjusted for lead and then put two rounds between the running man's shoulder blades. Tony was impressed with the shot. Three hundred meters, downhill at a running target and he'd seen fabric fly when the bullets tore into the man's back. Fucker went down like a wet sandbag. Collapsing the stock with a satisfied grunt, Barnes told Hoyt to check the dead gook out and led Bravo Two into the village of Pham Xa Vi.

The villagers couldn't hear it over the cackle of hens and the grunt of pigs, but there was a time bomb ticking.

While the leading squads fanned out through the poor village full of thatch hooches reinforced with rusting tin and American C ration boxes, Bunny stomped off alone, idly working the piston action of his pump shotgun. There was something comforting in the oily snick of the weapon's bolt and Bunny needed that just now.

This fuckin' shit's beginning to piss me off, he thought. People ain't playin' fair around here. Bunny bashed the butt of his shotgun into a tall pottery water jar and grinned. Shards flew and water cascaded into the hard-packed clay of the village street. Sergeant Warren had made him leave the RPG rocket launcher in the bunker complex. What kind of shit was that? Bunny wanted to take that to the rear and have it in his hooch so he could show dudes when they came around rappin' about all the combat they seen.

Yeah, Bunny mused, these people been takin' too much shit off the gooks lately. We ought to be givin' it back in double doses. The fuckin' gooks would shit if he opened up on them with one of their own rockets someday. It would serve the sneaky fuckers right after what they did to Sanderson, Sal and Manny.

We don't fight like that, Bunny thought indignantly. You want to kill a fucker, you look him right in the eyes and blow his ass away. That's when Bunny spotted the snuffling pig tied to a stake near a hooch at one edge of the ville. He jacked a round into the chamber of his shotgun and shouted at the imaginary point-man whose life he was saving.

"Gook pig! Watch out!"

The heavy 12-gauge slug jolted the porker directly between his beady eyes and he collapsed in a twitching pile at Bunny's feet. Bunny grinned, ejected the spent shell and caught it before it hit the ground.

"Payback's a motherfucker."

O'Neill strolled toward the well that formed the centerpiece of Pham Xa Vi. He was not happy with the results of his reconnaissance. Spying Barnes on the radio near a muddy pigpen, he went to make a report.

"The ville stretches way to hell and gone over that way, Bob. We didn't see no young ones anywhere. All we seen is old men, women and kids. It's too much for two squads and the CP. Whyn't we wait until Elias gets here with Two Alpha?"

Barnes did not seem to hear. He stood staring, blinking out over the shimmering green rice paddies that supported the people of the ville. O'Neill didn't care for that one damn bit. Wherever Barnes was in his mind, the man needed to come back to the here and now. Something smelled about this ville above the pig shit and fermenting fish sauce. Barnes should be calling the shots.

"We gonna wait for Two Alpha, Bob?"

"We ain't waitin' fer shit. You and Warren have your people shake this ville down from top to bottom. Ah want you to turn this place upside down and inside out. Them fuckin' NVA been here. Ah kin feel it."

Barnes spotted the interpreter squatting, talking to a gaggle of kids, and shouted to get the show on the road. "Lerner! Get away from them kids. Find the head papa-san of this shit-hole and bring him to me."

Barnes was back in charge and his hard, flinty voice echoing around the ville carried the ominous ring of an avenging angel.

"You people get crackin'! Ah know these zipperheads been supportin' the NVA . . . but that shit has just come to a screechin' halt!"

It may have been the dizzying heat of the day, the irritating whine of Vietnamese peasants protesting their innocence, the stinging memory of mutilated buddies or any combination of those ingredients, but the grunts of second platoon fell to carrying out their orders with a particular vengeance.

The family bunker that served to protect the occupants of the hooch from marauders of all nationalities had been dug under a dirt mound and the entrance covered with round, woven baskets that the villagers used for winnowing rice. The deception didn't fool Barnes, who had seen it many times before.

"They're in there and we're gettin' 'em out." He motioned for Big Harold and Hoyt to back away from the bunker entrance and flipped away the rice baskets with the muzzle of his M-16. The high-pitched wailing in Vietnamese began immediately. Hoyt thought he could hear the platoon sergeant's teeth grinding as the man knelt to one side of the bunker entrance, out of the line of fire, and tried to peer inside the dark interior.

"Sounds like they'se just wimmen and kids, Sahge."

Barnes turned a cold glare on Big Harold. "Well, we ain't gonna know 'til we get 'em out, are we fat-ass?" The black soldier shrugged and went back to poking at the roof of the hooch with a bayonet fixed to the end of his rifle.

Hoyt was only mildly surprised when Barnes shouted in Vietnamese. Shit, the sarge was full of surprises these days.

"*La dai! La dai! Di, mao lin!* Come on you slab-sided cocksuckers, get up outa that bunker!"

The gabbling died down a bit at the sound of Vietnamese being spoken and Hoyt thought he saw movement inside the bunker. It wasn't enough for Barnes. He fired two rounds into the top of the dirt mound and was rewarded with a set of slim brown hands that appeared at the bunker's entrance, waving as if to ward off further shots. An emaciated Vietnamese woman emerged dragging two sobbing children.

"Harold, stop fuckin' with that hooch and take these zips down to Lerner in the pigpen. Tony, gimme a flashlight."

Barnes studied the interior of the bunker from an angle for a moment and then snapped off the light. "There's two more of them down there at least. Ah cain't tell what variety."

"How we gonna get 'em out, Sahge?"

"We ain't gonna get 'em out, Tony. You heard me tell them assholes to get up outa there. They don't wanna follow orders, they pay the price. Gimme yer willy-pete."

Hoyt shrugged and unclipped the cylindrical white

phosphorous hand grenade from his radio harness. While Barnes pulled the pin, Tony backed off from the bunker entrance to avoid the sizzling spears of phosphorous that would come flying out after the detonation. Once a piece of willy-pete got on your skin, there was no way to put it out. Unless you were able to smother it, the stuff burned right through to the bone.

Barnes tossed the grenade in the bunker and walked calmly away from the muted explosion and star-burst of phosphorous that shot out the entrance. He didn't seem to hear the animal wail of unspeakable pain that followed.

Parker had been about to ask Fu Sheng if his good-looking sister gave head when they found the arms cache. Both men had been waist-deep in a hole for about twenty minutes, struggling to hand heavy rice urns up to Ace, Lieutenant Wolfe, Sergeant Warren, Bunny and Morehouse. Each of the four-foot urns contained enough rice to feed the village for a week. It was too much, as was the resemblance between the urns they'd found in the village rice cache and the one they'd discovered at the NVA bunker complex.

Fu Sheng shouldered one of the urns, lifted it toward the surface and felt his foot break through wood at the bottom of the hole. Unstrapping e-tools they went to work on the false floor of the storage hole. Beneath a layer of bamboo and green plastic waterproofing, they found the first bundles. Yelping with glee, the men began handing up plastic-wrapped bundles containing AKs, SKS carbines, RPG launchers, Chinese light machine guns and bundles of fresh NVA uniforms.

Then they got to the heavy stuff. In a second layer, they found explosives, rocket rounds, mortar tubes and ammo and a disassembled heavy machine gun with anti-aircraft sights.

Lieutenant Wolfe felt sure this treasure trove would set him right with Captain Harris again and ordered Ace to construct a careful inventory. He reached for the handset to report their find as Sergeant Barnes stormed into the center of the village. The troopers backed away from the hole while Barnes calmly stepped around and over the huge pile of enemy weapons and ammunition. When the man stopped pacing and knelt to examine one of the machine guns, Sergeant Warren directed one of his outsized boots at a rice urn. The contents spilled with a hiss.

"And they had enough rice down there to feed a whole damn regiment!" Barnes rose angrily to his feet and located Huffmeister, who had been saddled with carrying C-4 demolition blocks and detonating chord.

"Rig this shit for demo. Warren, you put 'em back on it. Turn 'em loose! Ah want to know what else they got in this garbage pit! You hear me? Ah'm goin' down to the pigpen to see if Lerner's found the honcho."

Taylor's arms ached from jabbing and poking at things with the bayonet on the end of his rifle. Since the arms cache had been found and Sergeant O'Neill had discovered him sitting under a tree smoking a cigarette, he'd gone back and torn apart three of the hooches they'd already searched on the first sweep. The sun was making his head throb painfully and the angry cackling of the villagers was setting his teeth on edge.

Didn't these ignorant assholes understand they'd been caught with their pants down, for Christ's sake? The snivelling cocksuckers had been supporting the NVA and that meant they had a direct hand in killing Americans. Enough of this "poor rice farmer" bullshit, man!

Chris followed Francis into a rickety hooch, glad to

be out of the killer sun for a moment. The heat was boiling his brain under the steel helmet. It didn't look like the people who lived here had much to offer the NVA. There was a pile of sleeping mats in one corner and a dirt-mound Buddhist altar in the other. On the altar was a faded photograph of a young Vietnamese man. A small vase before the photo contained incense sticks that still smoldered.

The place was clearly unoccupied but Chris could hear Sergeant O'Neill outside yelling about checking everything thoroughly. He began to poke around the hooch with his rifle. Francis spotted a neat pile of baskets under the low structure the Vietnamese family used for cooking and motioned toward it. "That ain't right."

Chris poked his bayonet under the bottom basket and flipped the pile aside. He was staring into a tunnel entrance. There was a definite contrast of movement in the gloom. "You're right, man. There's somebody in there."

Francis moved to his side to take a look but Chris angrily shoved him aside. "I can do it, man! *La dai! La Dai!* Get the fuck up outa there!"

The anger and frustration he'd been feeling since they entered the ville came boiling to the surface from deep in his belly like a hot jet of vomit. These rice-eating bastards had been helping to kill good soldiers, his brothers! Chris remembered what three of his brothers had looked like in the past few hours when they died: Sal a mangled lump of charcoal; Sanderson, armless and bloodless like some obscene Venus de Milo, and Manny, viciously slashed across the gills and staring goggle-eyed in wounded shock. Soldiers shouldn't die like that, man. And assholes who helped make it happen should get a dose of their own poison.

Chris screamed again for the Vietnamese to come out of the bunker. Francis seemed surprised at the venom in his voice.

"Take it easy, man. They're scared."

"They're scared? They're fucking scared? What about me, man? I'm sick of this shit! I'm sick to death of it! They don't want us here! Who do you think they're fighting for? Huh?"

Chris swung the butt of his rifle and knocked the cooking platform across the hooch. There was no dignity earned or deserved in the kind of shit these gooks had been supporting. Weren't the NVA supposed to be the bad guys in this horror show? Wasn't the whole war supposed to be something about self-determination? These gooks didn't seem determined about anything except helping the NVA kill Americans in the most horrible ways possible. So why are we over here half-stepping around the area and looking out for their sorry-ass dignity?

"You people get the fuck up outa there or I'll waste your ass!"

Hands pressed before her in supplication, a wizened old woman with no teeth suspended from her purple gums crawled out of the hole. She was followed by a one-legged younger man who shakily rose on his remaining leg and retrieved a gnarled, homemade crutch from the hole. The cripple had a loose, unfocused grin on his face. Francis marked him as feeble-minded, probably inbred by some horny relative in the ville. Bunny bumped his shoulder as he moved forward to get a better look at Taylor's catch.

Chris was trembling with heat, but it was a different

sort of flush; not at all like the one he'd felt during his first days humping in the jungle. Bunny noticed the knot of muscle distorting Taylor's sweaty jaw and laughed.

"What you got here, Taylor? Looks like Ma and Pa Kettle. That's a real pair of greasy gook motherfuckers, man."

Taylor's rifle struck like a black serpent and caught the one-legged Vietnamese in the ribcage. He dropped with a grunt but quickly recovered his grin and began to stand.

"Why didn't you come up out of there, goddamnit? I didn't want to hurt you! Why didn't you come out when I called? Why don't you listen, you stupid shit?"

The cripple bobbed his head and widened the vacant grin. His mother wailed and tried to grab his arm.

"What the fuck is so funny, gook? What the hell are you laughing at? Huh?"

Chris seemed to have no control over his body. He couldn't stop the shaking and he couldn't stop the rifle as it came up into firing position. Bunny stepped aside and howled.

"Oh yeah, Taylor! Do 'em, man! Do them gook motherfuckers!"

Chris snorted hot air and tried to concentrate on the sights. He growled at the grinning Vietnamese face he could see centered on the front sight-post. He could feel the slack coming off the trigger and fought his rage to lower the muzzle.

"Dance, you one-legged motherfucker! Dance!"

Taylor stared over the rifle sights in amazement as his rounds kicked dirt in the area where the Vietnamese cripple's other foot should have been. The old woman moaned and collapsed on the dirt floor while her son hopped around like some insane toad. His heavy crutch made a drumming sound on the hard dirt floor of the hooch that could be heard long after Chris had stopped shooting.

The man seemed content to hop. His grin had faded into a look of resignation. The cripple was not angry, not resentful, not even fearful. He would dance for the Americans and then he would die.

But Taylor had lost interest. His bloodlust was expended when the bolt of his smoking M-16 slammed to the rear and caught on an empty magazine. He lowered the rifle along with his head and turned silently to leave. Bunny caught at his arm.

"You're chickenshit, Taylor Look at them fuckin' faces, man. See that? That's the way a gook laughs. They're laughin' at you, Taylor. You gonna let 'em get away with that, man?"

Chris was exhausted and confused. Jesus Christ, what's happened here? I had it all worked out, all rationalized, until I pulled the trigger. Now Francis is looking at me like I'm some kind of demented asshole. Why did I do that, man? He heard the old mama-san moaning *"Xin loi, Xin loi"* in a sobbing singsong voice.

"Yeah, you're real sorry ain't you, bitch?" Bunny advanced on the woman and muscled her son to the ground with his shotgun. "You fuckers are just cryin' your hearts out about Sal and Sanderson and Manny, ain't you? Look at this shit, Taylor. Their family is out in the bush blowin' us away and these two are laughing at us. I don't have to take that shit!"

Bunny cycled the action of his weapon viciously and raised it toward his shoulder. Sergeant O'Neill finally stepped out of the shadows near the door where he'd been resting and watching the other troops clear hooches. "Give it a rest, Bunny. We got better things to do."

Maybe O'Neill's comment registered and prompted Bunny to modify his action. Or maybe the muzzle end of the weapon simply seemed too impersonal. Bunny gave no indication as he deftly flipped the shotgun in the air and brought the butt savagely against the side of the cripple's head.

O'Neill winced as he heard a sound like someone thumping on a ripe watermelon. "Give it up, Bunny! This ain't what it's all about, man."

Bunny stood staring at the cripple's crushed skull. He grinned over his shoulder at Taylor who stood riveted by the grisly scene.

"Bunny, give it up, man! Stop now and we'll say the fucker tried to attack you or some shit. Stop, Bunny. That's a direct order, man!"

When Bunny made no response except to raise his shotgun again, O'Neill ducked out of the hooch and walked quickly away. He'd tried, goddamnit! Taylor could be a witness. He'd ordered that crazy fucker to stop.

Chris wanted to follow but his boots seemed to weigh a hundred pounds apiece. Bunny examined his work and decided a second stroke wouldn't be necessary.

"Hey, Taylor, man. Looka dat shit. You see his fucking head come apart? I never seen brains like that before, man."

Wailing in anguish, the old woman cradled the body of her dead son and began rocking back and forth. Bunny turned cold eyes on her tearful face.

"Bet the old bitch runs the whole show, man. She probably helped 'em cut Manny's throat. And she'd cut my balls off too, if she had half a chance. We shouldn't

give her that chance, Taylor. We should do her right
fuckin' now, man!''

He raised the butt end of the shotgun and smashed it
repeatedly into the old woman's face and chest. Her
wails turned to moans and then there was no sound in
the hooch except for the wet thud of the shotgun hitting
pulpy flesh. "Let's waste the whole fuckin' village. Let's
waste all these gook motherfuckers!''

In stunned silence, Chris watched Bunny at work and
wiped ineffectively at the gore which splattered onto his
face and uniform. Somewhere in a numb corner of his
brain, he knew O'Neill was right. This wasn't what it
was all about.

Bravo Two had herded twenty-five or thirty villagers
into the muddy pigpen. Three of the older men and two
middle-aged women had failed to produce identity papers and Lieutenant Wolfe had ordered them segre-
gated. Tubbs and Ace had roped them around the neck
and forced them into a squatting position. They'd be
questioned later after Barnes and Lerner got through
with the old papa-san who said he was the village chief.

When the old man arrived, in the company of his
chattering shrew of a wife and waving identity papers,
Barnes had seemed mildly amused. After fifteen minutes of sullen silence from the man and angry cackling
from his wife, Barnes got angry. Very angry.

He tore the ID papers from the man's hands and
threw them over his shoulder. He had Big Harold grab
the woman and hold her out of the way as he tore the
village chief's ragged black shirt down over the man's
shoulders. There were long, ugly scars on the man's
chest and back.

"Lerner, find out where he got them wounds.''

The interpreter asked the question, waited for the response and then turned to Barnes. "He says he got them in a bombing raid, Sarge." Hoyt laughed and moved forward to examine the scar tissue more closely.

"Bullshit, Sarge. At least one of them's a bullet wound. This fucker's a dink for sure."

Barnes paid no attention. His eyes were riveted on the village chief. "Ask him what those weapons are doing in his village."

Lerner was feeling more and more uncomfortable in this exchange. Barnes did not look at him when he asked a question and the old man did not take his eyes off Barnes when he answered. The chief seemed to be telling the truth. He didn't appear to be hiding anything.

"He says they had no choice, Sarge. The NVA killed the old honcho . . . the guy before him . . . when he refused to store their weapons. He says he didn't want to get killed, so he let them bury the stuff. He also says all that rice is theirs."

"Bullshit!" Barnes broke eye contact for the first time and slowly scanned the soldiers who had clustered around the pigpen. "Who was that gook we nailed on the riverbank?"

When he heard the question, the old man simply shrugged. "He says he doesn't know," Lerner translated. "He says the NVA haven't been around in a couple of months. Maybe it was one of their scouts or something. . . ."

With an angry growl, Barnes regained eye contact and leaned into the old man's frightened face. "Bullshit, pap-san! What about all that rice and them weapons? Who they for? Huh?" He didn't wait for Lerner to translate.

"This cocksucker knows what I'm sayin'. Don't you,

pop?'' Barnes did not react to the shouts from the assembled troopers. He held the village chief locked in a penetrating glare.

"Waste the fucker, Sarge. Then see who talks!"

"You bet yer ass he knows what yer sayin'!"

"The dipshit's lyin' through his teeth, Sarge."

The old man mumbled something and glanced furtively at Lerner.

"He says he doesn't know anything. He swears it, Sarge. He says he hates the NVA, but they come and go when they want and . . .''

The translation was interrupted by a shriek as the village chief's wife broke free from Big Harold's grasp. She shook her finger angrily at Barnes and began to shout.

"The old bitch is just goin' on, Sarge. She's pissed off about . . . I don't know, man. She says why are we shooting the pigs and hurting the women. They're just farmers. They got to make a living. Crap like that. . . .''

Barnes merely blinked. His rifle was in his shoulder before Lerner realized what he intended to do. The steel-jacketed M-16 round snapped the woman's head back violently and left her with an oozing black caste mark in the center of her forehead. The back of her skull was blown off and she collapsed backward into a pile of brain and gore.

Barnes calmly lowered the weapon and turned his gaze onto the startled and sobbing village chief. "Tell him he talks . . .'' Barnes made a sweeping motion toward the assembled villagers with the muzzle of his rifle, ". . . or ah'm gonna waste more of 'em."

Lerner found it tough to make himself heard over the high-pitched keening of the village chief who had his wife's bloody head in his hands. He turned his attention to several of the other villagers and elicited a gabble of negative response.

"They all swear they don't know anything, Sarge! Shit, I think they're tellin' the truth. I mean, these people can't refuse the fuckin' gooks when they . . ."

Hoyt and Ace interrupted. They raised their weapons and moved toward the cowering crowd of squatting peasants.

"Bullshit, Lerner. You speak that fuckin' gook talk and you startin' to act like a fuckin' gook. I say we waste all of these fuckers . . . one by one . . . until they tell us where the NVA are!"

"Yeah, let's go for it, Sarge. Let's waste this whole fuckin' gook ville. It's time for some payback!"

Doc Gomez began to back away from the pigpen and the infected jungle sores on the arm of the little girl he'd been treating. He bumped into Chris Taylor near the gate.

"Back off, Chris. I seen shit like this before, man. There ain't no controllin' it. They'll kill everyone, man. I've seen it happen."

Chris watched in horrified fascination. That's number three, he realized. I'm an accessory to three murders . . . I think. Barnes scooped up a pretty little six-year-old girl and clasped her squirming, screaming body to his side. The platoon sergeant unholstered his .45 pistol, cocked the hammer and held it to her head.

"Lerner! This is the old fart's little girl, right? You tell him he either tells me about them fuckin' NVA or I'll blow her brains out!"

Taylor winced at the painful prickly heat irritating his scalp under the webbing of his helmet. He understood that the snakes were loose now and the killing was about to begin in earnest. There was nothing he could

do to stop it. And maybe he shouldn't stop it. Maybe
Sergeant Barnes knew best how to obtain the information that would help them locate the NVA. Then they
could kill them to prevent more killing. In the stupefying
heat near the pigpen that day, it seemed somehow
reasonable.

On his way into the ville after meeting the engineers
back at the NVA bunker complex and failing to find
Manny out in the jungle, Elias realized it was dumb to
send second platoon into a village. Captain Harris should
have sent one of his other elements—one that hadn't
spent the past month in angry frustration or just lost two
of its members to a gook boobytrap. Bravo Two was in a
twisted, angry mood and Elias knew that could be
dangerous.

He'd seen it happen before . . . with the 196th up north
of where they were now, in some ville near the coast.
His unit had been mauled by mines and boobytraps.
Scattered sniper fire from a village in the area brought
on the killing rage. It had swept through the unit like
some obscene plague infecting everyone and driving
them to a wanton slaughter of men, women, kids and
animals. No VC had been found among the corpses and
the company commander had covered it all up with an
air strike.

Elias had almost left Vietnam shortly after that. He'd
had the first glimmerings that the Americans were going
about fighting the war all wrong. Yet there was something perverse in his nature that made him stay; convinced him he could do something about preventing
such errors and get the war—at least the people he led
into it—back on the right track.

There was nothing wrong or dishonorable about soldiers on any side fighting for a cause. That's the way it always had been and that's the way it would be long after Elias was gone. But there was a line you needed to walk, man. It was a thin line, especially in a war like the one in Vietnam, but you needed to walk it. Otherwise, you might as well call in the B-52s with the nukes and turn the whole fucking battlefield into one big parking lot.

He could almost feel the tension as he led his squad into the empty ville and quickened his pace when he saw the mob of soldiers and civilians down by the pigpen. Where was that asshole Lieutenant Wolfe . . . and why wasn't he doing something to control this? Elias bulled his way through the soldiers at the edge of the pen and spotted Barnes holding a pistol to the head of a screaming child. His eyes darted to the corpse of the Vietnamese woman and he realized someone would have to put the brakes on here . . . fast.

"Hold it, Barnes!"

The platoon sergeant turned an ugly glare on his first squad leader, but he put the girl down and allowed her to run screaming to her father.

Elias shoved his way forward to confront Barnes, carefully placing his body between the man and the child. "What the fuck are you doin', man?"

"You stay out of this, Elias. This ain't your show."

"And you ain't a fuckin' judge, jury and firin' squad, Barnes!"

"Ah'm warning you . . ." Elias could tell from the icy flecks in the man's eyes that there was no reasoning with Barnes. The man had gone over the edge into an area where violence was the only appropriate response.

Elias threw his rifle at Barnes and aimed a punch at the man's startled face. Barnes staggered backward un-

der the force of the blow and then recovered to land a
kick on Elias's hip. The two NCOs collapsed in a
shower of mud and angry blows. The platoon quickly
separated into two cheering sections. The majority wanted
Barnes to win so they could revenge themselves on the
villagers.

Ace, Lieutenant Wolfe's RTO, hooted when his officer tried to break up the fighting titans and was rewarded with a bloody nose from an errant punch. He
was laughing so hard he almost missed the radio call
from the company commander.

"Bravo Two, this is Six. Be advised, Recon has a
new fix on the NVA that unassed your bunker complex.
Bravo One and Bravo Three are following them at this
time. Get a solid count on the weapons and torch that
ville ASAP. There is an ARVN unit moving in your
direction. Meet them outside the ville and turn the villagers over to them. How copy? Over."

Factions from the Bravo Two ringsiders had managed
to separate Barnes and Elias. Both enraged men stood,
prevented from clashing by their seconds, and glared at
each other. Ace relayed the new orders to Lieutenant
Wolfe and the officer leaped on the chance to restore
order. He needed time to concoct a story for Captain
Harris that would convince the man they'd been justified
in killing the old woman. Elias was bound to report that.

"Awright, troopers, we move out of here in two-zero
mikes. Lerner, Taylor, Harold and Doc. You start moving these people out down by that rice paddy. We turn
'em over to the ARVN. The rest of you start torching
the hooches. We leave nothin' for the NVA."

Nguyen Thi Thai was just four days beyond her
fourteenth birthday when the Americans came to her

village. Since she considered herself old enough now to make personal decisions, she walked away from her mother and went to see what the sweating, white-faced ones wanted here. It would be good to have the foreigners leave so the people of Pham Xa could get on with their work. Her father was always speaking of his one trip to Saigon. Thai wanted to earn enough money to go there herself one day.

The smiles on the pale faces of the three Americans she encountered on the edge of the village seemed friendly, in an odd sort of way. One of them seemed very young, perhaps not much more than her own age. Thai greeted him politely and did not scream until one of the foreigners grabbed her, forced her to the ground and tore off her shirt.

Morehouse slapped a hand over the struggling girl's mouth and forced himself between her legs. He'd have to make it quick. Bunny, Hoyt and Junior were all waiting for their turn. It wasn't easy to maintain a hard-on with people watching, but the more this juicy little gook broad squirmed, the harder he got. He maneuvered himself downward, holding the girl still with the weight of his upper body, and made contact.

Morehouse closed his eyes and thought about the Chinese chicks he'd stuck it to on R&R. He ignored Hoyt's suggestion that they roll the girl over and take her up the ass.

"Shit, man. It's hard enough gettin' in this way. She's tighter'n a tick!"

Stumbling along a paddy dike, staggering away from the heat of burning bamboo and from the memories of Bunny in the hooch and Barnes in the pigpen, Chris felt sick and helpless. He clung to the vision of what Elias had done as a solitary float in a sea of madness. At least

Elias had pulled the plug before the full crackle of murderous rage could pulse through the platoon.

Still, it had been too little too late. Chris wanted out of the ville. Every turn he made to escape brought a new question. Bravo Two was losing control of their actions in this place. Even Elias was too busy trying to save civilians to provide guidance.

Should he care how gooks died? Should he give a shit if Bunny bashed in the heads of an old lady and her half-wit son? What difference did it make in the face of what happened out there in the bush?

Was he a real soldier now . . . or just an animal waiting for an opportunity—any opportunity—to tear out someone's throat? How far should it go . . . and how far should he go with it?

In his muddled state, Chris barely heard the sound from the other side of the slight rise to his right. It sounded like a struggle. He walked to the top of the high-ground hoping he would not discover another question with no apparent answer.

He spotted Bunny, Hoyt and Junior crouched in a tight circle. They were watching a pair of white, pimpled buttocks bounce up and down. Chris could see the muddy soles of jungle boots and a pair of green GI underwear shoved down around them. He heard a muffled scream and then noticed the slim, dirty legs that thrashed beneath the pistonlike movements of the buttocks.

He could watch the rape in stunned silence as he'd watched Bunny murder the two villagers. Or he could do something; take some responsibility for what was happening in this insane asylum as Elias had.

"Let her go! You hear me, assholes? I said let her go!" Chris ran forward, pointing his rifle at the stunned men, and kicked an angry Morehouse from his position between the sobbing Vietnamese girl's legs.

Morehouse reached to pull up his trousers, eyed the muzzle of the M-16 pointing at his bloody crotch and wondered why this scumbag couldn't have waited just ten seconds more.

"What the fuck's your problem, Taylor? Shit, it's just a gook broad."

Chris pulled the girl to her feet and swung the rifle to cover all four men. Clutching him desperately, Nguyen Thi Thai reached to pull her trousers up and wrap her torn shirt around her shaking shoulders.

Taylor eyed the expressions of mild surprise and amusement on the faces in front of him. They seemed like dogs wondering why the master was angry. They think *I'm nuts*, Taylor realized. They don't understand that they're the ones who are acting crazy. We can't just walk into this ville and kill people and rape little girls. No war . . . nothing justifies that. Don't they understand?

Chris backed away from the smirking troopers, covering them with his rifle and sheltering the Vietnamese girl. No, he decided as Bunny, Hoyt and Junior began to kid Morehouse about missing a nut, they don't understand. And they don't care.

Flame and smoke pumped into the muggy air over Pham Xa Vi. The searing heat from burning hooches turned the soldiers' exposed arms and faces red, but they hung in with the task of leveling the ville. King watched in amazement as Parker, the normally passive son of a Nebraska preacher, whooped and tossed a willy-peter grenade into the village well. Rodriguez was singing some song in Spanish as he tossed a frag into a rice storage bin and then poked a bamboo torch at the roof of a hooch.

They'd do a thorough job, King decided. They wouldn't need his help and he needed to get away from the heat. Taking a side path to avoid being caught by one of the NCOs and put to work, he spotted Rhah sprawled under a tree and sucking on a joint.

King flopped down beside him and reached for the smoke. He inhaled and felt the muscles in his neck relax. "Good shit, Rhah. Where you get it, man?"

Rhah reclaimed the joint and jabbed it at the blazing village. "While them fuckers was decidin' who to kill, I scouted around, man. Found this shit growin' in a garden plot. Them gooks should have stuck to growin' dope 'stead of hidin' stuff for the NVA, man."

"That was some heavy shit in there, man. Ah thought fo' sure Barnes was gonna waste that little kid."

Rhah grinned and held his fists up in front of King's eyes. "These two was fightin' for control in there, man. Love and Hate was both tryin' to control Barnes. Which one you think won?"

King retrieved the joint and inhaled deeply. "Who the fuck knows, man? Let's just do the dope. It beats the shit out of burnin' hooches."

"There it is, man. You got to fight a war, stoned is the way to be."

Bravo Two's troopers didn't turn back to look as they left Pham Xa Vi. Even when Huffmeister's huge demolition charge erupted to destroy the NVA weapons, no one looked back at the mushroom-shaped cloud rising over the village. They herded the villagers

across the muddy paddies toward a rendezvous with
the ARVN and wondered when the NVA would stand
and fight. It couldn't be long now. Both sides had
drawn blood.

8.

Captain Harris winced inwardly as Elias unfolded the story of death in the ville. Bravo Company didn't need this kind of trouble just now. Goddamnit, weren't there enough NVA out here to kill? Why did the troopers have to start blowing away villagers—guilt or not?

Elias finished recounting events in Pham Xa Vi and stood before the company commander defiantly, as if he were waiting for Harris to convene an immediate court-martial. The clatter of inbound re-supply choppers headed for their position provided a welcome break. Harris shouted for his field first sergeant.

"Top, we got birds inbound. I'm going down to the LZ and check on the re-supply. You get down to second platoon and tell Lieutenant Wolfe and Staff Sergeant Barnes I want to see 'em up at the CP. Elias, you come with me."

On the way to a huge bomb crater that served Bravo Company as an LZ, Harris spoke quietly to the squad leader. "You been over here longer than I have, Elias, so you know the score. It's a different war in 1968 than it was back in '64 or '65. Everybody knows the NVA are in it up to their assholes and the VC have long since faded back into the bushes. We're bein' forced to play it more like a conventional conflict now.

"People who help the enemy these days are making a conscious decision about which side they're on; not just lending a hand to some country cousin who's pissed off at Saigon. . . ."

"That ain't a license to kill women and kids out of hand, Captain. It was shit like that that made the ARVN such a gang of maggots. We step in and start doin' the same thing, where's it all gonna end?"

Harris wanted to tell Elias he'd often wondered the same thing, but the roar of two Hueys flaring into the LZ made further conversation impossible. He watched sweating troopers unload water, rations and ammo and thought about the Brigade Commander's briefing he'd attended just after the new year. He'd come away confused, unsure for the first time in his career of just how to lead his people.

In a speech full of football lockerroom analogies, the brigadier general had urged them all to compile an impressive bodycount in 1968 and let nothing stand in the way of accomplishing the mission. On the other hand, he said, we must be extremely careful about the welfare of the local people, especially with their Tet Lunar New Year celebration coming in February. He concluded by saying that MACV was becoming very concerned over reports of American field troops mistreating villagers. Verified cases would be dealt with severely.

So there it is, Captain Harris had thought as he walked away from the briefing and back to his line company, we've got to slap the shit out of 'em with one hand and pat 'em on the ass with the other. And if you get confused, we'll hand you *your* ass on a platter.

As he walked with Elias back toward his CP, Captain Harris spotted Wolfe and Barnes waiting for him on the edge of the LZ. Best defense is a good offense, he thought, as he noticed Wolfe pacing nervously like a man with a full bladder and no place to pee. Barnes seemed calm as usual but there was no mistaking the venom in the man's eyes as he spotted Elias. Harris glanced over his shoulder and noted a similar sentiment from the squad leader, who still bore a puffy lip and a bruise under one eye from the fight. Thank God someone stopped it or there would have been more KIA to report on this fucked up operation.

Harris sighed and stopped when he reached Lieutenant Wolfe. Why did they have to bring this to him now, just when he'd received new orders?

"Okay, Lieutenant Wolfe, what's your version of this incident in the ville?"

"I didn't see anything illegal, sir."

Elias gave the officer a disgusted look. "I sure as hell did!"

Wolfe's hairy eyebrows were working across his forehead like two angry caterpillars. "That dink woman was reported to me as confirmed NVA by Staff Sergeant Barnes, sir! I didn't actually see it, but I'm told she attacked him while he was interrogating a prisoner, sir."

Elias stared directly into Wolfe's eyes. "My report, sir, will indicate Lieutenant Wolfe was an eyewitness to the shooting."

Harris badly wanted a cup of coffee, a smoke and an end to this bullshit. He turned to Barnes and noted the look of calm on the man's disfigured face. Was it the mask of a murderer or the look of a professional NCO who knew exactly where he stood?

"Staff Sergeant Barnes, I want a full, written report on this incident from you as soon as we're out of the field."

Barnes allowed a small grin. H'ed been given some slack. "You got it, *Dai Uy*. And that report will include plenty of eyewitnesses who can testify to what really . . ."

Harris had heard enough for now. There was still a war to fight out here. He interrupted the platoon sergeant angrily.

"Not now, Sergeant Barnes. Later . . . in your report. We'll get into this completely when we get back to base camp. I'll promise all three of you one thing. If I find out there was an illegal killing in that ville, there *will* be a court-martial.

"Meanwhile, I need every man in the field. You people are going to stick together. You hear me? This is no time for fighting with each other! Barnes . . . Elias . . . you hear me?"

Both men locked on the company commander's eyes and nodded silently. It would be an uneasy truce at best, Harris realized, but at least they could get on with the mission. He thought both were professional enough to do that.

"All right, tomorrow we're going back into that bunker complex. This time we approach from the jungle side. S-2 thinks the gooks may try to get back in and reclaim what we left for 'em. First platoon will lead and you'll be on a flank. Get some rest and be back up here at the CP by 1800 for a briefing."

When the men from second platoon left his CP,

Captain Harris pulled out his message book and re-read the intelligence estimate he'd been provided by the battalion commander. The 141st NVA, including an independent heavy mortar company, had crossed the border from Cambodia in full force. They were headed toward the Saigon corridor and MACV wanted them stopped. There were only seven days left until the Tet Ceasefire period.

Maybe it'll all get sorted out in a week, Captain Harris thought as he heated water for C ration coffee. Maybe it won't make any difference who did what to who by that time.

Wolfe tried to leech confidence from Barnes's calm demeanor as they walked back to the platoon area. If an old soldier like Barnes wasn't worried about a court-martial, why should he sweat?

"We got it dicked, Sergeant Barnes. Elias can't prove a thing. He's a troublemaker, but he can't prove we did anything wrong."

Barnes sighed and shook his head. Where did they get these assholes? If Brigade or Division got a hair up their ass and decided to look closely into what happened in the ville, they could all wind up in LBJ. He'd have to make sure the platoon knew the score.

"They can't prove anything's wrong, lootenant, because we didn't do anything wrong. When it's wrong to blow away a dink, we playin' the wrong game. Elias is a waterwalker . . . like them fuckin' politicians in Washington. They want to fight this war with one hand tied around their balls. Ain't no time . . . or need . . . for a courtroom out here."

Wolfe gave his platoon sergeant an irritating pat on

the back as the man walked toward his hole. Sergeant O'Neill and Bunny were waiting there for him.

"How'd it go, Bob? Is there gonna be an investigation or something?" Barnes accepted a light from O'Neill and merely grunted.

Bunny laughed at what he presumed was a negative response. "Shit, man. There ain't gonna be nothin'. You worry too much, O'Neill."

Sergeant O'Neill lit the wrong end of his filter cigarette and began to worry even more.

On an edge of the company perimeter near the blackened berm of the bomb crater, Junior, Francis and Big Harold had hacked out a clearing and dug their foxhole. While Harold cooked a C ration meal for them, Francis and Junior filled sandbags. It was an unusual grouping. Francis normally dug in with another squad, but this night—with memories of what had happened to Manny and the events in the ville still strong in their minds—the Brothers sought kindred spirits.

Francis viciously packed a sandbag with the blade of his entrenching tool. "Dig it, bros. You got to understand this is the real thing. Manny's only the first. And that shit in the ville, man. That was a number one bummer. What Bunny and Barnes done, man . . . that could have been my mother."

Harold scraped a chunk of boned chicken onto a round C ration cracker. "I never seen nothin' like it, man. The way they killed Manny . . . shit, next week it might be one of us."

Junior snorted and lit a Kool. "Shit, Harold. You think these chucks give a fuck about you and me, man? We could have gotten crosswise wit' Barnes yestiddy and he'd of blowed us away too. And that Bunny, man, he a crazy mothah-fuckah. Dat dude scares me, man. He just fuckin' scares me."

Sergeant Warren had been out checking the holes on his section of the perimeter. He wandered into the conversation with a glazed look in his eyes and a vague smile on his black face.

"You dudes gettin' too hung up on that shit. Them gooks are a lot smarter than you think. Barnes knows his shit. They was NVA . . . every last one of them. You just gotta get on with it, brothers. You just gotta pray and get on with it. Barnes and the Lord . . . they taken care of you this far. They'll take care of you the rest of the way."

Junior threw down his e-tool and stared up into Warren's dead eyes. "Listen heah, man. Christians don't go 'round a village and cut off people's heads. This shit is definitely gettin' out of control . . . and it seem to me you too high on that shit you shoot to know the difference."

A flicker of light appeared in Warren's eyes. "It comes from a higher place, home-boy. It was God give me morphine."

Francis stood and stared into the dusk settling over the jungle. The night sounds were beginning to build. It would soon be hard to hear an enemy approaching through the bush.

"Ain't none of it right, brothers. Not the war . . . or the way we fightin' it."

On a slight rise above the platoon CP, Chris and Rhah were finishing a four-man fighting hole. Lerner and King sat on the edge cleaning weapons. Rhah paused to wipe sweat from his brow and then stood up on a pile of sandbags as though it was a pulpit. His hoarse growl brought work to a stop.

"I know Barnes seven, eight months now and I'll tell you somethin'. The man is *mean*. He's red in his soul like a dick on a dog."

King grinned and went back to reassembling his machine gun. "There it is. If they ever manage to kill Barnes, his jaws would just go on clackin'."

Chris recalled that he knew practically nothing about his platoon sergeant. "Where the hell's he from anyway?"

Rhah snorted and leered at Taylor. "You got it, man. Barnes's from hell!"

Lerner corrected the comment. "He's from Tennessee. Somewhere in the hill country. The place probably doesn't even have a name."

Rhah moved closer to Chris and jabbed a dirty finger dangerously close to his eye. "Barnes took a bullet right there. He was with an outfit in the Ia Drang Valley . . . and the cocksucker *survived*, man. That's some baaaaaaad shit! That's his high, dudes. Barnes is high on war!"

"He done a year in the hospital. While they workin' on his face, he married some Japanese woman. Nevah could figger out how a lady could wake up next to somethin' like that every mawnin' . . . anyway, first thing he does when they let him out, he re-ups in the Army and gets his ass sent back to the Nam. Don't know what happened to the Japanese lady, but Barnes been out heah four yeahs now . . ."

"And you know how many times he's been shot?" Rhah had a strange, glazed expression on his face as though he were about to reveal some magical mystery.

"Seven times, Taylor! Barnes been hit seven times, man."

Chris glanced from face to face searching for a mischievous smile. Surely they were kidding. No one survives being hit seven times . . . not even Barnes. There were no smiles.

"And he still wanted to come back to the field?"

Lerner giggled and lit a cigarette. "Does Howdy Doody have a wooden dick?"

Rhah could see no humor in the tale. "The Good Lord works his revenge in strange ways, man."

Slamming the feed cover on his machine gun, King said what they were all thinking. "There it is, man. And Barnes must be His revenge on us!"

Chris recalled the tic he'd seen near the bullet scar on Barnes's forehead. "Someone said he's got a metal plate in his skull. Is that straight?"

"You mean is he crazy?" Rhah coughed and spat phlegm into the mud. "Barnes ain't no crazier'n the rest of us been out here in the bush too long."

"Well, he ain't normal . . ." Lerner stood up and relieved Rhah of his e-tool. "That's for sure."

Rhah raised his right fist in front of Taylor's face and flexed the knuckles. The "HATE" tattoo wiggled into focus.

"That's what he is . . . and he's filled with it. He's out there roaming these jungles lookin' for little yellow devils to kill. You got to remember, the Devil does God's work too."

Lifting his left hand, Rhah displayed the "Love" inscription across his knuckles. "And this here's what Elias is. . . ."

Lerner lifted his eyebrows in an exasperated gesture

and shook his head at Chris. "Don't pay that no mind, Taylor. He's seen too many movies."

Rhah swung on him and squealed. "Baaaaaaaa! Rhah got no time for movies, man. Love and Hate too busy fightin' for possession of my soul."

Chris frowned in confusion. Both Elias and Barnes had seen more war than the average Cossack. How could they come through such similar experiences with such dissimilar results?

"You got to remember about Elias, man . . ." King lit a smoke and pondered for a moment. "He come over here runnin' from that actress chick in L.A. . . . the one that blew all his bread and then turned him in on a dope rap. When dat judge offer to reduce the sentence, that's when Elias skip over to the Nam. Now, Barnes, he been steady headin' for the Nam all his life."

"Okay . . . so why doesn't he go on home?"

"It's just that sometimes a man plain don't want to go back. Look heah, how you gonna talk to civilians, man? People back in the World, they don't give a shit. Y'know? To them you just a fuckin' animal."

"I was home on leave one time when my Dad died. . . ." Lerner seemed to be recalling a particularly upsetting period. ". . . and everybody back in the World is just concerned with makin' a buck, y'know? Everybody's out for themselves. They don't even want to talk about it, man. It's like the fucking Twilight Zone back there. You wouldn't even know there's a war on. My sister even asked me why I had to go back to the Nam . . . like I had a fuckin' choice or somethin'."

Rhah exploded back up onto his sandbag pulpit. "Baaaaa! Fuck it, man! They sold us out. So what? What did you expect? Civilian life is all phony bullshit.

They all robots, man. They watch their fuckin' television and they drive their fuckin' cars . . . and when they fuck up, nobody dies.

"It don't mean nothin', man. Civilians keep fuckin' up and politicians keep lyin'. None of that shit matters. You ain't gonna get no parade, man. No grunt in no war no time ever got no respect . . . til he was *dead*. And then it don't mean shit! You're fightin' for yourself, man. You're fightin' for your soul and dat's all. Remember dat!

"We all wrestlin' wit' dat angel, man. Love and Hate . . . the whole fuckin' shootin' match. Dat's the real war! That was the story then . . . that's the story now . . . and it ta ain't hardly gonna change."

King arched his eyebrows and grinned at Chris. Yeah, Chris thought reflecting the whimsical expression. There it is, I guess. Maybe Rhah has got it right. Maybe there is a sort of Biblical simplicity: Good versus Evil; Cain versus Abel. He shook his head and thought back to earlier times, back to school days when he could afford the luxury of deep contemplation.

Maybe it's like in Melville's great book, he thought, recalling a teacher who had stood at the front of the class and rattled on about metaphors. Chris had listened and supposed the Real World was not like that. Now he wondered. The world is pressing closer and I'm being forced—as Hemingway said—against my will into history. I'm dealing with the biggest stakes I've ever known: life and death.

Now maybe I understand what it really means, Chris thought. Maybe that English teacher was right. There is a Good and there is an Evil. And their forces—like great Atlantic waves—can roll you up inside them and twist you and turn you . . . and you'll never be the same again.

Somehow, Chris knew at that moment, his innocence—the aura of innocence anyway—had disappeared forever. It had faded when Bunny—at his instigation—crushed the skulls of the two villagers. And Chris knew whatever innocence was, it was something he would never get back. It saddened him.

It was not his turn on watch, but Chris could not force himself into badly needed sleep. Several times he'd nearly made it, but every time his mind started to switch off, the slide projector would click. Another frame from his recurring dream would appear and the concentration it took to focus on the image would keep him awake.

For the past week, Chris had been spending fitful nights staring at what looked like a platoon snapshot in his mind. With maddening regularity, the view would fade to black and then reappear. Each time it did, more of the familiar faces were missing. It was as if the platoon was melting away before his eyes.

Chris slipped out from under his poncho liner and stood, careful not to silhouette himself against the skyline. As he stretched and stared around the perimeter, he caught sight of Elias on watch outside his hole.

Flopping down next to the man, Chris offered to stand guard. "I can't sleep, man. Why don't you go ahead and sack out?"

"Can't sleep either . . ."

Chris followed the squad leader's gaze up toward the stars.

"Beautiful night . . ."

"Yeah. I love this place at night. The stars are so

clear, man. There's no right or wrong in 'em, y'know?
They're just there.''

Elias reluctantly pulled his eyes away from the stars
and stared at Chris. The kid was pensively studying the
sky but Elias knew his mind was elsewhere. He's caught
in the trap, Elias determined, studying the taut worry
lines creasing Taylor's forehead. He's thinking too much;
trying to figure out the modern American Army and
Vietnam.

The smart ones all want to solve the puzzle in a burst
of brilliant insight about the nature of man and the
inhumanity of war. That's bullshit. It's all so simple
. . . and all they have to do is look in a mirror to see it.
The worm has turned on Taylor. Now the damn thing is
twisted and convoluted and strangling him.

Chris sighed and relaxed against a tree root. ''Barnes
has got a real hard-on for you, doesn't he?''

''Barnes believes in what he's doing.''

''And you . . . ?''

''I did when I first came here . . . back in '65. Now?
I don't know. What happened today's just the beginning. We're gonna lose this war. . . .''

It seemed inconceivable to Chris. The military might
of America . . . foiled by a gang of gooks running
around in the jungle?

''You really think so? You really think we're gonna
lose over here?''

''We been kickin' other people's asses for so long
now, I guess it's time we got our own ass kicked. The
only decent thing I can see coming out of this mess is
the survivors. Hundreds of thousands of guys like you,
Taylor. They'll be going back to all the big cities and
shit-heel burgs back in the World knowing what it's

like to take a life . . . and understanding what it can do to your soul.

"You guys will understand that shit can twist you like a corkscrew . . . like it's done to Barnes and Bunny, made 'em die inside. And if you got half the brains God gave an eggplant, you'll spend the rest of your life fighting against that kind of shit.

"It's cheap, Taylor. Killing is cheap. It's the cheapest thing I know and when some drunk like O'Neill starts glorifying it, you're gonna puke all over him, man. And the next time the politicians start trying to sell you and your generation a used war, Taylor, you're gonna tell them to go fuck themselves. Cause you know. You've seen it and you'll have the memories deep down there. . . ."

Chris grunted in pain as Elias jabbed him sharply below the ribcage.

". . . and that shit will be with you until the day you die. That's why the survivors remember. Because the dead won't let them forget."

Chris couldn't think of anything to say. It was the first time since the Underworld party that he'd heard Elias string this many words and thoughts together. And it was certainly the first time he'd contemplated an unsuccessful end to the war.

Elias revealed a shy grin and shook his head. "Ah, shit. Maybe it's too much grass. Sometimes it does that to me. I get all fucked up like a crazy Indian. . . ."

"Do you believe that stuff . . . about knowing you're gonna die?"

"Yeah. Those are the ones that live. . . ."

Elias seemed amused by the thought of death; not at all frightened or anxious. Chris thought maybe it had something to do with the man's heritage. He'd heard that Indians believed they came back to earth in the form of an animal.

"Do you believe in reincarnation . . . all that stuff?"

Elias spun sideways and wrapped steel claws around Taylor's shoulders. There was an eerie flash in the man's eyes. It was deep . . . back beyond the pupils where no one sees but anyone can feel. Chris stiffened with discomfort. Elias's hands were like bear-traps on his shoulders. The look was riveting; demanding yet softened by a strange supplication.

Chris froze and watched Elias's face as it moved slowly to within inches of his own. The move had been slow and determined, enlarging to fill his field of vision like a subject seen through a zoom lens. He was reminded of the fierce glare Elias had used to halt Barnes in the ville.

"Reincarnation goes on all the time, man. Maybe a piece of me's in you now. . . ."

Chris slid backward when Elias released the tension and let him go. He understood. Maybe that little piece of Elias was what gave him the strength to stop the rape out there just as Elias had stopped a murder. Elias brought back the lop-sided grin and shook his head.

"Who knows? Sometimes I think I'm gonna come back as wind or fire . . . or maybe a deer. Yeah, I think maybe a deer. . . ."

Chris nodded and touched Elias lightly on the shoulder. He stood to leave but the squad leader grabbed his hand.

A shooting star flickered and fell across the night sky. Chris followed the arc and wondered about Elias.

"They say when you see that, someone has died somewhere."

"Go to sleep, Taylor. If that was true there wouldn't be any stars left over the Nam."

Like huge green buoys covered by ponchos, the soldiers of Bravo Two stood waist-deep in a jungle stream. Rain was falling in wet sheets making a monotonous series of dimples on the murky surface of the green water. Lerner, walking point for the platoon, had signalled the halt. He was forward now, somewhere up in that jungle with Sergeant Warren and Sergeant Elias checking for a trail that would take them back into the NVA bunker complex.

In the stream, men were using the pause to check each other for the leathery black leeches that swam through the water or dropped from the dripping foliage to suck their blood. Rhah had spotted a bloated specimen on Taylor's lip and used the lit end of a soggy cigarette to force the leech to release its grip. Taylor watched Rhah squeeze blood out of the slug and wondered if anyone ever fucked up badly enough in a first life to be reincarnated as a leech.

Big Harold, Francis and King stood talking quietly beneath a tree. They were in no hurry to move out and head into the jungle. There was something ominous about the rain and the quiet it seemed to bring to the area.

Harold reached underwater, stuck his paw through a long rip in the crotch of his trousers and held up a fat leech.

"Look heah. Dis fucker's been sucking on my dick."

Francis examined the leech with clinical interest. "Don't look like he got much, Harold. You should have left him there, man. Leech on the dick might be a medevac, dude. You could have got out of the field."

King shifted his machine gun and remembered an earlier conversation. "What the fuck you doin' out here anyway, Harold? I thought you was gettin' that laundry job back in the rear."

"Shit, I got to paint myself white to get one of them jobs, man. But it don't mean nothin'. I got my request in for a circumcision. De Army got to give you one if you asks for it."

"What you gonna do, Harold . . . become a rabbi?"

Francis mopped water from his face with a towel and grabbed the leech. "You let 'em start cuttin', man, and your dick will wind up lookin' like this."

"Dat's all right with me, man. Better to have a little dick than no dick at all."

"There it is. Only way to be sure some gook don't blow your dick off is get the fuck out of the field."

"All I got to do is stretch that circumcision out to fifteen days in the rear, man. I'd be short under fifteen days and the Beast wouldn't dare send me back to the bush."

"Shit, Harold. How you gonna act, man? What you gonna do back in the World?"

"Ain't no problem, dudes. First I eat all the hamburgers and french fries and steaks I can find. Smother them bad-boys with ketchup and onions. . . . Sheeeeeeit! Den I'm gonna grab hold of my main squeeze and fuck til I drop. Then I'm gonna sleep for two weeks. When I wake up, I'll think about what comes next. . . ."

Up on point, Sergeant Warren was checking his lensatic compass. The lieutenant had said the bunker complex should be on a heading of zero-three-five degrees when they emerged from the river. He pointed in the general direction and watched Lerner move out toward a small hill crested by a clearing.

Elias was squatting beside a cluster of spider holes that had been dug near the ruins of an old Catholic church. The church was overgrown and wasted by time and neglect, but the one-man fighting holes had been dug relatively recently. He didn't know whether it was worth mentioning the abandoned position or not. Elias decided to let it go as he watched the platoon trudge wearily toward the high-ground. He moved away from the flank and started back toward his squad.

Lerner was looking at a tall cluster of anthills and thinking that they resembled muddy Indian teepees when he emerged from the jungle and into the clearing at the top of the hill. Had he stopped and looked beneath a mossy log that appeared to have fallen into one side of the clearing, he might have been able to warn Sergeant Warren.

The distance to the bunker was only twenty-five meters, but Lerner never saw the NVA trooper shift his RPD machine gun and squeeze the trigger. The first burst cut Lerner's legs out from beneath him. The second stitched Sergeant Warren in a neat line just below his navel.

Fifty meters to the rear, O'Neill heard the gunfire and dove for the cover of a gnarled mangrove tree as a gunner from another bunker rose to trigger a rocket-propelled grenade. The shrapnel from the bursting round tore through the trees and stung O'Neill's legs. He curled up into a tight ball and screamed back down the trail.

"Doc! Get up here. We got two down. Warren's hit!"

Like fireflies in the clearing, O'Neill spotted the wink of several more muzzle flashes. For once, S-2 had been right. The NVA had reclaimed their turf. This time they did not intend to run.

Like everyone else in the platoon, Taylor had thrown himself prone when he heard the firing. He watched Doc Gomez reluctantly rise and rush forward just as another rocket roared over their head and slammed into the wall of the old church. The platoon was sprawled in the mud, stretched out in an irregular pattern between the clearing and the churchyard.

Something odd . . . frightening yet thrilling was building inside Taylor as he crawled forward in the mud. Chris thought it must be a lot like this when you sat with a loaded gun in your hand and contemplated suicide. Another rocket blast shook the trees and the odd feeling got the best of him.

Taylor rose from the mud, dropped his pack and poncho and rushed forward toward the clearing. He slammed into the tree next to O'Neill, who had begun to slither backward. "What the fuck's goin' on?"

"Ambush, man. They was waitin' for us to cut trail. Rockets and machine guns. Lerner and Warren been hit!"

Chris watched O'Neill push backward through the muck and tried to stop him. They'd need all the fire-power they could get up front.

"Where you goin', man? Doc's on his way up. . . ."

O'Neill never stopped crawling backward. And Doc Gomez never made it to the clearing. He was busy about halfway back with a rapidly dying Flash, who had been under a tree when a rocket struck and turned the trunk into a storm of deadly splinters.

• • •

Tubbs, the angry former clerk who had been sent to a line company as punishment for stealing beer from the PX, tried to move forward under covering fire from Morehouse, who had inherited an M-60 when Tex was wounded. He nearly made it to the clearing before a low, wicked burst from the NVA machine gun broke both his thigh bones. After that, no one was willing to move in any direction.

Barnes had seen this kind of thing many times. Troops in shock from the impact of a well-planned ambush were more than happy to simply remain pinned down by fire. It was natural. It was the safest thing to do. And it was the surest way to die.

He stood calmly, dropped his poncho and walked toward the clearing, hoping his example would inspire some of the others to move forward and bring some of their own fire to bear on the enemy. When that didn't work, he began kicking and screaming. Tony Hoyt followed his platoon sergeant, forced into movement by the umbilical attachment of his radio handset.

Barnes motioned for him to use the set and Hoyt ducked behind a tree, glad to be out of the line of murderous fire. "Get Two Bravo and the CP up here ASAP, Tony. And tell 'em to bring their fuckin' gun. Let's go assholes. Get some firepower out there. Pick your target. There's plenty of 'em out there."

A close burst of AK fire shattered a branch near his head and an RPG roared through the bushes on his left but Barnes did not seem to notice. He caught sight of Elias and Crawford trundling forward on his right and waved to them. He had to yell to be heard over the steady rattle of fire from Bravo Two which seemed to have recovered some of its shattered integrity.

"Move it out on the flank, Elias. Try to get an angle on the bastards!"

Increased firepower from his rear gave Chris a chance to look out from behind his cover and into the clearing. He could see at least four bunkers beyond a clump of deadwood that provided slight cover for the wounded Sergeant Warren. The man was sitting up and fumbling with a pile of steaming intestines that had spread across his bloody thighs.

Behind a clutch of three conical anthills, Lerner lay on his back and tried to squirm more deeply into the mud. Bullets from an AK wielded by an NVA in a spider hole nicked around him and Chris suddenly realized the gook did not want to kill Lerner . . . not just yet. If he could keep the wounded man in place out there, some unwounded American might be foolish enough to try and rescue him.

Warren would never make it, but Gator didn't look too bad. He'd live if someone went out there and pulled him back to the Doc. Someone who? Chris raged at himself as a machine gun burst chewed into the tree trunk near his head. No one is going to help Gator . . . and no one is going to help me! It's time, Chris screamed at himself urging his leg muscles into action. Soldier or stay home! Shit or get off the pot! The time for rational observation and academic distancing is gone.

Chris fired a burst and began to crawl forward. He paused beside Warren, winced at the coppery stench of blood and punctured bowel, and then sprinted around the woodpile. He flopped down beside the kid from the Florida Keys just as a vicious burst of AK fire carved three inches off the top of the anthills. Chris burned through another magazine and glanced at Lerner. The man's eyes were screwed shut against the pain in his legs.

"Lerner! Can you hear me, man? Lerner, it's Taylor!" Lerner groaned and opened his eyes. "I'm fuckin' dyin', man. Can we get out of here?"

Chris jammed a full magazine into his rifle and put a reassuring hand on Lerner's shoulder. He had absolutely no idea if they could get out of there.

"Hang tough, Gator. I'll get you out. Just hang in there, man!" Poking his muzzle through a slot between the anthills, Taylor aimed and blew three rounds into the firing embrasure of the spider hole. The occupant fired two rounds in return and then disappeared into the dark, fumbling with the weapon's long, curved magazine.

It was either a stoppage or the gook was changing magazines. Either way, Chris knew he didn't have long to take advantage of the clear air. In a moment it would be filled again with high-velocity lead. Eying the fifteen meters between his cover and the spider hole, Taylor ripped a grenade off one of his magazine pouches and pulled the pin. Rolling onto his side, he let the safety lever fly, breathed deeply twice and levered himself up on one knee.

The toss was perfect. Chris knew it when the grenade left his right hand. It had the feel of a well-thrown peg that would scream low and hard into the first baseman's glove for the double play. Still, it marked the first time Chris had ever heaved a hand grenade in combat and he watched in wonder as the woven cover blew off the spider hole and wisps of smoke rose into the wet air.

Squirming through the mud, dragging Lerner back

toward the edge of the jungle, Chris paused for breath behind the pile of deadwood and noticed Sergeant Warren was dead. The fire had been so heavy in this area that two neat holes had been blown in the man's big feet.

The firefight that followed the ambush was gradually getting organized. Morehouse and King had moved their machine guns forward. Fu Sheng had followed Elias out on the flank and managed to kill the rocket gunner's assistant with two good shots. Big Harold had been sent to the rear to get more machine gun ammo and Lieutenant Wolfe was working diligently on calling an artillery fire mission.

It was tough going in the rain and incoming fire. Lieutenant Wolfe couldn't seem to match the hill they were on with the squiggly brown lines on the map. He thought it must be this area here . . . but they all looked alike. He guessed it was better to do something quickly than to let his men see him struggle with the map any longer. He winced at hot splinters which peppered the area following an RPG detonation and reached to retrieve the handset from Ace.

"Redleg, Redleg, Ripper Two Bravo Actual. Fire Mission. Grid six-four-niner . . . four-zero-two. Direction six-one-zero-zero. Dinks in bunkers. Danger close. Adjust fire, over."

The disembodied voice in the field artillery fire direction center repeated the data. "Rog, Two Bravo. Solid copy. Stand by for shot. Redleg out."

Hoyt slogged into the CP area and flopped down beside the lieutenant. He had been monitoring the battalion command frequency. "Sir, Bravo Three is inbound from the Sierra Whiskey. They should be here in about two-zero mikes if they don't run into any shit.''

Wolfe's face lit up. The cavalry was on the way. Now if they'd just hurry up with that fire mission, he'd be back in control of the situation. Hell, there might even be a medal in this thing.

He turned a smug grin on Elias as he ducked the blast from another RPG and flopped into the slight depression that served as the platoon command post. Elias did not seem to think the picture was quite so rosy.

"Lootenant, they're kickin' our ass up there. They know we're gonna bring some heavy shit on 'em pretty soon, so they'll be movin' in tight under arty. I spotted a cut over there on the right. Lemme take some men and roll up that flank. I can work right up on 'em.''

Wolfe thought it was safer and saner to wait for the fire mission. So what if the gooks left their holes and began to close? If he'd gotten the fire mission on the money, he could shift the fire as they pulled back and nail the fuckers.

"I don't know, Elias. Let's wait for Barnes. . . . I . . . we got four or five down already. If I split you off, we . . .''

The rationale for refusing Elias was lost in a roar and a curse as Barnes splashed into the CP. "Where the fuck is third platoon? Tony, you get 'em on the horn and tell 'em to get their asses up here!''

For the first time, Barnes seemed to notice Elias. He glared at the squad leader in silence for a few seconds and then growled.

"What the fuck you doin' here, Elias? Round up your assholes and move 'em forward. We're gettin' chopped to pieces out there while you sit here bullshittin'.''

Elias did not look up; he was sketching something in

the mud with a knife. "Barnes . . . just listen to me.
There's five or six spider holes back by that church.
You got third platoon comin' up right through that area
to reinforce us. If the gooks get some snipers in those
holes, they'll be in position to open up on both of us.
They'll start a crossfire between us and third. We'll
shoot each other to shit, man, and the gooks will come
pourin' out like crap through a goose."

Barnes squinted down at Elias's sketch but Lieutenant Wolfe did not bother. He didn't see why everyone
couldn't just calm down and wait for the artillery.

"It sounds pretty far out to me, Elias."

"Maybe . . . but I seen it happen. We were in the Ia
Drang in '66. First Cav. They got in between two units
and cut us to pieces. Give me three men. If I'm wrong
about the spider holes, I can still roll up that flank and
bust the ambush."

Barnes seemed to agree with the plan. He nodded
once and waved his hand at Elias. "Take off . . . but
tell Crawford to leave the radio here with us."

Elias took a step to sprint away from the CP, but
paused to glare at Barnes.

"You make sure those fuckin' troopers keep up the
suppressing fire. I don't want to be caught out there
with my ass hanging out."

The muscles in Barnes's neck tightened and he
snatched Elias by the collar. "Don't you tell me how to
fight my fuckin' war, Elias. You go cryin' to fuckin'
Brigade when we're in the rear. Out here you belong to
me. Now collect shit and move out!"

Elias saw the rage in the man's eyes and felt a
chill run up his spine. He wanted to change his mind;
to stay here and keep an eye on Barnes, but someone
had to occupy those holes and stop the gooks from

getting at their backs. It was either that or die in place.

Ace dropped the handset from his ear. ''Sir, shot out. Arty's on the way. . . .''

Elias took the opportunity to get moving. Barnes stared at his back with a grudging respect. Elias was right about the gooks getting between two American units. Barnes had seen it happen himself. You had to hand it to Elias. The man had his shit together in combat. Only trouble with Elias, Barnes decided as he ran forward to watch the big rounds blow away gooks, is the fact that he's fucked up inside. Too much heart and not enough belly.

When Lieutenant Wolfe had sent him forward after Barnes to relay adjustments for the artillery mission, Ace thought the officer was just too chickenshit to do it himself. Now he realized the problem was much more serious. The first round screamed in and detonated *to their rear*! Short! The arty wasn't falling on the gooks. It was falling on the platoon. That asshole had fucked up the fire mission!

Ace was trying to shrug the radio off and change frequencies so he could call off the fire mission when something slammed into his back and knocked him gasping into the mud. He was thankful to be prone at first . . . and then he felt the burning near his right shoulder blade. Shrapnel! He must have been hit. Ace wailed with pain and bucked frantically trying to throw the sliver of hot metal out of his back.

Barnes realized immediately what had happened. Wolfe had called the arty short. Any organization they had gained over the past few minutes would be lost to blind panic if someone didn't check the fire. He glanced to his rear and saw Ace squirming on the ground. Slipping his bayonet out of the sheath, Barnes crawled toward the wounded man, put a knee in the middle of his back and began to dig the smoking metal out of shredded muscle. A glance at the man's discarded radio told him most of the shrapnel had impacted the set. It would be useless for calling off the artillery.

Over the roar of incoming rounds, Barnes heard someone calling his name. Big Harold was stumbling away from the clearing in wild-eyed panic. He'd lost his helmet and weapon. A long belt of linked machine gun ammo was dragging behind him through the mud.

"Sergeant Barnes! Tell 'em to check fire! The arty's short!"

Barnes saw the man pause in full flight, glance at the base of a tree on his right and begin to scream something. It took only a second for him to determine what had attracted the man's attention.

A huge blast threw Big Harold into the air. He landed flat on his back and Barnes noticed a blackened stump where the lower half of the man's left leg had been. Satchel charge rigged to a tree, Barnes calculated. The fucking gooks had boobytrapped the escape routes from the ambush site.

He grudgingly acknowledged the effectiveness of the tactic, slapped a field dressing on Ace's cauterized wound and headed for the CP with murder in mind.

Morehouse had burned through all the available ammo for his machine gun. He was shouting at Fu Sheng who was busily reloading magazines behind a mound of dirt when he saw Big Harold trundling through the trees at his rear. The man carried another five hundred rounds, which would get the gun back in action.

When Harold hit the boobytrap, both Fu Sheng and Morehouse spun around ready to go to the man's aid. A sound froze them in place. It was a strange chuffing like the sound they'd heard before when arty shot directly overhead. But this was too close. Something instinctive in their ears picked out the sound over the bursts of small arms fire and sent information about the trajectory to their brains.

"Short! Short-round!" It was the last thing Fu Sheng said before an evil ball of black smoke engulfed him. Morehouse stared in shock at the red fireball that marked the Hawaiian's death by friendly fire and wondered calmly if it was just the marking round for subsequent adjustment. Or would there be more short artillery?

He had the answer in seconds. Morehouse heard the roar of the second 155 mm artillery round and looked upward through the trees. If he could see it, maybe he could get away from the blast.

He couldn't. The sound told him that. Morehouse was curled into a tight ball with his hands over his genitals when the short artillery round hit near his knees and turned him into a fine red mist that was spray-painted on the nearby trees.

Chris Taylor had chosen a flanking route to get Lerner to the rear and that unconscious decision kept him out of the pattern of impacting artillery rounds. He spotted Doc Gomez twisting a tourniquet below Big Harold's knee and made a hard right turn toward medical aid for his friend. He dumped Lerner in the mud near the medic just as Elias, Crawford and Rhah emerged from a hedgerow. They knelt in a tight circle with Elias at the center as though he where calling plays for a pick-up touch football game.

Lerner moaned and grabbed for Taylor's hand. "Don't leave me, man. It's bad. I know it's bad!"

Chris glanced at Lerner's legs and knew the man was right. The enemy rounds had shredded flesh and bone. If Lerner didn't bleed to death before he got evacuated, they'd likely have to take both limbs off above the knees. Huge chunks of hamstring had literally been blown off the back of Lerner's legs.

Feeling impotent and ashamed, he returned the desperate pressure of Lerner's grip and mopped sweat from the man's forehead. "Hang in there, Gator. It ain't so bad, man. We're gonna get you out of here in just a little while. Hang tough, Gator."

Doc Gomez began to work on Lerner but interrupted his ministrations to bat Chris on the arm. "Just leave him with me, Taylor. Take off. Elias is yelling for you over there."

Elias led Crawford, Taylor and Rhah on a broken field run through the thick jungle vegetation. Laboring for breath to keep up, Taylor marveled at the agility of the squad leader. The man seemed to dart left or right instinctively, without looking at the ground. His legs and hips swiveled around obstacles while his eyes tracked the muzzle of his rifle in a searching pattern.

Suddenly, Elias ducked out of sight and the three men who had been following him nearly collided trying to stop short. He'd found a stretch of jungle that provided cover and good observation of the spider holes. Taylor could see the shattered spire of the church through the foliage. Elias pointed at the tangle of mangrove trees at the rear of the fighting holes. He shut his eyes for a moment and seemed lost in concentration.

"They're coming. They should break cover right over there. No tellin' how many they'll send. I'll work around the other side and see if I can take 'em from the flank."

Chris was still pumped up from Lerner's rescue and wanted another piece of the action. "I'll go with you. We can take 'em from two sides."

Elias looked into his eyes and let his mouth twist into a quizzical grin. "Ain't you the big-time bush-beast?" He patted Taylor lightly on the helmet and motioned toward a large tree. "You stay here where the extra firepower will do the most good. I do better out there alone."

Lieutenant Wolfe was straining to spot the solution among the confusing lines, loops and squiggles on his tactical map. The artillery was clearly landing short of the intended target and among his own troops. It must be the FDC, he thought as another round tore through the trees over his head. They must have put the wrong dope on the guns! I couldn't have been that far off!

He was reaching for a handset to let the artillerymen know they had made a mistake when his helmet banged painfully across the bridge of his nose. Wolfe thought he had been hit by a piece of shrapnel until he peered out from under the dripping helmet rim and spotted Barnes. The man must be crazy. He was screaming something disrespectful.

"You ignorant asshole! What fuckin' coordinates did you call? You killed a bunch of people with that fucked-up fire mission. You know that?"

Wolfe worked his mouth in paralyzed fear. Didn't Barnes understand that it wasn't him? Didn't he know it must be the fire direction center?

Barnes grabbed a handset from Tony and pressed the transmit switch. He ran a thick finger over his own map and then locked hate-filled eyes on the platoon commander. His every word banged into Wolfe's brain.

"Redleg, Redleg . . . Ripper Bravo Two. Check fire, check fire! You're short on our pos! I say again, check your fire! Initial mission was incorrect. From Registration Point X-Ray, add one-five-zero, left five-zero. Fire for effect, over!"

He threw the handset at Lieutenant Wolfe and leaned in close enough to spit in the petrified officer's face.

"Thanks to you, we ain't got a whore's chance in hell of overrunnin' them gook positions now. The arty will have to do the work for us. Now do somethin' useful and get these people back outa here. We'll link up with third platoon and sweep back through here once the artillery has beat the shit out of 'em for a while."

Lieutenant Wolfe was gradually regaining control of his voice. Something was wrong with that plan, but Barnes seemed committed to it. He watched as the platoon sergeant issued instructions to get it underway.

"Tony, you push Two Bravo and Two Charlie. Tell 'em to haul ass back toward that church. We'll regroup there."

While Hoyt began transmitting, Wolfe recalled what was bothering him about a tactical retreat. "We can't pull back now. Elias is out there. If we head for the rear, he won't have any fire support!"

Barnes caught him with a glare. "Great time to start thinkin' like a fuckin' leader, lootenant! You get these troopers movin'. I'll go out and bring Elias back in. . . ."

Lieutenant Wolfe watched Barnes slip into the jungle on a dangerous solo mission. Maybe that rotten bastard will be killed out there, he thought. The platoon was

down to fifty percent strength with today's casualties.
They might bring in a new platoon commander before
rebuilding it . . . especially if the platoon sergeant was
KIA.

Crouched between the roots of a mangrove tree, Elias
shut his eyes and dialed in the filters which allowed him
to separate sound in the bush. As he concentrated, the
rattle and roar of the firefight at the clearing faded. He
heard the muted rattle of equipment shifting on a body
and picked out the sound of a branch wiping across a
uniformed leg.

At least two . . . maybe three, coming at me abreast.
Take 'em left to right and let the natural swing of the
rifle carry you through it. Two rounds for each and use
the off eye to pick up their movements after the shooting starts.

The first NVA trooper broke cover slightly ahead of
his two companions. He was wispy-bearded and bush-
wise. He'd seen a lot of Americans in the two years
he'd been fighting in the south and he knew they were
no good for this sort of war. They didn't know how to
move silently or take advantage of the natural camouflage built into the terrain.

Such thoughts made him slightly careless and he
completely missed seeing Elias's still form wrapped
around the mangrove tree like a large snake. Shortly
after he motioned his comrades up toward the clearing,
he died from two M-16 rounds that tore into his heart
and lungs.

Elias caught the flash of movement as the second
NVA dove for cover and it gave him a point of aim to
put two more rounds through the man's neck and cheek.
He caught the third man between the shoulder blades

before the NVA had taken two steps back in the direction from which he'd come. Elias unwrapped himself from the tree and sprinted easily into the jungle. He didn't even slow down to put the sixth bullet into the wounded NVA's skull.

Morning rain had fallen off to a drizzle and the warm earth of the jungle floor was once again covered by a drifting mist. Rhah, Crawford and Taylor peered through the spun-cotto wisps and waited.

Artillery and small arms fire from the clearing at their rear was tapering off drastically. Maybe Elias was wrong. Maybe the gooks had decided to run away from the American firepower. They considered the six rounds they'd heard fired shortly after Elias melted into the bush. All had been M-16 reports. There were none of the larger, characteristic cracks that indicted AK fire. Maybe Elias had cut the gooks off and killed them before they could reach the spider holes.

Hell, maybe that was Elias coming in now . . . no! Taylor spotted the shape of a Soviet-style helmet beneath the moving clump of bushes. He could clearly make out a pair of frightened oriental eyes shifting left to right, right to left. When the tubular shape of an RPG launcher came into view, Chris shouldered his rifle, shifted the front sight onto the center of the man's chest and squeezed the trigger.

Rounds from a wall of return fire snapped past Taylor's ears, but he kept the weapon in his shoulder and concentrated on bringing the muzzle to bear on a target. He was sure he'd nailed at least two and Rhah and Crawford, banging away to his right, probably got some also. It was invigorating, reassuring to be in control of the situation for once. He roared with passion and release as what was left of the NVA patrol faded back into the jungle.

"I got two of the bastards, man! They're runnin' now!"

Rhah smiled with undisguised delight. "I nailed three . . . maybe four, man! Dem fuckers ain't gettin' in no holes today!"

Taylor and Rhah looked to the right, expecting a similar accounting from Crawford. They heard only a gasp and a rattling cough.

Crawford's helmet had fallen off when they reached him. His back was braced against a tree and his long, blond hair was matted to his forehead with sweat. Rhah slashed away at the wounded man's equipment with a fighting knife he carried and spread the panels of his flack jacket. A ragged hole, bubbling with blood, had been punched in Crawford's ribcage. Chris could see gristle and bone through the ooze of blood.

"Looks like a lung, babe." Rhah was biting the wrapping off a field dressing. "But you're gonna be okay. You only need one of them."

Crawford seemed more surprised than hurt. "Oh, man . . . after all we been through. I never thought I'd get hit, y'know?"

Chris poured water from his canteen onto Crawford's face. "You be cool now, man. Sounds like the gooks are breakin' contact. We'll carry you out of here."

"Goddamn right you will. . . ." Barnes broke into the clearing and glanced briefly at the wounded man. Chris stared in amazement at the anger burning in the man's face. Was he pissed off at Crawford for getting wounded? ". . . and you start carryin' him back to the church right now. We're pullin' back."

Taylor thought the platoon sergeant should know

about the gooks who tried to get to the spider holes and how they had spoiled the plan.

"Sarge, about five or six gooks tried to come through here . . ."

Barnes was staring out into the jungle clearing but he was not looking at the NVA casualties. "Where's Elias?"

Rhah made a gesture toward the tangle of bush behind the spider holes. "He's out there somewhere. He hit 'em first and then we . . ."

Spinning abruptly to stare at the trio as though they had been stupid rather than heroic, Barnes inclined his head in the direction of the ambush site. "Didn't you hear the arty shift? We're pullin' back to link up with third platoon. Now get that casualty on his feet and get outa here. Wolfe is gonna set up an LZ near the church for the Dust-Offs."

Taylor rose to his feet and motioned toward the jungle. "But, Elias is still out there . . ."

Barnes took a threatening step forward. "He wouldn't be if he'd stayed here where he belongs instead of actin' like a hotdog. Ah'll get Elias. You two get that casualty to the rear. Do it now! Or ah'll nail both yer asses with an Article 15!"

Elias had a good view of four NVA knees through a crack in the hollow stump where he crouched. They were only fifteen meters away now. He smiled and drew a deep breath. Letting half of it out silently, he told himself he'd let them get this close to be sure there were no more than two. Or maybe, he realized as he tensed his leg muscles to rise, I let 'em get close because I want to catch a glimpse of their expressions.

It didn't matter, Elias supposed. This was the way the fight should be. Warriors facing warriors in the bush where no one was ever boss and you survived by instinct. He sprang up and shouldered his rifle in one easy motion. The first NVA froze in his tracks but the second man moved to raise his SKS carbine into firing position. Elias shifted aim and blew away the threat immediately. The first man had not completed his escape turn before he fell across his partner with an M-16 round lodged in his brain.

Adrenaline was coursing through Elias's system. His thigh muscles were bunched so tight that his knees flexed involuntarily and he began to bob up and down in a weird war dance. He barked triumphantly into the jungle and slipped away to maintain the high.

Barnes heard the shots and the shout. Pausing to range on the noise, he recognized the tinny spang of an M-16. Elias was killing gooks out there, about seventy-five meters away in the direction of 2:30. Barnes turned slightly right until he was facing the way the hour hand of a clock would point at that time and sprinted off after Elias.

Taylor carefully laid Crawford down among a growing number of casualties being attended by Doc Gomez and a Medic from third platoon. O'Neill was spacing the remaining members of second platoon in a tight circle around the church ruins. The flat churchyard would serve as an LZ. Rhah motioned for him to cover an open spot in the perimeter but Chris ignored the gesture.

Gooks would be pouring down off that high-ground in a short time. They'd hear the helos and rush to see if they could shoot one down. A helicopter was a much more valuable target than a single grunt . . . even a grunt like Elias.

There would be no loiter time in the LZ. They'd have to unass the area in a hurry. Barnes knew about the choppers. He'd make it back in time whether he found Elias or not. Would they leave without Elias?

Chris decided he shouldn't take the chance and sprinted off into the jungle to locate his squad leader and bring him back to the fold.

Barnes was crouched near a moss-covered tree, listening for another fix on the man. Goddamn Elias and his solo act! The man is fuckin' up mah fightin' machine. Ah got to leave things to that dipshit lootenant while ah chase his ass . . . and when we get to the rear, he makes me waste time writin' up some bullshit report. Dammit! C'mon, Elias. We got a war to fight and you ain't helpin'.

The rustle of vine against metal caught his attention. Someone was approaching from behind that hedgerow. Probably gooks, Barnes thought. They'd have good enfilade position to hit the troops pulling back from the ambush if they got into that clump of jungle. He silently squatted into a stable firing position and shouldered his M-16, aiming at the spot where the noise indicated the gooks should emerge.

Over the front sight Barnes watched Elias step cautiously through the hedgerow and smile in recognition. Barnes expelled the remainder of the breath he'd been holding and started to lower his weapon. Now that he'd finally found Elias, they could stop all this cheap shit and get on with the war . . . or . . .

Something painful snapped in a space behind Barnes's eyes. A warm surge flooded his neck and shoulders. There was a hollow booming in his ears. His right eye fell back naturally behind the rear sight and he squeezed the trigger.

In the instant it took for Barnes's cheek to lock into the stock of the rifle, Elias realized the man intended to kill him. Why? My God, he's finally lost control. He can't stand the thought of being sent out of the fight. Barnes has reached a point where he'll kill anything that interferes with his killing.

Unable to take his eyes off the incredible sight, Elias leaped backward into the bush. It was not soon enough to escape the rounds. He knew that when he saw the evil wink from the muzzle and felt the first painful impact deep in his chest.

Chris bulled past soldiers headed toward the LZ. Most of them struggled under ponchos rigged as litters for wounded. He spotted a man he knew from the third platoon and inquired about Elias.

"I ain't seen him or anyone else, man. If he's still out there, he's in a world of shit. Choppers spotted a fuckin' swarm of gooks headin' in this direction. We *all* getting the fuck outa here soon's the birds can get into the LZ. My lootenant said we was gonna let the arty and ARA take care of the bastards."

He pushed on. There was little time left. He could hear the beat of chopper blades coming from somewhere behind the church ruins. Chris had to reach Elias before the helos began chewing up the jungle.

Breaking suddenly into a small clearing, Chris spotted Barnes. The platoon sergeant spun on him and they both stared for a moment over rifle sights. Barnes was first to drop his weapon from the shoulder. He seemed disturbed, upset, distracted. The network of scars gleamed under a layer of sweat in a white-on-white mosaic.

"Where's Elias?"

"Elias is dead. . . ." Barnes's voice was shaky. It lacked the usual iron edge Chris had come to recognize. The man kept glancing back toward the LZ.

Dead? Elias was dead? Where was the body? Didn't Barnes even have the decency to carry him out? Or was he just trying to get out of here; to save his own ass and the hell with Elias?

Barnes craned his neck and glanced at Taylor from the corner of the near eye. "Thought I told you to get back and join up with the platoon, Taylor. . . ." Some of the edge was returning to Barnes's tone.

"What the fuck do you mean Elias is dead? Did you see him?"

"Yeah. I saw him . . . or what was left of him. He's back there about a hundred meters. Just about where the gooks are now. Ain't nothin' to be done, Taylor. Get back to the LZ."

Rounds were beginning to pepper the trees at their rear. Barnes turned abruptly and headed toward the church. He disappeared quickly in the heavy bush and left Chris very alone.

I should go get Elias, he thought. I should go on back in there and bring him out . . . bring his body out . . . something. A close round cracked by Taylor's head and sent him sprawling to the ground. Gooks have got Elias's body by now. They'll sure as hell get mine if I don't get out of here. Elias was out of it; maybe even *better* out of it. Maybe he was somewhere else now . . . as a better thing.

Taylor tore himself off the ground and sprinted for the LZ.

• • •

Bravo Company's third platoon and what was left of the second fought a retrograde action, delaying the NVA long enough for the evacuation helicopters to dip into the tight LZ, gobble a load of wounded and spin off into the overcast sky. Chris was firing and falling back. He had no identifiable targets but he expended anger over Elias's death on the foliage. On his way back to the LZ, he blew away every likely looking bush on the off-chance there might be a gook behind it.

When he reached the clearing and fell in with a group that would just about make a single helo-lift, he got an idea of the carnage. Tubbs and Crawford were unceremoniously dumped into the belly of a Huey. Before the bird could lift, he saw two men carry Big Harold toward it. King tossed his machine gun in after the litter and climbed aboard followed by Doc Gomez. If the Doc was going out, they must have gotten all the casualties. Now the whole members of Bravo Two could make their escape.

Chris caught the frantic signal from the helicopter's left door gunner. He passed the word to Rhah and both men sprinted toward the chopper. King extended a powerful arm and pulled Chris in beside Big Harold. Groggy with morphine, the big man was lying propped up on his elbows.

A RPG blasted into the church ruins and peppered the helo with concrete shards. Chris heard the rattling impact against the skin of the aircraft just before the sound was covered by a ripping burst of fire from one of the door gunners. The gunner on the other side was waving his arms at Lieutenant Wolfe and Barnes, who were headed for the bird, running in a crouch.

Even before Wolfe had managed to scramble off the skids, the Huey broke contact with the ground, stagger-

ing under a heavy load and began to lift out of the LZ.
The pilot made a hard right bank circling to gain altitude and Chris got a dizzying panoramic view of the
church ruins. Expended cartridge casings winked in the
bright sunlight that had burned through the overcast.

They made it! They were whole and on the way out
of that fucking meat-grinder! King gave a triumphant
whoop and shouted at Big Harold over the rush of air
blowing through the belly of the helo.

"All right, Big Harold! You gonna be in Japan this
time tomorrow!"

Harold strained for a last look at the LZ swirling
below them. "I'm lucky dis time, man. I give a leg
anytime to get the fuck outa there!" He struggled higher
on his litter and screamed at the NVA out there somewhere in the bush. "Eat mah shit, you mother-fuckers!!!"

Doc Gomez pushed the man back on the stretcher
and Chris scooted toward the edge of the compartment
to give him room. That's when he saw it. Lieutenant
Wolfe and Barnes caught the incredulous look on his
face and leaned over to peer down at the ground.

Elias was staggering out of the jungle. He wasn't
dead! From altitude, Chris could see that he soon would
be if they didn't go back and pick him up immediately.
Figures in dark green uniforms flowed through the bush,
moving the foliage where they brushed it in full pursuit
of the wounded American. Blood stained the front and
back of Elias's uniform. He had no weapon and he did
not appear to be in any shape to use one. Taylor winced
and screamed at the aircrewmen as Elias staggered
under the impact of AK rounds and collapsed slowly to
his knees.

Barnes and Wolfe exchanged startled glances as Elias
slowly, painfully raised his arms at the departing chop-

per in mute supplication. Chris spun on the pilot and
screamed to be heard over the noise. Both door gunners
were now blazing away at the ground. Wolfe was shouting at the co-pilot and tugging on his arm. The pilot
turned in his seat and looked at the startled infantryman
in the belly of his aircraft. His eyes were unreadable,
masked by the dark visor of his helmet. With a gloved
hand, he pushed his microphone toward his lips and
mouthed something.

"Dragon one-niner, this is Stingray outbound from
the LZ. Be advised there's one on the deck down there
but they just blew him away. Bring on the gunships. . . ."

As the evacuation helo dipped its nose and headed away
from the LZ, Chris scrambled for the door to get a last
look at Elias. The man was sprawled on the ground and
surrounded by NVA who were now firing up at the
approaching helicopter gunships. He watched the body
disappear in a geyser of dirt and flame as the high-
explosive rockets spewed into the churchyard.

He wanted someone to explain it to him. How could
this happen? How could Barnes have left Elias wounded
out there without trying to evacuate him? Chris looked
around at the soldiers riding with him, in search of an
answer. He saw only shock and more questioning looks.

And then his glance fell on Barnes. The man showed
no emotion at all. He was unloading his rifle and
staring contentedly out into space . . . like a skilled
laborer contemplating a good day's work. Chris knew
the answer to his questions.

Barnes could say what he wanted after the choppers
had driven the NVA away from the area and returned to
pick up Elias's shattered body. There would be no
investigations this time. No one would notice three
smaller entry wounds on a corpse riddled with AK

rounds. Like a cautious engineer, Barnes had removed a malfunctioning part to keep his war machine functioning smoothly.

Staring with cold hatred at the man who had saved second platoon's mangled asses during the ambush, Chris understood that the rule book had just been shit-canned. Using Barnes as a bad example, he could forget rhyme, reason and form in this war. All that remained was substance and the substance of war was killing; cold, efficient elimination of the enemy.

Given the painful boil of emotions surging through his veins, Chris didn't know if he could ever be as cold as Barnes . . . but from now on, he could sure as hell be as efficient at war.

9.

"Gentlemen, I am heartily sick and tired of the 141st NVA and all their shenanigans. . . ." The Brigade Commander had an irritating way of pausing to play with a collapsible pointer before he dropped the other shoe. Captain Harris waited with the other company and battalion commanders for the bad news. He wondered how a man who had only seen the jungle from the relative safety of a helicopter could stand before them and call an engagement that had cost fifty-some casualties—including ten from Bravo's second platoon—"shenanigans."

"I have come up with a plan that should put an end to enemy activity in this sector. . . ." The general vaguely indicated a stretch of border area to their west. ". . . and more importantly for the short run, keep the 141st from coming on the Saigon corridor before the Tet Ceasefire, which begins day after tomorrow."

What's the rush, Harris wondered. The war would still be there after Tet. His people needed time to rest, re-supply and receive some replacements. But time was tight, according to the general.

"You all understand that if we let the NVA slip through, they'll have a good two weeks to set up between us and the national capital defense forces for subsequent attacks on the Saigon perimeter." Harris stared wearily at the huge situation map that dominated a wall of the briefing tent. God forbid that anyone serving in the rear areas for their tour in the "combat zone" should hear a disparaging word . . . much less a genuine shot fired in anger.

The Brigade Commander waited while an assistant erected a larger scale map-sheet which centered on a valley about two thousand meters from the Cambodian border. "You all know by now that Alpha Company was hit hard last night in this area. Bravo Company also suffered casualties and had to be lifted out before they were able to close on the NVA bunker complex that guards the approaches to this valley. After that evacuation, Charlie Company spent the night responding to probes all along their perimeter on this high-ground.

"Obviously, what we require to settle the issue in this area is a fixed battle in which we can bring all our supporting arms to bear. Therefore, we are going to use an old deep-sea fisherman's trick and chum a little to make Charlie rise to the bait." The general smiled as though he was letting them in on some delicious secret and tapped the map with his pointer.

"We're going to do something that will seem tactically stupid to the NVA. We're going to set up a two-company perimeter in this valley. Bravo and Charlie will man the perimeter with Alpha in mobile reserve out here with elements of third of the Twenty-second Armored Cav. For once, we're gonna let Charlie have

the high-ground. When he takes the bait and comes
pouring out of those hills, we call arty, ARA, TacAir
and everything else at our disposal to nail him. When
that's been accomplished, we bring in the other two
maneuver battalions by APC from the east and west and
seal up the survivors.''

Harris flicked a nervous glance at the Charlie Company commander. The man's mouth was hanging open
and all the blood in his face seemed to have settled in
his ears. He knows, Harris thought. He understands.
The bad thing about being bait is that you generally
wind up getting eaten long before the big fish is landed.

The general noted lift-off time was dawn the next day
and called for questions. Harris had a number of them
but they involved details that could best be handled by
brigade staff officers.

''No questions? Good. Operations in the valley will
be controlled by my S-3, Major Stone, in a jump CP.
Gentlemen, before we break this up and let you get
some sorely needed rest, let me make my intentions for
this operation perfectly clear. This is an aggressive
tactical deception with only one objective in mind: to
erase the 141st NVA from the enemy order of battle. Is
that clear?''

It's clear, Harris thought as he left the tent and
headed back to his own CP, as is the fact that if we
fuck it up out there, the American order of battle is
liable to contain one less Bravo Company. He glanced
at his GI wristwatch and calculated only about eighteen
hours until dawn. He was badly understrength and stood
no chance at all of getting replacements before tomorrow's lift-off.

Investigations of the shooting in the ville and that

bungled arty fire mission would have to wait for another time.

Showers, hot chow and mail had helped Bravo Two's morale significantly. Doc Gomez had learned that Big Harold, Crawford and Lerner made it out alive. Both men were on their way to hospitals outside Vietnam and would not be returning. The company clerks had quietly and efficiently removed all traces of Morehouse, Fu Sheng, Tubbs, Flash, Warren, Sanderson and Sal from second platoon's hooches. Only memories and naked canvas cots remained to mark the departure or death of a third of the unit.

By the time weapons had been cleaned, equipment replaced or repacked and everything made ready for the trip into the valley, night had cloaked the base camp area. Lanterns and electric bulbs kept the demons away from some, but Chris needed a different sort of solace. He was seething inside and wanted to focus on the hatred he felt for one man to compensate the sorrow he felt for the loss of another.

He sucked noisily on a joint and glanced at the faces illuminated by the flickering candles in the silent Underworld. King, Francis, Doc . . . even Rhah seemed subdued and shocked by what they'd been through over the past week. Chris finally broke the silence for the first time since the Heads had assembled at sundown.

"He killed him, man. I fuckin' *know* he did! I saw that look in his eyes when he came back in. . . ."

Rhah sucked savagely on his Montagnard pipe and swallowed smoke. "Don't be lame, Taylor. How do you know the gooks didn't get Elias? You got no proof, man."

Reaching in his trouser pocket for a grenade, Chris

held it up for all to see. "The proof's in the eyes. You were there, Rhah. I saw what you were thinking. I say we frag the fucker tonight!"

King stared at the weapon. He missed Elias but he was thinking of Big Harold and a man trying to farm a piece of Mississippi bottomland with only one leg. "Ah go wit' dat. Sometimes it got to be an eye for an eye."

While he'd been at the Bravo CP closing medical records, Doc Gomez had seen the papers the company commander had drawn up ordering an investigation of Lieutenant Wolfe, Barnes and the shooting in the ville. "He ain't gonna get away with shit, man. I say let military justice take care of Barnes."

"Military justice is shit!" Chris put the frag down gently and stared at it for a long moment. "How they gonna prove something when all the witnesses are corrupt?"

Rhah grabbed the grenade from in front of Taylor's face. "Baaaa, you been out in the sun too long, boy! You try to pitch to Barnes and he'll shove the bat in your ass and break it off."

"Okay, dude. What the fuck do you suggest?"

"I suggest you all watch your asses very carefully 'cause Barnes is gonna be down on 'em hard out there in the bush tomorrow!"

In the glow of a short joint, Francis's dark face lit briefly with fear. After Lieutenant Wolfe had told them about the planned operation, Francis had tried every ploy he knew to get himself excused from the field. Nothing had worked. "How you figure that, man? Barnes gonna need every man he's got out there."

Rhah flashed the knuckle inscribed "Hate." "Shit, you ain't talkin' 'bout need, man. You talkin' 'bout human nature."

"Then you just gonna fergit about it, man?" King thought about all the tough times Elias had led them through in the bush so they could live to relax in the Underworld. "You just gonna fergit about Elias and all the good times we had right in here?"

It had taken Rhah some time to arrive at the conclusion and he felt it was time to announce it. "You got to figger it dis way, man. Elias dug his own grave out there."

Chris jumped to his feet and jabbed a finger at the man on the makeshift throne of the Underworld. "That's bullshit, Rhah, and you know it, man! Any way you cut it, Barnes is a fuckin' murderer!"

Rhah calmly refilled his long pipe and pointed the stem around the bunker. "You dudes are tryin' to cure the headache by cuttin' off the head. Elias didn't ask you to fight his battles. And if there's a heaven and a God—I hope there is—I know Elias is sitting up there fucked up and smokin' shit and groovin'. That's 'cause Elias done left his pain and hurt down here, man!"

Chris listened but he could not seem to shake any of the heat that was causing his heart to pound. "Fuck that shit!"

Rhah lit his pipe and smoked for a moment in silence. "Taylor, I remember when you first come in here and you was tellin' how much you admired that bastard. You said you thought he was one helluva soldier."

"So, I was fuckin' wrong, man!"

"*Wrong?* Taylor, you ain't ever been *right* . . . about nothin'. Now dig this, you assholes. Barnes been shot seven times, right? And he ain't dead! That tell you somethin'? Only thing that can kill Barnes *is Barnes!*"

•   •   •

Staff Sergeant Robert E. Lee Barnes stood just inside the entrance to the Underworld, watching and listening in silence. He tried to exhale the alcohol fumes that he'd amassed to cloud his consciousness. For once the whiskey had not worked to smooth out his anxieties.

Ah wasn't ever confused before, he thought. Why now?

The questions were more complicated, Barnes realized. It's harder for a soldier to fight as he should, on gut reaction. Barnes would be required to think more if he was to survive much longer in the bush. But, he supposed, he'd continue to do what he'd always done. Assess the situation and concentrate on those tactile sensations that told him what needed doing in combat. Fan the flames that made him burn with a murderous fire inside. Do what had to be done.

Didn't these dope-smoking assholes understand that's how it worked? That's how it has to work. When the feeling comes, you don't fight it, you use it. The feeling gives you power over the gooks . . . over anyone.

It was the feeling that told him to eliminate Elias. Barnes didn't understand the feeling—that painful pressure behind his eyeballs—but he knew it was his source of power in combat. When the feeling was there, he knew what to do, how to kill efficiently and not worry about his own safety. He'd had that feeling this morning when Elias threatened the safety of second platoon.

Why didn't these assholes understand that? And why did the feeling—for the first time since he could remember—seem unwelcome?

An errant clod of sun-packed dirt fell to the floor of the Underworld and the Heads looked up toward the entrance. They had forgotten to post a sentry and that had given Barnes a chance to slip into their world undetected. The blue eyes above his scarred cheeks blazed with alcoholic fire. In the shocked silence that heralded his arrival, the assembled Heads could clearly hear the gurgle of whiskey as Barnes drained a bottle and tossed the empty aside. He seemed to float in the haze, absorbing and enjoying the discomfort his intrusion had caused. There was no telling how long he'd been standing there.

"Y'all talkin' 'bout killin'?" Wrinkling his face into an ugly smile, Barnes floated through the Underworld haze and grabbed the long pipe from Rhah's hands. "Y'all experts? Y'all know about killin'?"

He dragged deeply on the pipe and swallowed the smoke with practiced ease. Rhah watched the performance in awe. So Barnes knew about the Underworld . . . and he apparently knew something about smoking dope.

"You pussies smoke this shit so you can hide from reality. Me . . . I don't need that shit. *I am reality!*"

Barnes began to circle the Underworld, holding on to the pipe and turning his twisted grin on everyone as he passed. "There's the way it oughta be . . . and there's the way it is. Elias was full of shit. Elias was a fuckin' crusader. Now, I got no fight with a man that does what he's told . . . but when he don't . . . the machine breaks down. And when the machine breaks down, *we* break down! I ain't gonna allow that. Not from any of you . . . not one. . . ."

As though it were nothing more substantial than a matchstick, Barnes broke the sturdy bamboo pipe stem over his thigh. "Y'all love Elias? Y'all want to kick my ass? Well, ah'm here, all by mah lonesome. Ain't nobody gonna know. They's five of you boys and only one of me.''

Barnes dropped his hands to his sides and stared at something in the haze that only he could see. His voice was soft, almost pleading.

''Kill me . . .''

The Heads had long since lost their high. Most were clearly embarrassed by the platoon sergeant's naked appeal. For the first time since any of them had known the man, Barnes seemed pitiful; pleading for an end to some ordeal they could not understand. King momentarily contemplated breaking the big NCOs neck. With his size he could probably do it, but the moment passed. Barnes might play God with other people's lives, but King could not presume the privilege.

When no one made a move against him, Barnes broke the spell with a contemptuous snort. ''Ain't a full set of balls among you people! Ah shit on alla you!''

The contempt was too much for Chris. He broke from his position near the wall with a scream and buried his head in Barnes's gut. The NCO lost his breath and fell to the ground. Chris straddled him and pummeled the man's distorted face with both fists.

Barnes was swinging his head from side to side, causing most of the blows to miss. His eyes seemed to dance with the excitement of it all. He was back in combat . . . at close range where the thrill was most vivid.

Chris could barely hear the assembled Heads cheering him on to kill Barnes. He was concentrating on trying to bury a fist in the puckered bullet wound on the man's forehead. Maybe he could drive it through to that evil brain and end all their miseries. He saw Barnes wince in pain as a blow finally landed in the chosen spot. And then he was flat on his back, staring up at the man he hated more than anything on earth at that moment.

Barnes had wedged a knee into Taylor's crotch and flipped the lighter man over and onto his back. Now he sat straddling a gasping Taylor and staring into defiant eyes. Instinctively, his right hand flew to the left shoulder strap of his webbing and whipped downward to within inches of Chris's face. An evil, spade-shaped push-dagger was in his hand. The gleaming blade emerged from between the middle two fingers and the point nearly rested on Taylor's nose. Barnes drew back the weapon and prepared to shove it cleanly into an eye socket.

He heard something before he could order the necessary muscle release and he paused to blink. Rhah was shouting into his ear.

"Easy, Barnes! Easy, man! Think about it, Barnes! You'll go *dinky-dau* in Long Binh. They'll give you ten years for killin' an EM, man! Ten years in LBJ, Barnes . . . don't do it! Don't do it, man!"

A wave of forced self-control washed over Barnes. Chris forgot the knife and watched in fascination as the facial muscles melted from rage to utter calm. Taylor thought he had escaped totally unharmed when he saw the tight smile lift the uninjured corner of Barnes's mouth.

But the platoon sergeant would not be completely robbed of his moment. He flicked the dagger downward with a controlled motion of his wrist and left a crescent slice under Taylor's left eye. The wounding was so quick and clean that it was seconds before the capillaries began to give up blood. Barnes rose to his feet and watched while Chris touched the cut and stared in fascination at the blood covering his fingers.

"Death?" Barnes chuckled and then shouted into the darkness. "Y'all don't know nothin' about death!"

The platoon sergeant left them in stunned silence.

Chris Taylor had learned a lot about jungle fighting since the day not so long ago when he'd nearly died from heat exhaustion and carrying too much weight. He'd learned that a bandanna like the one he had wrapped around his forehead was an invaluable tool in the bush. He'd traded his issue rucksack for a smaller pack that hung from his cartridge belt at the rear of his web equipment and learned to concentrate his load on ammo, chow and water. Everything else stayed in the rear. He'd learned to get rid of his rifle sling and tape the plastic parts to keep them from rattling. He'd even learned to modify his jungle fatigues; have the seamstress at the local gook shop cut them down so they could fit and did not snag when he was moving quickly in the bush.

All those things he'd learned from Elias, Taylor thought as he looked around the shuddering cargo compartment of the Huey helicopter. But Elias wasn't here today and no one on the bird seemed to miss him. In the hard light of dawn that poured into the helicopter, Chris counted survivors and wondered if they'd see another dawn.

It really didn't matter much, he supposed. Nothing mattered much anymore, if you cared to check it. Like an old, toothless lion, he'd lost the heart for the fight. Barnes had nicked his face, but the real surgery had been somewhere deep in Taylor's soul. Some vital ligament that linked his gut and his brain had been snipped. Now the brain was numb. There was only that smoldering fire in his gut . . . and Chris did not know if he would ever be able to fan it into a rage again no matter what the situation.

I should do something to get out of here right now, he told himself. If I don't, I'm a dead man. Even if I survive this operation, I'm a dead man. I wanted to emerge from Vietnam with all the answers, but I don't even understand the questions. It's too late. I've gotten myself into something I can't control.

Even if I could get control, Chris wondered, what should I do about this fucking mess? What *can* I do about it? What's right and what's wrong? Jesus, I thought I knew and that knowledge made me an adult, rational human being. But . . .

Who deserves punishment and who deserves reward? Should Barnes get a medal for killing more gooks than anyone else in the world . . . even if he had to murder Elias in the process? Is that right in the context of this war? Or is that insanity? Should the NVA be punished by fire and death for simply trying to do what we're all trying to do: survive this fucking meat-grinder? If not, he shouldn't kill any more gooks and that would allow the gooks to kill him. That could not happen. Chris would not *allow* that to happen. If there was to be justice, *he* would have to determine what form it should take.

Barnes was studying a map of the valley that lay somewhere below and ahead of them. Charlie Company had already been inserted and was busily digging into the area. Rodriguez was massaging a rosary and moving his lips in silent prayer. Bunny was working on a huge wad of C ration chewing gum and idly stroking the shotgun that rested across his skinny thighs. King was making some final adjustments to his equipment.

Francis was beating out a rhythm on his knees, lost in the lyrics of some soul tune.

Bunny glanced between his boots hanging out the chopper door and nudged Taylor. The ruins of Phan Xa Vi were still smoking, but he could see some villagers had returned and were poking through the ashes. Bunny prodded him again, placed the shotgun between his legs and made masturbating motions up and down the barrel. Taylor looked up in disgust and caught sight of four more Hueys stacked above them in a loose echelon. The flight was gaining altitude to pass over the tangled stretch of jungle high-ground before descending into the valley.

Chris was off the helo and striding away from the LZ before any of the other passengers had gotten their feet on the skids. He'd been designated to dig in with King and the machine gun somewhere near a key point in the second platoon perimeter. The automatic weapon position would have to be strong and well-constructed. He and the big black gunner had a lot of work to do before dark.

While the second platoon troopers stood and stared around the small perimeter carved out of the jungle on the valley floor, Barnes conferred with the Charlie Company platoon sergeants and was assigned a sector of the circle to defend. Their sister company occupied the ground across a small stream that ran through the center of the perimeter. Bravo would occupy the opposite side.

Captain Harris's CP was already under construction on the near bank of the stream. Four 81mm mortars had been emplaced in Charlie Company's area. The Jump CP for the Brigade S-3 who was in command of the entire defense was marked by a bristling ridge of high-power antennas that sprouted from a bunker in Bravo Company's sector.

Barnes led the troops up a muddy rise to a position facing the jungle and began pairing them off to dig their fighting holes. O'Neill and Huffmeister held the left edge of second platoon's sector. Next to them, Francis and Parker unstrapped entrenching tools and went to work on a hole. Chris and King were farthest forward on a corner where the line of defensive positions turned to flow away down the slope. Rhah dug in with Adams, Rodriguez with Ebenhoch and Bunny with Junior. To the rear of the line, Doc and Hoyt, who had been bumped up to platoon commander's RTO when Ace was hit, dug a four-man hole for themselves, Lieutenant Wolfe and Barnes. They were pitifully few to hold the piece of perimeter assigned to second platoon.

Below, near the Jump CP, Major Stone was pouring over a map with Captain Harris and the Charlie Company Commander. Under a tree nearby, a pair of nonchalant ARVN Rangers guarded three NVA who were squatting in sullen silence, their elbows bound behind their backs by lengths of commo wire.

Tony and Doc took a break from filling sandbags and glared at the POWs. Tony had heard the story of their capture over his radio shortly after Bravo Company arrived at the perimeter.

"Recon dudes workin' with the ARVN before we come in caught 'em somewhere up there on the highground." Tony waved his e-tool to encompass a sweeping hill mass that surrounded the valley like an irregular horseshoe. "They found maps on 'em, binoculars, all that shit. Dude up at the Jump CP told me they practically had every fuckin' foxhole and gun position mapped. He said the little cocksuckers had indicated where the treelines were, distances to the holes, Claymore locations and everything, man.''

Doc went back to shoveling. "So what the fuck are we doin' sittin' here, man? Why don't we move out? I got some bad vibes about this place, Tony. And we ain't got replacement one, man. You see how many dudes is left to hold this sector?''

Hoyt shrugged off the question. It wasn't something he wanted to think about with nightfall less than two hours away. "You know, Doc, these people are *so* fucked up. I heard we're inside Cambodia right now, man.''

Several men who had been digging nearby paused too look around at the green hills. Fear flashed briefly across their faces. Was it true? How could they know? They went back to their e-tools. In the end, what difference would it make?

Lieutenant Wolfe supposed he was obligated to go through the motions and appear to be in command. He sent Tony up the hill to get Rhah and tried to visualize the wire-diagram that was supposed to outline the organization of second platoon. There were more blanks than boxes containing names. It didn't matter much how he tried to shift things around either. Since the ambush and the short arty mission, Barnes had not bothered to speak to him. Barnes listened in silence while orders from higher headquarters were passed along, but any attempt Wolfe made to control things after that met with dull disregard from the troops or a withering glare from the platoon sergeant.

Carrying a long bamboo stick topped with a nasty coil of rusty barbed wire, Rhah approached the CP and found the lieutenant staring off into space.

"You wanted to see me, sir?"

Wolfe glanced up at what looked like a filthy pirate come ashore after a long voyage in cruel seas. Why the Army insisted on making NCOs out of obvious psychopaths he could not fathom.

"Your promotion is effective as of today, Jackson. Looks like you got Elias's squad."

Rhah glanced over at Doc and Tony with an evil leer playing on his face. "Squad, sir? I didn't know we was still referring to this platoon in terms of squads, lootenant."

Wolfe sighed and pointed at the edge of the platoon sector. "Those two holes over there are yours. . . ."

Glancing in the direction indicated, Rhah interrupted the orders. "Beggin' yer pardon, lootenant, but them holes are so far apart you could run a regiment through and nobody'd notice. I got only five warm bodies left. . . ."

Wolfe waved in irritation at his new squad leader. "I don't want to hear your problems, Rhah. You'll get replacements any day now. For the time being, you make do just like everybody else."

"Hey, lootenant, I didn't ast fer this job. . . ."

"I don't want to hear about it, Rhah." Wolfe picked up his weapon, motioned for Tony to follow and started off toward the Company CP.

"You don't want to hear about it?"

"That's right, Rhah. I don't want to hear about it. And you know why? Because frankly, Rhah, I don't give a shit. Okay? I just don't give a shit anymore!"

Rhah leveled an incredulous glance at Doc Gomez who had been watching the entire exchange while resting his chin on an entrenching tool. He finally shrugged and smiled at Rhah.

• • •

When their hole was deep enough and solidly ringed
by firmly packed sandbags, King left Chris to heat a
couple of meals and wandered twenty-five meters down
the jungle hillside to emplace the Claymores. He was
unraveling the connecting wire and working his way
back up the slope when he spotted the reinforced squad
from first platoon snaking their way through the perimeter. He warned the squad leader about the two Claymores beside the trail, got an approximate position for
their night ambush site and joined Chris sitting on top
of the bunker. He considered the frightened looks on
the faces he'd seen pass outside the perimeter and
plugged the electrical lead into the Claymore firing
device.

"Glad it's them and not us goin' out on that ambush,
man. Somewhere out dere is de beast, Taylor, and he
hungry tonight. Dis shit's a stone bummer, man. Ah
got ten and a wake-up and ah'm still out heah dealin'
wit' dis shit. . . ."

King couldn't tell if Chris had heard him or not. The
heat tab beneath their meal had gone out, but he made
no move to relight it or do anything but stare into the
jungle at the backs of the ambush party.

"What's yo' problem, Taylor? How come you ain't
writin' no mo', man? You used to be writin' home all
de time. Ain't dey nobody back in de World? No
parents or girl or nothin'?"

Chris made a futile gesture with one hand and reached
inside his pocket for a plastic bag full of pre-rolled
joints with the other. King grabbed the bag from his
hand.

"You doin' too much of this shit, man. And dis ain't

no time for it. You smoke too much of dat shit and it bring you down.''

Chris ignored the comment and turned his attention to several bandoliers of loaded magazines and a pile of hand grenades which would need to be organized inside the hole before dark. King shrugged and began to sing "Tracks of My Tears" in a soft falsetto.

Before he could get to the chorus, Chris interrupted. "King Pin, you ever get caught in a mistake and you just can't get yourself out of it?''

Striking a match to avoid a cold C ration supper, King looked up from the makeshift stove and grinned. "They's a way out of anything, mah man. You just gots to keep yo' pecker hard and yo' powder dry. What dat Elias used to say? De worm *will* turn. . . .''

"That's what's bothering me, King. It ain't just me, man. It's the way the whole thing works. People like Elias get wasted and people like Barnes just go on making up their own rules and doing anything they want. And what do we do? We just sit around in the middle and try to figure how many days we got left. We don't amount to dogshit, man!''

"Does a chicken have lips? Whoever said we did, man? Make it outta here . . . it's all gravy. Every day of the rest of your life, man . . . gravy. . . .''

Before Chris could argue further, they heard the strident tones of O'Neill coming up the hill. He was calling for King.

"What de fuck Super Lifer want now, man? Ain't no shitters to burn out heah.''

For once in his life, O'Neill was bringing happy news, but they would never have guessed that from the hangdog expression on his freckled, sunburned face.

"Get yer shit together, King. Yer orders just come through."

King spilled a steaming glob of ham and lima beans onto his crotch but did not seem to notice the heat as he jumped and stared into the noncom's face for any sign of a joke.

"You ain't shittin' me, is you? My orders really come through? Oh shit, Taylor, the Lifers done made a mistake and cut me some slack, man!"

O'Neill shook his head at the display. "You ain't on yer way anywhere unless you catch that last chopper in ten minutes, King. And don't take up too much room with yer shit. . . . I'm comin' along if I kin get myself hooked up. Francis is comin' up to take yer gun. Move out if you want to make it."

King stood paralyzed by indecision or disbelief. His wide, white eyes shifted between his pack and a willy-peter bag containing extra uniforms, odds and ends. Chris smiled at his friend and took the initiative. He grabbed the WP bag and put a reassuring hand on King's twitching elbow.

"It's for real, King Pin! You're gettin' out of here. Leave the gun for Francis. Grab your pack and I'll walk down to the LZ with you."

O'Neill checked at his hole to be sure his gear was packed and then shuttled down the muddy hill to find Barnes. The platoon sergeant was near Bunny and Junior's position. The black man had his feet up on a sandbag to make ministration easier on Doc Gomez, who was rubbing ointment on the pale, blistered soles.

The squad leader arrived in midconversation just as Barnes knelt, leaning on his rifle, to take a closer look at Junior's feet. He spat on the ground and turned to the medic.

"So, what's his problem?"

"Inflamed feet, Sarge. Says he can't walk."

Barnes pursed his lips and nodded. Junior did not like the cold, calculating look on the man's face.

"Where's his squad leader? Where's O'Neill?"

Doc Gomez nodded over his shoulder and Barnes stood to look at O'Neill. "This nigger o' yours says he cain't walk, Red. What we gonna do about that?"

In the distance, O'Neill could hear the steady chop of an inbound helicopter. He didn't have much time.

"Junior, get up off yer lazy ass and get yer boots back on. I know what you did, asshole. I seen you puttin' mosquito repellent on yer feet so they'd get tender. You get up from there or I'll court-martial yer ass!"

Junior threw both his jungle boots in the hole beside Bunny in an effort to smash the grin off the white boy's face.

"Den you court-martial me, man! I don't give a fuck! Bust mah ass. Send me to Long Binh, mothah-fuckah! I ain't walkin' no more. De white man done got his last klik outa me. Get some chuck dude to hump dis shit!"

Barnes grinned at O'Neill, wondering vaguely why the man was sweating in the chill of dusk. "Red, go on back by the CP and get me that centipede."

The sound of the chopper was beginning to echo around the hillsides. O'Neill was confused and anxious to end this charade. "What centipede, Sergeant Barnes?"

"You remember, Red. That big orange and black bastard I found in that ammo crate. I believe we'll just put him in this asshole's pants and see if he wants to walk.''

Junior's eyes got wider. He glanced nervously at both NCOs. Was Barnes serious? He'd seen men bitten by the huge centipedes and wind up swollen with so much pain they couldn't use their arm for weeks.

"No! Wait! Ain't no call to be puttin' no fuckin' bugs on mah ass, man! I'll walk. I don't need dis shit! I'm warnin' y'all. . . . I don't need dis shit!"

Bunny tossed the man's boots out of the hole. "You ain't warnin' shit, Junior. Lookit the pussy, Sarge. How come I got to have him on my hole?"

Barnes turned away from the problem and found himself caught by O'Neill's hand on his elbow.

"Uh, Bob . . . can I talk to you for a minute." The last supply chopper of the night was circling the perimeter, ready to flare for a landing.

"Look, Bob, I got Elias's R&R when we was back in the rear. I'm gonna take a trip to Hawaii and see Patsy. Anyway, the plane leaves in three days and I was just wonderin' . . ."

There was no understanding in Barnes's cold eyes. O'Neill would have to say it all.

"I was just wonderin'. . . . I never asked you for a break before, Bob . . . but I was hopin' you'd send me in on that last chopper with King. What do you say, Chief? Can I take off?"

Barnes applied painful pressure to unwrap O'Neill's fingers from his elbow. " 'Fraid ah cain't do that for you, Red. We need every swingin' dick out in the field. Sorry 'bout that. . . ."

O'Neill shivered involuntarily. His chances of survival were getting slimmer with each passing second.

"Hey, Bob . . . come on. Talk to me here, huh? It's your buddy, Red. I'm only askin' for three days!"

"Ah am talkin' to you, Red . . . and ah'm tellin' you to get back to your position." Barnes began to walk off toward the CP. He had to duck flying debris from the landing chopper.

O'Neill shouted over the whine of the engines. "I got a bad feelin' about this one, Bob. I . . . I'm tellin' you, I got a bad feelin'. Bob! I don't think I'm gonna make it outa here. You know what I mean, man?"

Barnes turned his head slightly and caught O'Neill with a sidelong glance. "Everybody's gotta die sometime, Red. Get back to your foxhole."

King's worn white jungle boots beat a steady tattoo on the dirt of the LZ. He was waiting for a signal from the crew chief to approach the helicopter. That would come as soon as the last water can was unloaded. The huge black machine gunner had only moments left in the field.

"I'm really happy for you, man!" Chris grabbed his buddy by both massive shoulders and stared up into his face. "You take it on home for all of us now. Hear? I got your address back in the World. And you sure as shit know where you can reach me. Right? I'll miss you, man!"

"Ah gotta di-di, Chris. Got to make dis bird, man. Ah'll send you a postcard . . . soon's ah gets me some. And . . . and ah'll send you some tapes too, man . . . for de Underworld. Dey got dis new cat name of Jimi Hendrix. He's outasight, man. Shake it slow now, Taylor. Don't think too much, man. And don't be no fool. Ain't no such thang as a coward out here, mah man. It don't mean nothin', dig? You jist keep on keepin' on. Mah man . . .''

King and Chris executed the ritual of the Dap and got it all in just before the helo crew chief waved King and several others onto his bird. Chris spun away from the helicopter without a final wave. King would think he was just trying to avoid the blast of rotor-driven debris but Chris knew the real reason. He didn't want King to leave the Nam remembering the sorrowful, envious look on a buddy's face.

At the stream crossing, just before he entered his own company's area, Chris paused and peered at the gloom descending over the jungle. Something was irritating him; telling him to do something and he didn't know what it was. What can I do . . . other than take it like it comes? He decided to have a last cigarette before the dark and the need to remain invisible to the enemy made smoking impossible.

Chris had left his smokes in the foxhole with all his other gear when he walked King to the LZ but someone in the thinning crowd of soldiers around the stream crossing should have a cigarette. He squinted into the gloom and spotted a soldier sitting on a pile of sandbags. There was something familiar about the man.

"Got a smoke I can borrow, man?" Chris stared into the soldier's haggard face and felt embarrassed about asking for anything from a guy in such pitiful condition. Whoever the man was, he should have accompanied King out of the field wearing a medevac tag. His skin had the pasty pallor of a malaria victim. Lesions from cold sores surrounded his cracked lips. Sweat and dirt had fused with the stubble covering his cheeks and chin.

The man looked cadaverous. It was almost as if some

ghoul had hung a set of tattered jungle fatigues on a
skeleton and mashed a filthy bush-hat down on the
skull. The man stuck two fingers in an upper pocket of
his shirt and fished out a C ration four-pack of Win-
stons. There was one crumpled cigarette left in the box.
Chris nearly refused to accept the man's last smoke but
he was afraid to do that.

There was something ominous in the man's tortured
eyes. Beyond the deep velvet of the pupils, they seemed
lifeless. Chris had seen that sort of unfocused stare
before among casualties who had the misfortune to die
with their eyes open.

He accepted the smoke as the man stood to cross the
stream, but Chris could not bring himself to rummage
for matches. He was mesmerized by those eyes and an
icy serpent that seemed to crawl up his spine. As
though sensing Chris's discomfort, the man shifted his
gaze to the impenetrable jungle that seemed to squeeze
in on the perimeter with the approach of full dark. He
sighed deeply once and stepped away from Chris.

"Later . . ."

Even the voice had an odd, eerie sound . . . as
though the man was speaking from a small tiled room
. . . or a mausoleum.

Chris had to walk parallel to second platoon's line of
foxholes to reach the one that would be occupied by
himself and Francis. He had paused at Rhah's and
Parker's position to borrow a match when the thump of
grenades and the rattle of small arms split the silence
out in the dark jungle at their front. All three men
instinctively jumped in the hole.

Rhah raised his head and eyed the bush warily.
"Whoa, dudes. Watch out now! There goes that fuckin'

first platoon ambush. Somebody done stepped on their dick this time. Them gooks ain't *even* waitin'. They hungry now. You better get back to your hole, Taylor.''

When Chris passed by down the line, Bunny and Junior were staring at each other from seated positions on either side of their hole. Junior was glaring at the teenager, tense with anger, but Bunny was calmly baring his soul . . . as though he was sitting beside an intimate friend.

"Y'know, Junior, some of the things we done . . . I don't feel like we done something wrong . . . but sometimes, y'know, I get this bad feelin'. It ain't all that shit the Chaplain's tryin' to jam up our ass about the Good Lord. It's just a fuckin' *bad feelin'*, y'know? I don't know why, man. I told the Chaplain the truth is I really like it here. You do what you want. Nobody fucks with you. Only worry you got is dyin' . . . and if that happens, you don't know about it anyway. So what the fuck? You know what I mean, man?''

Bunny lapsed into an eerie giggle as Junior glanced nervously over the top of the hole at the sound of small arms echoing in the jungle. The ambush had been popped and he was stuck with a stone lunatic!

"Mothah-fuckah, man! I gotta be on this hole with you? I jist know I shouldn't have come out here!''

Bunny chuckled and began to cram rounds into his shotgun. "Don't you worry about a thing, Junior. You in a hole with Audie Murphy, man.''

Outside his cramped CP bunker, Captain Harris was pacing back and forth, forcing his primary RTO into a complicated form of close-order drill to keep up with him.

"Bravo One Alpha, Bravo One Alpha, this is Six. Send me a grid. I say again, send me a grid, over."

Harris resumed pacing and waited impatiently for a response. It was too soon. The ambush should not have hit anything yet unless the S-2 had been wrong about the last reported position of the 141st NVA. If lead elements were already down in the valley, things would get very heavy in very short order. Alpha Company and the other two maneuver battalions were not in place. They would not be until 2300 hours. Thank God the major had spent time plotting pre-planned artillery fire. Now, if he could only get the ambush squad leader to send him a grid or reference point.

"Bravo One Alpha . . . send a grid and I'll get Redleg to the rescue, over!"

A confused breathless voice shouted into Harris's ear through the radio handset.

"We're pinned down, sir. They're in the trees . . . the fuckin' trees for Christ's sake!"

Trying to ignore the persistent visions of what it must be like out there in the jungle, Harris breathed deeply and tried to force calm reassurance into his voice.

"Okay, One Alpha . . . calm down now, boy. I'm gonna get you a fire mission ASAP. Smoke will be first . . ."

The deranged voice rattled on before the company commander could finish his instructions.

"Sergeant's dead, sir. Radioman looks like he's had it. I don't know where the map is, sir! They're all around us, Captain! They're moving. Hundreds of 'em. I can hear 'em talkin' gook! Jesus Christ, sir!"

Harris studied his map and placed a finger on the spot where the ambush should be. Did the squad leader make it all the way? Did he manage to find the right

position in the dark? There was no way of knowing.
And there was nothing to do but call the mission and
hope whoever was on the other end of the radio could
adjust the rounds onto the gooks.

"Fire mission comin' up, son. Just spot the rounds
and tell me where to shift. Just tell me too long, too
short, left or right. We'll get you out of there. Hang
tough and tell me where the rounds hit, over."

Mashing the transmit key of a second handset, Harris
called a fire mission for his beleaguered ambush party.
The rattle of small arms fire had died down to an
occasional burst of AK, echoing like a woodpecker
through the jungle, before Harris heard the distant boom
of outgoing artillery rounds. As soon as the marking
round crashed into the jungle some five hundred meters
outside the perimeter, the company commander was
back on the radio.

"Bravo One Alpha, Six. How about that round, son?
Can you adjust fire?" The hiss of undisturbed air waves
was maddening. Captain Harris had an uncomfortable
thought.

"One Alpha . . . if you can't talk, just key the
handset twice, over."

Their faces lit momentarily as Harris and his primary
RTO heard static interrupted by someone keying the
handset. They waited anxiously for fire corrections.

After his senior corporal killed the last American,
Captain Pham Van Phuong picked up the radio handset
the man had been clutching and depressed the transmit
switch. For the first time in his life, he wished fervently
that he spoke English. It would be rewarding to lure
more of the soldiers out of their perimeter. But Captain
Phuong did not speak English and had to shout his

defiance into the radio in his native tongue. Perhaps some Saigon puppet serving with the foreigners would translate.

"Leave this valley, Americans! You will all die tonight! I am Dai Uy Phuong of the fourth company, 141st Regiment of the People's Army. You won't live to see another day!"

Standing with his Tokarev pistol in hand, Captain Phuong nearly put a bullet through the hissing radio set and then thought better of it. He motioned for the senior corporal to pick up the set and bring it along so he could monitor the American's radio transmissions. Phuong might not understand what was being said, but he felt sure he could tell from the tone of voices when their morale was about to collapse.

Soldiers from Captain Phuong's company and five others were preparing for an all-out assault on the Americans. Whatever had prompted the Americans to occupy this valley in such meager strength would be their undoing. The senior officers had planned an attack that would send elements of the 141st through the enemy units like lightning bolts and leave them in position for the great Tet uprising. If they were lucky, men from the 141st would be among the first troops to enter Saigon after it fell. What a glorious moment that would be!

But first they would have to deal with the enemy in this valley and avoid the artillery and planes that were sure to be loitering in the area. The plan called for assault elements to move forward under cover of an extended mortar barrage and close with the enemy inside his own perimeter before the deadly supporting arms could be brought to bear. Once inside the enemy positions, the big guns and planes would be of no use. They would not fire for fear of hitting their own troops.

Even now, Phuong thought as he watched his men string wire and post luminous arrows to guide the assault troops, sappers were wiggling through the Americans' perimeter wire. These heroes would detonate the explosives strapped to their bodies as they ran into strategic positions to blind and confuse the enemy forces. The shock effect would be devastating.

To the rear of their position, Chris and Francis could hear the cough and clang of the 81mm mortars spitting illumination rounds into the air over the perimeter. The light was reassuring at first but the eerie shadows cast by the burning fires swinging under parachutes and the unnerving whoop of the empty canisters falling to the ground made them wish for darkness. It was a simple law of survival. What you couldn't see probably couldn't see you.

Artillery from their fire support base was still pounding into the jungle in a futile attempt to cover the withdrawal of the ambush party. All the small arms they could identify in the periodic lull between rounds was AK. Their battle-tuned ears indicated the people firing those AKs were doing so from an ever-decreasing distance.

Francis had urinated outside the hole twice in the last half-hour. He returned from a third relief expedition and checked to insure there was a round in the chamber of his M-16.

"Oh, shit, Taylor. This is gonna be a motherfucker, man! I wish I was back in Memphis now. I'm tellin' you, man. This is gonna be a stone motherfucker!"

Chris concentrated on the growing crescendo of fire and realized Francis was right. This night would be

terrible. Somehow that seemed entirely satisfactory. In
the end, it all boiled down to something like this; some
night when both sides laid it all on the line in the full
knowledge that only one side would live. Maybe that
was the only real question worth pondering in war.
Maybe the only answer was not to question . . . only
fight well and survive.

But could he fight well or had it all become too much
for a rational man to handle? Was he rational? More
questions. Chris decided not to ask.

He'd heard something faint off to their right, somewhere in front of the hole that housed Rodriguez and
Ebenhoch. Both men flinched at an explosive pop from
that area. They squinted and ducked as a trip-flare
sputtered into light. When Rodriguez's machine gun
stuttered into action, Chris raised his head. It was hard
to see anything through the wash of light from the flare
and the muzzle flash from the gun.

Suddenly Chris saw a third bright light and heard the
roar of an incoming rocket. A ripping blast from
Rodriguez's hole sprayed them with dirt and debris.
The machine gun stopped and Chris swore he heard
some NVA Lifer issuing orders in Vietnamese. You
could always tell by the tone of voice. The nationality
made no difference.

"Jesus, RPGs. They got one on Rodriguez, man!"
Francis shook his head nervously and tried to identify
the voice calling for a medic off to their right.

"Sounds like Ebenhoch made it. We ought to get the
fuck outa here, man!"

Small arms rattled all across the perimeter and it was
hard to hear. Rhah had to call three times before he
found Taylor's hole and identified himself to keep from
being shot. Taylor was glad to see someone at least

nominally in charge. They'd had no orders or contact with anyone else since nightfall.

Rhah caught his breath quickly. He nodded toward the smoldering ruins of the hole on their right. "They cuttin' loose with rockets all around the perimeter. Here it is. One: They got through Charlie Company's positions. That means anything behind you don't identify itself, blow it away. Two: We got an air strike comin' in. They gonna lay snake and nape right on the perimeter so stay tight in your holes and don't be wanderin' around out there. . . ."

A fresh string of mortar illumination rounds lit the sky. The jungle glowed a luminous lime green in the flare light. Rhah, Chris and Francis ducked below the rim of the hole to keep from being silhouetted. A wicked burst of Ak fire drew their attention to the left.

"They probin' us. Gooks be runnin' up and down this line all night tryin' to get through. I got to check on Rodriguez and Ebenhoch. You two stay cold. I'll be back."

Rhah thought the perimeter was spookier than anything he'd ever seen. The eerie whoop of flare cannisters falling into the jungle set his teeth on edge. The dancing light made his eye muscles ache from the pupil expansion and contraction required to see. Shadows loomed and receded like goblins in a lurid cartoon.

He bolted to his left, heading for the CP to request reinforcement, when one of the shadows knocked him sprawling. Rhah scrambled to his feet and tried to make out the other man collecting himself up off the ground after the accidental impact. Both men were panting, their faces just two feet from each other for a moment.

Rhah detected a sour, fishy odor which he attributed to fear. I must have scared the shit right outa that guy!

It wasn't until both men had turned to continue their errands inside the perimeter that Rhah realized he'd bumped into a live gook. There were no reinforcements to be had at the CP and Rhah decided not to mention the incident with the gook inside the wire.

That asshole Wolfe might not give a shit now . . . but he would very soon.

Chris turned his attention back to the hillside in front of their hole. He thought he'd heard something crashing around in the bush out there. In a moment Francis also identified the sound. He shouldered his rifle while Chris grabbed the Claymore firing devices. Chris strained to see in the swooping shadows and thought he picked out a flash of jungle fatigues. He put a hand on Francis's and told him to hold his fire.

"Who is it?" There was no response to Taylor's loud whisper. He flicked a safety off the Claymore and prepared to squeeze the handle as he watched the form lurch and stagger toward the perimeter. Surely, a gook would have more control in the assault. When the trip flare outside their hole sparkled into a flush of blue light, Chris made out a bloody American face. The man was covered with blood and clearly terrified to be caught in the flare light. He had no helmet and no weapon.

"Don't shoot! Don't shoot!"

The bloody soldier stumbled and clawed his way up the hill. Chris yelled for him and ducked out of the way as he crashed into their hole on top of Francis. The man moaned for water and Chris reached for a canteen while Francis scrambled out from under the panting figure.

"They're all over the place, man. Hundreds of the

cocksuckers movin' this way! They wiped us out, man! We never had a fuckin' chance!''

The man swilled the contents of Chris's canteen and recovered some of his shattered composure. He was bleeding freely from a dozen shrapnel wounds but had no time for treatment.

"Which way's the CP, man? I got to tell 'em what's out there! You dudes better di-di outa this fuckin' hole too! I'm tellin' you. They're right on my ass and they ain't stoppin' for shit!''

Nearly tearing the top off their carefully constructed hole, the terrified soldier bolted for the center of the perimeter. Francis began to gather equipment frantically until he noticed Taylor was calmly sweeping the hillside to their front over rifle sights.

"C'mon, man. Didn't you hear what that dude said? The fuckin' gooks are comin' right through here. Let's di-di!''

No, Chris told himself. This is not the time to run. This is the time to fight; to face whatever the night and the war and the gooks might bring. He would live or die . . . or live *and* die . . . in this hole; in the place where he'd come to prove something. Now the test was at hand and he could do no less. The smoldering fire in his gut died with a final flicker. Chris felt an icy cold spread outward to his fingertips.

He picked up a grenade and straightened the pin for easy removal. "You go on, man. I'm stayin'.''

Francis stared back toward the center of their perimeter for long moments. He could see muzzle flashes winking in the night. There was no way to know who was killing who back there. And he'd be all alone if he left Taylor in the hole.

"Sheeeeeeeeeeeeeeit!'' Francis dropped his equipment,

picked up his rifle and made solid shoulder contact with Taylor.

Bunny had been in a grenade fight with the NVA for the past fifteen minutes. He heaved his last frag with a maniacal yelp and then picked up his shotgun to make things a little more personal. There were plenty of targets out there, flitting through the shadows just outside his hole.

Junior sat in the bottom of the position, scrunched into a tight ball and twitching with fear. His round eyes were locked on the three ChiCom potato-masher grenades that had fallen into the bottom of the hole. Three direct hits on the hole and three duds? It seemed impossible. One of them had to go off soon! And that crazy white boy hadn't even noticed. He was up there holding a conversation with the gooks!

Bunny ducked shrapnel from an incoming rocket round and returned the compliment with three shotgun slugs. "Come on, you gook motherfuckers! Come on! You can do better than that!"

Junior stared up at Bunny's face. Firelight from burning timbers distorted his features. Junior reached for his rifle and thought of the hideous gargoyles he'd seen perched on high corners of old buildings. They always looked ready to pounce on a man and devour his very soul. This white devil would get him killed and then devour his soul!

Junior edged toward the entrance to their bunker. "Fuck dis shit, man! I ain't dyin' in no white man's war. I'm gettin' outa dis mothah-fuckah!"

He bolted for the escape hatch, trying not to step on the NVA grenades and ignoring Bunny's insane cries.

"Junior! Get back here, you gutless shit!"

A stream of golfball-sized green tracers sent Junior
sprawling as he scrambled out of the foxhole and he
lost his helmet. He had nothing but a bandanna covering his head when he regained his feet and rammed
painfully into a solid teak tree about fifteen meters to
the rear of the hole. He staggered on wobbly legs and
then fell painfully onto his back. A shadow loomed
over his prostrate form and Junior was able to focus
glassy eyes on a glint of moonlight off something that
looked like an icicle.

When the NVA bayonet skewered down through his
belly, nudged aside a kidney and drove through the skin
of his lower back to pin him in place like an insect on a
display surface, Junior drew his knees up to his chest
and heard a strange noise.

It sounded like the hiss of air that the buses made
when they stopped and opened their doors to pick him
up back in the World.

Bunny spun to nail the gook that had bayonetted
Junior and howled when he saw the man blown backward by the impact of the shotgun slug. He heard the
thud of someone dropping into the hole at his back and
thought maybe they had finally gotten reinforcements.
He spun to welcome a new partner in the game and
found himself staring into the beady eyes of an NVA
trooper.

He tried, but there was just no time to swing the
shotgun and divert the muzzle of the gook's AK. Two
rounds knocked the breath out of Bunny and he collapsed to the floor of the hole trying hard to complain.
He stared up at the gook and felt the man's sandal-clad
foot on his chest. Tobacco-stained teeth cracked and
splintered as the enemy soldier worked the muzzle of
his AK into Bunny's mouth.

The heavy slug tore through the brain stem and popped the skull cleanly off the spinal column leaving Bunny's head at an odd angle to the rest of his corpse.

Chris had only four full magazines and no grenades remaining. He was about to ask Francis about his situation when he heard the noise. There it was again! Gooks talking calmly with each other. They must be close! Chris wished desperately for some longer range weapons but they'd fired both Claymores in nervous reaction to the tinny loudspeaker voice and scratchy patriotic music that had been broadcast from somewhere out in the jungle a half-hour ago. It was about that time the outgoing fire from holes on their left and right had begun to dwindle.

Chris didn't know if they'd managed to kill any gooks with the Claymores, but they'd put the loudspeaker out of commission. And that's when the strange noises started. There were chirps and whistles that both men believed were NVA signals.

Straining his ears to discern a pattern in the sound, Chris clearly heard something thud into the mud in front of their hole. He barely had time to duck below the rim and pull Francis after him before the grenade blast spun his helmet off his head and knocked him reeling toward the back wall of the bunker. Chris could see Francis screaming at him but it was a moment before his ears stopped ringing and he could hear what the man was saying.

"They're movin' up, man! I heard 'em talking gook out there!"

Chris crawled to his feet and peered out into the darkness. When the buzz in his head had completely subsided, he was able to pick out Vietnamese conversation and the telltale scrape of metal against metal. Somewhere out there a gook assistant gunner had just rammed a rocket round into a launcher.

"Out of the hole . . . fast!" Chris was halfway out when he realized Francis was not coming. The man was quaking and hugging his rifle.

"Goddamnit, Francis! Get out of there. They're gonna blow the hole!"

Francis finally responded to an angry jerk and slithered away into the dark behind Chris. They held up and turned around near the broad roots of a teak tree. From the new angle they could clearly see NVA troopers moving to flank the position they had just left. They heard a whistle blast followed by a loud bang as the RPG gunner sent a warhead directly through the firing aperture of their foxhole.

Huffmeister looked dead but O'Neill could feel a feeble heartbeat through the gore that matted the man's chest. He could hear the heavy fighting on his left over by Bunny and Junior's hole. O'Neill smeared blood from Huffmeister's wounds on his own face and neck as he cautiously raised petrified eyes over the rim of his hole. He listened to the vicious rattle of gunfire and smeared more blood onto his uniform.

He should go over there and help whoever was still alive. Or run to get help for Huffmeister. Or something. Before he could finish applying a third handful of blood, he spotted the two gook flankers headed for his hole. They were approaching cautiously, headed for O'Neill's position and glancing nervously in the direction of the battle to their right. They seemed no more anxious to get involved in that fight than O'Neill was.

When the gooks were no more than twenty meters

from his hole, O'Neill silently slipped out of sight and wedged his body under Huffmeister's. He held his breath and hoped the wounded man covering him would not moan or cry out, forcing the NVA to deliver a killing burst into the foxhole.

He heard a bolt snatched roughly to the rear and prayed for the first time since he'd faced that general court-martial in Germany. A voice uttered something in Vietnamese. That's right, O'Neill pleaded in terrified silence, these two in this hole are dead. No need to waste valuable ammunition on them.

The NVA troopers apparently agreed. They moved on and O'Neill sobbed out his relief when he could no longer hear running footsteps outside the hole. He crawled stiffly out from under Huffmeister, grabbed a field dressing from his equipment and began to bandage the man's wounds.

Nobody ever called Red O'Neill a welsher, he thought staring at Huffmeister's pale face. You saved my life and now I'm gonna save yours. Red O'Neill pays his debts.

Master Sergeant Melman had sure as hell not wanted to come out here on this crazy boondoggle, but after twenty-two years in the Army it seemed about time he qualified for the Combat Infantryman's Badge. Maybe if he got a CIB, the major would get off his ass about the beer-belly he'd been carrying around since Christ was a corporal.

It sounded okay back at the base camp. Good tight perimeter. Plenty of protection in the Jump CP. All the arty and air in the world on call. He'd spend a few days out here, get his ticket punched and get the hell back in the rear with the gear. Now everything was turning to shit in short order.

Someone said the damn gooks had got through the wire and Charlie Company was falling back. The major said he did not want that to happen. What he did want was for Master Sergeant Melman to leave the safety of the Jump CP and head off any soldiers from Charlie that tried to leave their positions.

Melman's eyes were never very good. He squinted into the inky night and saw two figures running toward the center of the perimeter, heading for the Jump CP. They seemed to be wearing steel helmets. Gooks didn't wear steel helmets, did they? Melman thought all the dinks wore conical straw hats. That would mean the two running figures were probably a couple of turds from Charlie running away from the gooks. He would, by God, put a stop to that!

"Hey, you boys! What company you two with?"

His question was never answered. In response to the authoritarian tones, an NVA Sapper put four rounds into Master Sergeant Melman's chest and continued to head for the bunker with all the whip antennae sticking up into the night air.

Major Stone was trying to make some sort of sense out of the confused gabble of reports that was pouring into the CP over the radios. Harris seemed to be holding his own on this side of the perimeter.

"Get me Bravo . . ." Before the RTO could make contact, another operator shouted above the din to relay an incoming message.

"Sir, Charlie Company reports hand-to-hand on the perimeter. Three holes are down and they're calling for help!"

Turning to his young assistant operations officer the

major pondered where to get reinforcements. "Okay
. . . get over to Weapons Platoon and have them pull
some people off the mortars to reinforce Charlie." The
first lieutenant picked up his weapon and turned to push
through the poncho that covered the entrance to the
Jump CP. He paused just long enough to hear the
major's final remark.

"Where the hell is that air strike? If we were the
goddamn First Cav, they'd be here by now. . . ."

A dark green blur ripped off the poncho covering the
Jump CP entry and flew inside among the startled
Americans. The first lieutenant tried to throw a cross-
body block and wound up bowling over a map table.
The major was trying to formulate something short and
sharp to say about the need to maintain light discipline
at night when he discovered that the disturbing blur was
an NVA Sapper.

Major Stone had just enough time to stare into the
fanatical eyes of the enemy before the man jerked on a
lanyard near his chest and detonated the four full pounds
of Composition B high explosive material contained in
bags strapped to his back.

At his CP less than a hundred yards from the de-
stroyed command bunker, Captain Harris peeked out
from under his helmet and felt a very heavy weight
descending on his aching back. His primary RTO poked
a handset in Harris's direction and confirmed the officer's suspicions about the nature of that weight.

"Sir, Brigade's down and we can't get Charlie Six
on the horn! You got command net and air net now!"

Harris swept the perimeter with weary eyes. Dark
figures seemed to cavort in the flickering light of fires
and flares like demons from some deep, dark level of

hell. The circle was tightening rapidly. He knew what would have to be done.

Harris drew his pistol and laid it on the edge of the hole. "Get me TacAir," he told the primary radio operator, "and then you and the other RTOs get on out of here and reinforce the perimeter."

Before the debris from the RPG round had settled to the jungle floor, Chris saw six NVA appear beside the smoking hole and begin firing their weapons into the ruins.

There was an angry buzzing in his ears that suddenly dropped pitch and became an ominous hum. He tried to think but he was so angry . . . so fucking pissed off . . . that the thoughts could not congeal into a plan of action. But there was no *heat* to his anger. He clenched his jaw muscles and swallowed what felt like a cold drink of ice water. Real justice, he knew somewhere in a corner of his mind, demanded the death penalty for these gooks who would otherwise never learn not to try and pull this shit on Chris Taylor.

He threw off Francis's restraining grip and jumped to his feet. He triggered several bursts into the startled NVA. Running forward to regain the hole, Taylor caught two more NVA trying to escape the madman who should have died. One was blown forward as rounds from Chris's M-16 broke his spine. The other tumbled backward into the hole. The man was still squirming when Chris jumped back in the foxhole and landed on his chest. He rested the muzzle momentarily on the man's flat nose and pulled the trigger twice.

Francis watched Chris kill enemy soldiers like some crazed robot and felt a giddy exaltation swell in his chest. He leaped to his feet, sprayed rounds in the

direction of two darting figures down the hillside and
ran for the safety of the hole. He would not make it
alone this night. And there was something about being
with Taylor. Francis watched Taylor take control of the
firefight and felt for the first time that they might live.

Taylor had no intention of staying in the hole and
letting the gooks come to him. He bolted over the edge,
ticking off rounds at every shadow as he disappeared
into the jungle, and screamed his farewell to Francis.

"It's beautiful, man! It's fucking beautiful!"

Doc Gomez flopped into the platoon CP dragging a
badly damaged Parker by the equipment straps. The
man was near death and a wide-eyed Tony Hoyt counted
at least ten bullet holes at various places on the upper
torso. Gomez was gasping and Tony found it hard to
tell if it was anguish or exhaustion. Doc suddenly groaned
and rolled Parker's lifeless form off his bloody lap.

"I can't help him! I can't help any of them anymore!
There's gooks all over the place out there. You can't
even stand up outside a hole without getting cut to
pieces!"

Lieutenant Wolfe nervously digested the comment.
He'd suspected holes were falling like dominos. There
was nothing more any of them could do. They'd have
to pull back off the perimeter and find shelter somewhere. He grabbed for the handset of Tony's radio.

"Bravo Six, this is Bravo Two Actual . . ."

Captain Harris did not sound happy to hear from his
second platoon commander. "Yeah, Two . . . send
traffic or clear this goddamn net!"

"We . . . we've been overrun, sir. We're pulling
back, over!"

Captain Harris breathed deeply to gain some control

over his voice and let his eyes settle on the two bullet-riddled RTOs who had made it no further than ten feet outside the CP.

"Bravo Two, Six! Goddamnit, lieutenant, where the hell you plannin' to pull back to? They're all over the perimeter! Be advised, Lieutenant Wolfe, you *will* hold in place and you *will* fight. That means you, Bravo Two! Bravo Six out!"

Lieutenant Wolfe stared around the smoky bunker. He shakily handed the receiver back to Hoyt. No escape. They'd have to take their chances . . . unless . . .

"Where's Barnes?" The madman could have the platoon. He could have the whole misbegotten Army if he showed up and pulled them out of this mess alive.

The medic shook his head, breathed deeply and reached for his rifle. "I think he's dead, sir. I think they're all dead."

Hoyt slammed the radio handset against the wall of the CP bunker and added his confirmation. "Negative contact, lootenant. Can't raise Barnes or any of the squads."

Wolfe was gushing sweat under the angry glare of the medic and his RTO. What did they want from him? There was no magic incantation in his commission. He couldn't just wave a wand and make the gooks disappear. Barnes had always been around to point the way in the past. What should we do? What the fuck should we do?

Hoyt shoved by him and headed for the entrance to the bunker. "You're a complete asshole, lootenant!"

Doc Gomez and Tony Hoyt ran out into the fire to take their chances. Lieutenant Wolfe waited a few moments and then realized he was totally alone. He picked up his rifle and followed them out into the murderous night.

Tony killed one NVA charging across the top of the bunker before his M-16 jammed. He was struggling to pull the charging handle to the rear when an unseen second enemy soldier put two rounds through his pectoral muscle. Hoyt spun with the impact of the bullets and tumbled down a grassy slope. He cringed with pain and held his breath as two more NVA leaped over his body in their rush to get inside the perimeter.

Doc Gomez was afraid of killing his own troops. It was so hard to tell about the shadows. When a flare popped he thought he saw a gook and when the light diminished he swore it was an American. He fired between two shadows hoping the rounds would scare whoever was coming his way into retreat. A grenade blast knocked him off his feet and he hit his head painfully on an engineer stake. He passed out quite content that he would not be conscious when the NVA finally killed him.

Lieutenant Wolfe was crawling on his hands and knees away from the CP bunker and toward the river crossing. He'd already had to play dead several times while charging NVA hurdled over his body. It looked like he might make it and Lieutenant Wolfe thought he could afford to rest for a moment behind a collapsed mortar position.

He heard the sound of rushing water and stood to sprint for the stream crossing at about the same time an NVA trooper finished spiking the mortar tube at his back with a grenade. Wolfe and the NA stared at each other for a long moment. The lieutenant noted the fear in the man's eyes and thought perhaps they could both just turn and run.

The NVA, remembering the smoldering fuse on the grenade he had primed, bolted first. Wolfe barked in triumph and turned to run. He bumped into the muzzle of an SKS carbine in the hands of an NVA squad leader and lost his heart to a steel-jacketed 7.62-mm round.

Wounded by shrapnel in several places, Barnes was involved in a painful scramble to find cover somewhere along the slight rise between O'Neill's hole and the one being overrun next to it. He realized calmly that Bunny and Junior must be dead. The NVA were pouring through a gap they should be defending.

Trust the feeling, he told himself. Do what must be done. It will all be over soon. The important thing is to make 'em pay; to see 'em bleed and die. Barnes felt the pressure building. It was worse than it had ever been. A strong steel band behind his eyes was being heated and stretched. His head ached horribly and the pain made him feel like his ears were being pushed apart so that his skull would split down the middle.

And then the steel snapped.

Despite the dark, his hands moved mechanically and efficiently to strip and prepare the Light Anti-tank Weapon for firing. He'd plug the leak with high explosive and then get down there to tear the bastards' hearts out with his hands. They would not escape this time.

A nicely timed illumination round burst over the perimeter as Barnes brought the weapon to his right shoulder. In the distance over the crackle of constant firing he could hear the rushing whine of jet aircraft in tight orbit over the perimeter. He'd have to hurry to kill them all. The jet-jockies would be after their share very soon.

Through the oblong plastic sight of the LAW, Barnes

focused on an NVA in Bunny's hole. He squared the stadia line onto the man's steel helmet and pressed the firing switch firmly.

The rocket round roared into the hole, atomized the gook who had killed Bunny, and wounded several of his comrades with hot metal fragments. Barnes roared, reached for his rifle and ran down the slope to balance the scoreboard he'd been carrying around on his face since 1965.

Captain Harris had just returned to the CP from a quick, terrifying reconnaissance. His one remaining RTO thought he had encouraging news.

"Captain! Third battalion armored just came up on the net. They're inbound on tracks about two kliks west of us!"

Harris glanced at his watch. They'd never reach the perimeter in time.

"It don't mean shit! They can't reach us soon enough. The whole perimeter is flooded with gooks. We still got some people holding out but I'm damned if I know exactly where."

While his RTO burned through a magazine and turned back an NVA fireteam headed for the Bravo Company CP, Harris reached for the handset which linked him with a flight of F-4 Phantom aircraft that were circling the perimeter high in the inky sky. He wondered for a moment what the pilots could see of the carnage below from their altitude. They'd been circling up there for half an hour now waiting for clearance to pounce. Harris had ordered them in once and then called off the strike when the NVA flooded through the wire.

You didn't call a tactical air strike on your own

position unless you were desperate. Harris took a last look at the chaotic perimeter and decided he was desperate.

"Snakebite leader, Ripper Bravo Six. We're gonna need you soonest. Be advised I've got zips inside the wire down here, over!"

The calm voice of the lead pilot carried a midwestern twang.

"Roger that, Bravo Six. Be advised we're hot to trot packin' snake and nape . . . but we're bingo fuel. It's your call, Bravo Six."

Harris chewed painfully on his lip and tasted blood. The planes were sitting up there with Snake-eye general purpose bombs and napalm canisters. They were low on fuel after so much loiter time above the perimeter. If he wanted help from the air it had to be now.

"Snakebite lead, Bravo Six. For the record, it's my call as senior man on the ground. Dump everything you've got *on my pos*! I say again, I want everything you're holding *inside* the perimeter! It's a lovely fucking war . . . Bravo Six out."

Now that he was cleared to go to work, the pilot's voice took on an excited lilt. "Roger your last, Bravo Six. We copy it's your call. Get 'em in their holes down there. We're comin' locked and cocked at treetops from Whiskey to Echo . . ."

". . . break, break . . . Snakebite two, this is lead. Orbit for a pass on zero-niner-zero. Watch my smoke to target and expend all remaining!"

It would be a few minutes before the planes could line up for their run. Captain Harris thought for a second about his own situation. Would it be better to sit here and hope the napalm didn't seep into the CP? Or would he rather go down doing what he'd been trained to do for so many years of his life?

He tapped the RTO on the shoulder and led the charge out of the hold and out into the night.

Barnes buried his push-dagger to the hilt under the chin of a squirming NVA and grabbed an abandoned e-tool just in time to deflect the muzzle of the AK the man's comrade was pointing at his chest. Recalling the powerful stroke he'd used to split rails back in Tennessee, Barnes buried the sharp edge of the shovel in the man's face and scrambled to retrieve a discarded AK. He killed two more NVA with the remaining rounds in the magazine before a third man—hearing the familiar sound of the bolt slamming home on an empty chamber— rose from cover and blew a large chunk out of Barnes's right thigh.

The NVA trooper watched in amazement as the foreign monster crumpled slowly to his knees and felt around for a weapon on the ground. How could the madman not lay down and die? He was bleeding from several wounds. There were ugly burn patches on his left arm and shoulder. He appears to have been struck by at least three bullets before mine . . . yet he snarls through the old scars from other wounds and refuses to let death take him. The man reminded him of the ancient and venerable water buffalo on his father's farm. Too stupid and mean to die.

Barnes wrenched the bloody entrenching tool from the face of the man he'd killed with it and dragged himself painfully toward the one who had shot him in the leg. He howled in protest when the NVA trooper turned and bolted back into the jungle. Barnes roared again and raised the dripping shovel as two more NVA charged from a treeline to replace their comrade who had lost nerve in the face of this wounded foe.

Chris heard the screams and recognized the voice. Barnes was alive! He turned left, gliding through the bush easily, and crested a slight slope just in time to see the platoon sergeant flailing away at two charging enemy soldiers. Taylor shouldered his weapon and cut one of the NVA down. The second man spun toward the direction of incoming rounds and promptly lost his right kneecap to Barnes's scything e-tool.

As Taylor ran down the slope avoiding the litter of NVA corpses, he saw Barnes drag the remaining NVA under him and nearly sever the man's head with a vicious stroke. He skidded to halt less than six feet from the man and watched in revulsion as Barnes methodically hacked and chopped at the corpse.

Something about the primitive scene of Barnes butchering an enemy sent a strong, rational breeze through Taylor's system. He felt the heat of passion for the first time that evening and thought perhaps he should simply kill Barnes here and now. Maybe the man's death would somehow bring an end to all the killing. It seemed sensible. Where Barnes went, there was always killing.

No, Chris told himself as he watched the platoon sergeant rage and ram the bloody club into another corpse, all this is not Barnes's fault . . . just as it isn't my fault or anyone else's fault. All this is well beyond simple right, wrong and assessment of guilt. All this is something . . . something else that . . .

He heard the shuddering roar of the aircraft headed in to deliver their deadly cargo.

"Barnes!"

The man swung to face Chris, but rage had clouded his vision. Barnes could no longer see, speak, recognize or think. He could only kill. He would kill anything and everything in reach. There was no overdose level. The control rods had snapped and Barnes had melted down to pure, primitive instinct. In Chris's cringing form Barnes saw only another target, another fix for his blood lust. He raised the e-tool for a killing blow and Chris saw the fires of hell in the man's mad eyes. Chris Taylor had made it to this point with the fates forgiving an occasional lapse in judgment, but this was a fatal error. The hate in Barnes could never be controlled.

As he watched the bloody shovel reach an apex and begin to fall toward his head, Chris felt the air sucked from his heaving lungs by the hungry splash of napalm. His last vision was a roiling cauldron of smoke and fire forming a demented aura around Barnes's tortured face.

Making a final, low-level orbit over the perimeter before a dwindling fuel supply forced them to leave the fray, the Phantom pilots banked their aircraft and craned to see out the side of their canopies. Flying through the inky skies with their eyes off the instruments was dangerous, but neither man could resist staring at the spectacle below.

It was like watching the playing surface of an overloaded pinball machine gone berserk. Secondary explosions from the GP bombs lit and blossomed like bumpers struck by a pinball. The napalm flowed over the perimeter, darting left and right where it found something to consume, like neon coursing through tubing to mark a player's progression toward a free game. But there would be no free game this night no matter what the score. The pilots were familiar enough with death to understand that.

They noted no one was moving on the ground and that was the signal for them to point their aircraft toward home base. The battle was over in this valley.

10.

When Chris Taylor was able to unstick the glue that held his eyes shut and massage them slowly into painful focus with the swollen, bloody fingers of one hand, he decided the devil truly defied stereotype. Lucifer looked like a buck deer with mossy antlers and a snowy white bib tucked beneath his pointy chin. How could anyone with such soft, liquid eyes dispassionately rule the depths of hell?

At the sound of roaring engines and creaking tracks, the deer lifted its ears, twitched its nose and bolted away into the brush. The animal moved with fluid grace, Chris noticed, as Elias had moved before Barnes killed him. Chris Taylor rose from the depths and resettled in Vietnam. He should be dead, lying somewhere amid a pile of NVA corpses with Barnes's bloody e-tool growing out of his forehead. But he was clearly not dead. His senses told him that as he rose on shaky legs.

Chris could smell the high-octane stench of napalm

mixed with the musk of cordite from high explosives. His ears told him the distant roar came from the armored mounts of the cavalry coming to the rescue. His aching eyes squinted in the pale light of a new dawn and sent the message of survival to his brain.

Other senses screamed in agony as Chris began to move slowly, ignoring the carnal sprawl of American and Vietnamese bodies between him and his destination. He was bleeding freely from shrapnel wounds and other blast damage. As he moved he could feel patches of dried blood crack and flake from his body. Chris realized he must have been saved from the madman's wrath by the air strike. It only remained to see if the madman had also survived. It only remained to be seen if justice had finally been served. Bending painfully at a point near the hole where Bunny and Junior had died, Chris retrieved an AK-47 and slid the bolt part way to the rear to make sure a round was in the chamber.

Barnes lay in a pool of blood with his shredded back propped painfully against a tree. His body was puffy and swollen from blast damage and the visible wounds on his legs and torso were clotted with lumpy blobs of sticky blood and lymphatic fluid. Chris stood over the man and stared at the ice blue eyes, hoping they would not blink.

For the first time since Chris had known him, Barnes seemed helpless and vulnerable. But he was clearly not dead. The scarred half of his face contorted in a grimace of pain. A low, mournful moan rumbled from somewhere deep in Barnes's chest and ended in a cough that splattered blood on Taylor's shredded trousers.

Barnes rolled his head slightly and seemed to notice Chris for the first time. His eyes flicked upward to the

younger man's face. Chris made no move to help or
hinder the platoon sergeant's agony.

"Go on, Taylor. Get me a medic, will ya?"

A medic might save Barnes but nothing would ever
heal his wounds. Barnes had set the example for Chris
to follow. If you wanted to win this game, if you
wanted to make some sense of it all, you ignored the
conventions and made up your own rules.

Chris slowly and painfully tightened his grip on the
AK-47 and brought the muzzle to bear on the center of
Barnes's bloody chest. Without moving his head, Barnes
glanced at the weapon and back to Taylor's eyes. He let
the twisted smile play across his face and realized he
would never have to see it in a mirror again. To think,
Barnes told himself as he noted Taylor's cold eyes,
release should come from such an unlikely source.

He whispered softly, coaxing Taylor gently into action.

"Do it . . . do it . . ."

Chris fired three times into Barnes's heart.

Snorting and screeching like an angry dragon, the
Armored Personnel Carrier clawed through a pile of
NVA corpses and crested the rise behind the slope
where Barnes died. Chris turned toward the sound painfully. He was numb and unsure what to do now that the
fight was finally finished.

He stared uphill into a grinning set of dragon's teeth
that had been painted on the front of the vehicle's hull.
A human skull was mounted on the feed cover of the
.50 caliber machine gun manned by a greasy crewman
whose naked arms were covered with crude tattoos.

Chris stared in mute fascination and felt the pain of
his wounds seep back into his system. A German Shep-
herd with a matted coat and a twisted muzzle bounded out

from behind the APC. The animal sniffed anxiously at a
dead NVA, Barnes and Chris before his handler appeared.

"Bozo! Get back here."

With a whine of reluctance, Bozo trotted back toward
his master and a friend who had climbed out of the
armored vehicle. Chris thought for a moment that the
Hell's Angels had been sent to Vietnam. Both armor
soldiers were unshaven, greasy and covered with a
coating of the dust their machine raised from its grinding tracks. One sported a gold earring and a Thompson
sub-machine gun. The other pulled a large saw-toothed
knife from under a tattered flak jacket emblazoned with
a bloody skull, two crossed pistons and the words
"Death Korps." Over their heads a large Nazi flag flew
from the antenna of the APC.

While his partner began to strip the NVA corpses,
the dog handler approached. He eyed Chris with open
interest and scrutiny as a sailor looks at the lone survivor
of a particularly nasty shipwreck.

"Can you walk out of here, man?"

Chris didn't trust his voice. He'd been numb with
cold just a few moments ago. Now a heat was building.
He was beginning to cope with the fact of his survival.
Chris Taylor could quit the battlefield honorably.

He nodded and shifted his gaze slowly in the direction the armor soldier was pointing.

"They got an aid station set up back at the LZ. . . ."

Chris started painfully up the slope as the APC driver
goosed his vehicle farther along second platoon's line
of holes.

O'Neill had to wave his arms frantically to keep the
driver of the Armored Personnel Carrier from grinding
directly over his hole.

A crewman jumped down from the machine and grinned at the carnage that surrounded O'Neill. He went directly to work stripping the NVA corpses. "They's some great shit here, Sarge! You musta blew away a hunnert gooks or more."

O'Neill slipped and stumbled on shaky legs while trying to crawl out of the hole. He pointed at Huffmeister and the track soldier left his scavenging to lift the wounded man up to ground level.

"This all they is left, Sarge?"

O'Neill choked on his response and bit his lip to swallow a sob.

"Fuck yeah! They all left me. Bunch of fuckin' faggots!!"

The track soldier determined that Huffmeister would live and stood to shake his head at the blanket of dead bodies strewn around the position.

"Man, looka this shit! You gonna get yerself a Silver Star!"

Staggering toward the center of the perimeter, O'Neill did not pause to address his response. "Fuck the Silver Star. I need a drink!"

Francis sat on the edge of his hole trembling. This was just too much, man. He counted sixteen NVA bodies around the position and took personal inventory. He was unhurt and had four more months in the field to go.

If there was ever a time, he thought. If there was ever a situation in which they'd never question it, this was it.

Francis reached for his equipment harness and slowly extracted the K-Bar fighting knife from its sheath. It would have to be clean. It would have to hold up when he told them it was a bayonet wound inflicted by some maniacal NVA who hadn't stayed around to finish the job.

Holding the knife with both hands, Francis squeezed his eyes shut anticipating the pain, paused for just a moment more . . . and then drove the blade into his thigh.

He collapsed into the hole and tossed the knife away into the jungle. When he heard a track shift into low gear and begin to grind up the hill he started shouting.

"Medic! Medic! Wounded man over here! Medic!"

Rhah used the barbed wire on the end of his walking stick to pull the swollen NVA corpse away from the tree where it had been pinned by long slivers of bomb shrapnel. There was something about the last look in the gook's dead eyes. Rhah knew it took one to know one.

He sliced neatly through the rolled rice tube the dead man had worn across one shoulder and quickly found what he sought. Inside was a plastic bag full of snowy white powder.

Rhah licked a filthy little finger and dipped it daintily into the powder. The heroin the soldier had used to ward off the pain of wounds or psyche himself up to face death was pure and potent. Rhah considered himself amply rewarded for having survived the night.

"Baaaaaaaaaaa!" He addressed God with a lingering look up through the bomb-blasted treetops. "Thanks, man. That's gooooood shit!"

Choppers were bounding in and out of the LZ like grasshoppers in a wheatfield feeding frenzy. They flared in empty, gobbled litters and walking wounded swathed in bloody bandages, then staggered into the air headed for whatever nearby Army hospital had been tasked with handling the overflow from an operation the briefing officers at the MACV Press Center in Saigon were already calling "a classic use of deception to trap and annihilate an enemy formation."

In the face of huge battles being fought across the countryside—especially in the streets of Saigon and to the north in the ancient imperial capitol of Hue—the fight seemed almost like a footnote and did not receive much initial press play. A smart Information Officer solved that problem by leaking to the press that the company commander who bravely called an air strike on his own position was being recommended for the Medal of Honor.

Word of the reporters' arrival reached Captain Harris while he was listening to a first accounting of the cost of the battle being passed by a borrowed RTO. "We get 37 U.S. KIA, 122 WIA and we're still counting. Estimate 500 Victor Charlie KIA, 22 WIA and still counting them also. . . ."

The company commander walked slowly through the shattered remnants of his second platoon, staring at the wounded with dull, lifeless eyes and trying to force some credibility into an encouraging smile. A second RTO tried to get his attention and failed. "Sir, TV crew is coming in with the general. Some reporters want to talk to you. . . ."

Harris glanced to his right where an engineer bulldozer was scraping away at piles of enemy dead and dumping them unceremoniously into a bomb crater. He flashed momentarily on pictures he'd seen of the Nazi death camps at Dachau after World War II. So many dead and so little gained. Harris knew the remnants of the 141st NVA were out there in the bush even now licking their wounds and calling for warm bodies all along their replacement pipeline.

He turned his eyes from the long row of bloody ponchos covering the dead and tried to smile at the living. He listened to the happy chatter of the walking wounded and wondered vaguely what he was going to do about reorganizing the company. A gaggle of squeaky-fresh replacements had been brought in by chopper but there were no officers to replace his lost platoon commanders. Harris walked away to let them communicate their fears and joys without an officer eavesdropping.

Francis rose on one elbow and spotted Taylor resting on a stretcher. "Hey, Taylor! You okay, man?"

A medic had squeezed morphine into Chris less than fifteen minutes ago and he had trouble paying attention. He frowned up at a piercing blue sky and wondered if he was okay. He'd survive the wounds and blast damage . . . but would he ever be okay again? Had his experience in combat engendered some messianic complex within him that made it all right to mete out his own brand of justice? Was justice served? Did Barnes deserve to die and leave him alone with a scar that would never heal? He thought for a while longer, watching stringy clouds disappear from his field of vision like the doubts from his mind. Somewhere inside Chris Taylor's head, a gavel pounded.

"Yeah, Francis. How about you?"

"Jes' fine, man. Jes' fine! Ain't never felt better. Both of us got two Purples, man. We're out!"

The black soldier with the bloody bandage on his thigh slapped Taylor on the shoulder as bearers lifted his litter and headed for the Dust-Off chopper that had just landed.

"See you at the hospital, man. We gonna get *high-high*! Yessir!"

Taylor lapsed into a grin and dropped his head back onto the stretcher. He followed Francis with his eyes for a while and then found himself distracted by the visage of a huge black man staring down at him.

"That's your ride outa here, man. You ready?"

Chris nodded and felt himself lifted into the air. Just one more lift and I'm gone from this valley of death, he thought. Just one more.

Sergeant O'Neill stood on the edge of a bomb crater and watched the majority of second platoon lift out of the field on helicopters. I should be on one of those birds, he thought. They owe me. O'Neill turned slowly away from the agonizing sight and noticed Captain Harris approaching. The captain knows what I've been through, he thought, maybe he'll let me out of the field. Deep in his soul, where truth still sparked unobscured by bullshit, O'Neill knew he would not make it through many more such fights. Maybe one more ambush, maybe one or two minor firefights, but if he had to stay out here, he would never leave the bush alive.

"How you doin', Sergeant O'Neill?"

"Okay, sir . . . but I been meanin' to ask . . ."

The company commander nodded aimlessly and stared at the skylarking gang of replacements. They were clicking pocket cameras and ogling the dead enemy bodies.

"That's just fine, Sergeant O'Neill . . . cause you got second platoon."

Why did I bother, he wondered as he watched the stooped shoulders of the company commander shrugging under the weight of his pack. The Big Con was on me. I worked so hard at getting out of the bush that I missed my chance. Barnes could not help now. No one could.

O'Neill trembled and glanced at the replacements. They could sort themselves out, he supposed. There was no hurry to make an impression with this new command. He was, after all, a dead man.

Chris Taylor lay sprawled in the door of the vibrating helicopter and watched Vietnam drop away from him. Rhah's solitary figure seemed to dominate the ruined landscape near the LZ. He was waving, signalling for all to see that he was okay, that he'd survived and would continue to do so.

Chris waved weakly and tried to mirror the wicked grin on Rhah's diminishing features. From an ascending angle, Rhah looked as though he were spread-eagled, pinned to the jungle floor. He spread his arms, stick in one hand, M-16 in the other and raised his face toward the sky. Chris heard the faint roar over the chop of rotor blades.

"Baaaaaaaaaaaaaaaaaaaaaaaaaaaaaaaa!"

I can dig it, he thought, responding to Rhah's message. You are alive. You are Rhah. There is no one in the world like you. Good-bye, Rhah. Continue to live, man.

The helo gained altitude and the whine of the turbines dropped into a steady drone. The war—at least the agonizing, soul-shattering part of it out in the bush—was over for Chris, much sooner than it should have been. The Army would get a full measure of his time, but he could opt to serve somewhere in the rear now that he'd been wounded in action twice. Still the bush and the mindless, numbing violence that would always be associated with it in his mind would never disappear completely.

He'd always live with it. Always. No matter what came along to try and force the memories into retreat. He thought of Elias and Barnes. Both were dead now . . . and both would live on inside of Chris Taylor forever. They'd always be there, valiantly representing their two disparate schools of thought on the nature of man, both fighting for possession of his soul.

A cool gust of wind blew in the door of the helicopter. Chris closed his eyes, feeling the breeze as a cleansing rinse; a release. Now that he'd become closely acquainted with both sides of human nature, Chris supposed he'd spend the rest of his days wondering whether to call on Elias or Barnes for an appropriate response. He was an orphan of war; a child born of two fathers who was now abandoned to his fate.

Someday Chris Taylor would have children of his own, or an obligation to instruct the children of others. What would he say about all this? Could he provide answers when they posed the questions he had asked just a short time ago? He stared at the jungle, flowing like a green river below the helicopter, and considered the demons waiting there to taunt and terrify someone else.

In the end, he thought, we did not fight the enemy. Man has fought man since time began . . . but the only enemy is within man himself.